BOWDRIE ON THE CASE

"All right, Ranger, speak your piece. What business do you have with us?"

"Five men robbed the bank at Morales Monday morning, and one of them was ridin' a paint horse, a dead ringer for that one out yonder." Bowdrie gestured toward the corral. "Where was that horse on Monday?"

"Right where he is now. He ain't been off this place in a week." He looked up, scowling. "Who identified that animal?"

"A dozen people. He was right out in plain sight. Nobody could've missed him. One who identified him was Bob Singer."

"Singer?" Roway's eyes flashed. "I'll kill him!"

"No, you won't," Bowdrie said. "If there's any killin' done, I'll do it."

—From "A Job for a Ranger" by Louis L'Amour

LONE STAR
LAW

EDITED BY

ROBERT J. RANDISI

POCKET BOOKS

New York   London   Toronto   Sydney   New Delhi

Pocket Books
An Imprint of Simon & Schuster, Inc.
1230 Avenue of the Americas
New York, NY 10020

This book is a work of fiction. Any references to historical events, real people, or real places are used fictitiously. Other names, characters, places, and events are products of the author's imagination, and any resemblance to actual events or places or persons, living or dead, is entirely coincidental.

This Pocket Books paperback edition October 2020

POCKET and colophon are registered trademarks of Simon & Schuster, Inc.

For information about special discounts for bulk purchases, please contact Simon & Schuster Special Sales at 1-866-506-1949 or business@simonandschuster.com.

The Simon & Schuster Speakers Bureau can bring authors to your live event. For more information or to book an event, contact the Simon & Schuster Speakers Bureau at 1-866-248-3049 or visit our website at www.simonspeakers.com.

Manufactured in the United States of America

10 9 8 7 6 5 4 3 2 1

ISBN 978-1-9821-5306-9
ISBN 978-1-4165-1459-6 (ebook)

CONTENTS

INTRODUCTION

The Texas Rangers have always been of interest to the public. Television followed them from the series *Laredo* in the 1960s through the miniseries *Lonesome Dove* in the eighties to the recently completed run of Chuck Norris's *Walker, Texas Ranger*. The past few years have seen the publication of the nonfiction books *The Men Who Wear the Star* by Charles M. Robinson III and *Lone Star Justice* by Robert M. Utley (both of which I recommend, by the way).

The stories in this collection are meant to trace the Texas Rangers from their inception in the 1820s to the early days of the twentieth century—roughly the first hundred years of their storied history. The authors included represent the best the western genre has to offer, from the Louis L'Amour reprint (the only reprint in the book) right through to new writer Marcus Galloway's tale of a Ranger's pursuit of Bonnie and Clyde.

Having put together a fair number of anthologies over the years, I feel I can honestly say there's not a bad one in this bunch. Sit back and let these writers take you on a wild ride through history, and see if you don't agree with me.

—Robert J. Randisi
St. Louis, Missouri
May 31, 2004

LONE STAR
LAW

A Job for a Ranger
Louis L'Amour

—⋙⋘—

While the only true series Louis L'Amour wrote in novel form was his tales of the Sackett family, he did write a series of short stories that featured Texas Ranger Chick Bowdrie. Some of the stories were published in a collection called *Bowdrie*. Most of them were written between 1940 and 1947 and appeared in the magazine *Popular Western*.

The one I've chosen for this anthology shows Bowdrie acting not only as a Ranger, but as a detective as well.

There were two bullet holes in the bank window, and there was blood on the hitching rail where the cashier had fallen while trying to get off a last shot. Lem Pullitt had died there by the rail, but not before telling how he had been shot while his hands were up.

Chick Bowdrie stood on the boardwalk, his dark, Apache-like features showing no expression. "I don't like it," he muttered. "Either the holdup man was a cold-blooded killer or somebody wanted Pullitt killed."

He glanced up the street again, his eyes searching the buildings, the walks, the horses tied at the rails. Many men kill, but killing a game man when his hands were up . . . it just wasn't the way things were done in Texas. And Lem had been game or he would not have stumbled out there, dying, trying for a shot.

The bandits had come into town in two groups. One man with a rifle dismounted in front of the Rancher's Rest while the others rode on to the bank. One then remained outside with the horses, and three had gone inside.

When shots sounded from inside the bank, men rushed to the street; then the man with the rifle opened fire. He covered the retreat of the four men at the bank, but what had become of the man with the rifle? He had not run the gauntlet in the street.

Henry Plank, clerk in the stage station, had stepped to the door and opened fire on the fleeing bandits. He claimed to have winged one of them. Bowdrie pushed his hat back on his head and studied the street, scowling.

A large man with a blond mustache emerged from the bank and walked over to where Bowdrie stood. His face was florid and he wore a wide, dusty Stetson.

"Are you the Ranger?"

Bowdrie turned his black eyes on the man, who felt a sudden shiver go through him. There was something in those eyes that made him feel uncomfortable.

"Name of Bowdrie. Chick, they call me. You're Bates?"

"Yes. They call me Big Jim. I am the banker. Or maybe I should say, I was the banker."

"Is it that bad?"

Bowdrie's eyes strayed up the street. That was the direction from which the bandits had come. They could not have been seen until they were right in the street, and when they left, it was in the opposite direction, which put them behind some cottonwoods within a minute or two.

On the side of the street where he stood were the bank, a livery stable, a general store, and a blacksmith shop. At the opposite end, standing out a little from the other buildings, was the Rancher's Rest. Across from the Rest were a corral, two houses, a dance hall, now closed, and the Chuck Wagon, a combination saloon and eating house. Directly across was the stage station.

"Yeah," Big Jim said, "it is that bad. I've got money out on loans. Too darned much. None of the loans are due now. A few weeks ago I loaned ten thousand to Jackson Kegley, and I was figurin' on loanin' him the ten thousand they stole."

"Who's Kegley?"

"Kegley? He owns the Rest. Got a big cattle spread west of town. Runs eight, nine thousand head of stock. His place runs clean up to West Fork. That's where the Tom Roway place is."

"Roway's the man you think done it? Something to that effect was in the report."

Bates shrugged. "I ain't seen Tom Roway but twice in five years. He killed a couple of men in shootin' scrapes, then went to the pen for shootin' a man in the back.

"Three years ago he came back and brought Mig Barnes along. Barnes is pretty tough himself, or so they say."

"Why did you suspect Roway?"

"Bob Singer . . . he's a puncher around here, seen that paint horse. I guess everybody else saw it, too. The gent who used the rifle was ridin' that paint. Sorrel splash on the left hip and several dabs of color on the left shoulder."

"Did you send a posse after them?"

Bates looked embarrassed "Nobody would go. Tom Roway is mighty handy with a rifle and he's fast with a six-shooter. Bob Singer is pretty salty himself, and he wouldn't go, and after that, people just sort of backed off. Finally Kegley, Joel, an' me went out. We lost the trail in the waters of West Fork."

"Joel?"

"My son. He's twenty-one, and a pretty good tracker."

Chick walked past the bank. There was a bullet hole in the side window of the bank, too. When they started shooting in some of these towns, they surely shot things up. He walked on to the Rancher's Rest and stepped inside.

Aside from the bartender, there were three men in the saloon. The big, handsome man standing at the bar had a pleasant face, and he turned to smile at Bowdrie as he entered.

A man at a card table playing solitaire had a tied-down gun. The third man was a lantern-jawed puncher with straw-colored hair.

"You'll be Bowdrie, I guess," the big man said. "I am Jackson Kegley. This is my place."

"How're you?"

Chick glanced at the straw-haired puncher. He grinned with wry humor. "I'm Rip Coker. That shrinkin' violet at the card table is Bob Singer. Better keep an eye on him, Ranger, he's mighty slick with an iron, either shootin' or brandin'."

Singer glared at Coker, and his lips thinned as he looked down at his cards. Chick noticed the glance, then turned his attention to Kegley.

"You know Roway. Do you think he done it?"

"I wouldn't know. He's a damn good shot. We trailed him as far as the West Fork."

Coker leaned his forearms on the bar. His plaid shirt was faded and worn. "Roway's not so bad," he commented, "and I don't think he done it."

Singer was impatient. "Nobody could miss that paint hoss," he suggested. "Ain't another in the country like it."

Coker gave Singer a disgusted glance. "Then why would he ride it? If you was robbin' a bank, would you ride the most noticeable horse around?"

Bob Singer flushed angrily and his eyes were hard when he looked up, but he offered no comment.

"I'll look around some," Bowdrie said.

He walked outside, studying the street again. There was a suggestion of an idea in his mind, and something felt wrong about the whole affair. He went to the hotel section of the Rest and signed for a room, then strolled outside.

Something in the dust at his feet caught his eye, and he stepped down off the walk, running the dust through his fingers. He took something from the dust, placed it carefully inside a folded cigarette paper, and put it in his wallet.

Singer had come out of the saloon and was watching him. Bowdrie ignored him and strolled down to where his horse was tied. He was swinging into the saddle when Bates came to the door. "You ain't goin' after him alone, are you?"

Bowdrie shrugged. "Why not? I haven't seen any of his graveyards around."

He turned the roan into the trail. He was irritable because he was uneasy. There was something wrong here, it was too pat, too set up, and they were too ready to accuse Roway. "Personally," Bowdrie told the roan, "I agree with Coker. An outlaw using a horse everybody knew, that doesn't even make sense."

The trail was good for the first few miles, then became steadily worse. It wound higher and higher into rougher and rougher country. Skimpy trails edged around cliffs with dropoffs of several hundred feet to the bottom of dry canyons. Then, of a sudden, the trail spilled over a ridge into a green meadow, and that meadow opened into still another, each one skirted by borders of trees. At the end of the last meadow was a cabin, smoke rising from the chimney. A few cattle grazed nearby, and there were horses in the corral.

Chick Bowdrie rode up and stepped down. One of the horses in the corral was a paint with a splash of sorrel on the hip, a few smaller flecks on the shoulder. It was an unusual marking, unlikely to be duplicated.

"Lookin' for something?" The tone was harsh, and Bowdrie took care to keep his hands away from his guns.

The man stood at the door of his cabin not twenty feet away. He was a hard-visaged man with an unshaved face and cold eyes under bushy black brows. He wore a gun in a worn holster, and beyond him inside the door another man sat on a chair with a rifle across his knees.

"Are you Tom Roway?"

"And what if I am?"

Bowdrie studied him coolly for a long minute and then said, "I'm Chick Bowdrie, a Ranger. We've got to have a talk."

"I've heard of you. I've no call to like the law, but you want to talk, come on in. Coffee's on."

The man at the door put down his rifle and put a tin plate and a cup on the table. He was a stocky man with a pockmarked face. "Ain't often we have a Ranger for chow," he commented.

Roway sat down, filling three cups. "All right, Ranger, speak your piece. What business do you have with us?"

"Have you been ridin' that paint horse lately?"

"I ride that paint most of the time."

"Did you ride into Morales Monday morning an stick up the bank?"

"What kind of a question is that? No, I didn't rob no bank and I ain't been in Morales in a month! What is this? Some kind of a frame-up?"

"Five men robbed the bank at Morales Monday morning, and one of them was ridin' a paint horse, a dead ringer for that one out yonder." Bowdrie gestured toward the corral. "Where was that horse on Monday?"

"Right where he is now. He ain't been off this place in a week." He looked up, scowling. "Who identified that animal?"

"A dozen people. He was right out in plain sight. Nobody could've missed him. One who identified him was Bob Singer."

"Singer?" Roway's eyes flashed. "I'll kill him!"

"No you won't," Bowdrie said. "If there's any killin' done, I'll do it."

For a moment their eyes locked, but Roway was the first to look away. Mig Barnes had been watching, and now he spoke. "Do you reckon Tom would be so foolish as to ride to a holdup with the most known horse in the county? He'd have to be crazy!"

He gestured outside. "We've got a cavvy of broncs all colors an' kinds. He could take his pick, so why ride the one horse everybody knows?"

"I thought of that," Bowdrie agreed, "and it doesn't look like anybody with a place like this would want to steal. You boys have got yourselves a ranch!"

"Best I ever saw!" Roway said. "Grass all year around and water that never gives out. Our cattle are always fat."

"Has anybody ever tried to buy you out?" Bowdrie asked casually.

"You might say that. Jackson Kegley wanted to buy it from me, and for that matter, so did old man Bates. Then some of Kegley's boys made a pass at running me off the place a few years back. We sort of discouraged 'em, Mig an' me, we shoot too straight."

The coffee was good, so Bowdrie sat and talked awhile. The two were hard men, no doubt about that, but competent. Nobody in his right mind would try to drive them off a place situated like this. Bowdrie knew their kind. He had ridden with them, worked cattle with them. Left alone, they would be no trouble to anyone.

Neither of these men shaped up like a murderer. They would kill, but only in a fight where both sides were armed and where they believed themselves in the right.

The idea persisted that the bank cashier had been shot deliberately, and for a reason. But what reason?

Bowdrie was not taking Roway's word for it as far as the paint horse went, but he did not have to. He already had some thoughts about that, and an idea was beginning to take shape that might provide an answer.

It was a long ride back to Morales, and Bowdrie had time to think. The sun was hot, but up in the high country where he was, the breeze was pleasant. Bowdrie took his time. Riding horseback had always been conducive to thinking, and now he turned over in his mind each one of the elements. When he arrived at a point where he could overlook the town, he drew rein.

Morales, what there was of it, lay spread out below him like a map, and there are few things better than a map for getting the right perspective.

The paint horse was too obvious. Rip Coker had put that into words very quickly, but Bowdrie had been quick to see it himself. To ride such a horse in a robbery meant that a man was insane or he was trying to point a finger of suspicion at its owner.

"What I want to know, Hammerhead," he said to the roan, "is how that fifth bandit got away. More than likely, if he rode around behind the Rest an' took to the woods, he had to come this way to keep from sight. He had to know a trail leading him up to the breaks of this plateau without using the main trail."

For two hours he scouted the rim, returning to town finally with the realization that there was no way to reach the top without taking the main trail in full sight of the town.

"And if he didn't use the main trail, he just never left town at all!"

Several men were running toward the bank as he

rode into the street. Dropping from the saddle, Bowdrie tied his horse and went swiftly in the direction of the others. Hearing someone coming up behind him, he turned to see Jackson Kegley. "What's happened?" Kegley asked.

"Don't know," Chick said.

When they rounded the corner of the bank, they saw a small knot of men standing at the rear of the bank. Bowdrie glanced at Kegley. His face was flushed and he was breathing harder than what a fast walk should cause. A bad heart, maybe?

Bob Singer was there, his features taut and strained. "It's Joel Bates. He's been knifed."

Chick stepped through the crowd. He looked down at the banker's son. A good-looking boy, a handsome boy, and well-made. Too young to die with a knife in the back.

"Anybody see what happened?" Chick asked.

Rip Coker was rolling a smoke. "He was investigatin' this here robbery. I reckon he got too close."

"I found him," Henry Plank said. He was a small man, bald, with a fringe of reddish hair. "I come through here a lot, going to Big Jim's barn. He was lyin' just like you see him, on his chest, head turned sidewise, and a knife in his back."

"When did you come through here last?" Bowdrie asked. "I mean, before you found the body?"

"About an hour ago. He wasn't lyin' there then. I walked right over that spot."

Chick squatted on his heels beside the body. The knife was still in the wound, an ordinary hunting knife of a kind commonly used. There probably were as many such knives in town as there were men. This one was rusty. Probably an old knife somebody had picked up. He bent closer, lifting the dead man's hand. In the grain of the flesh there were tiny bits of white. His hand looked much as it would if he had gripped a not-quite-dry paintbrush.

Bowdrie stood up, thinking. Joel Bates's body was cold, and in this weather it would not lose heat very fast. Bowdrie was guessing that Joel Bates had been dead for considerably more than an hour, but if so, where had the body been?

Big Jim, stunned by grief and shock, stood nearby. Only that morning Bowdrie had heard Bates speak with pride of his son, the son who now lay cold and dead.

Chick Bowdrie was suddenly angry. He turned to face the group.

"The man who killed this boy is in this crowd. He is the same man who engineered the bank robbery. I know why he did it and I have a very good hunch who he is, and I'm going to see him hang if it is the last thing I do!"

Turning sharply, he walked away, still angry. Perhaps he had been foolish to say what he'd said, and this was no time for anger, yet when he saw that fine-looking young man lying there . . .

He walked back toward the barn and entered. It was cool and quiet in there, and sunlight fell through a few cracks in the boards. There were three horses in the stalls and there were stacks of hay. At one side of the old barn was a buckboard. Chick was following a hunch now, and quickly, methodically, he began to search. His success was immediate—a pot of white paint hidden under sacks and piled hay.

"Found somethin'?"

Bowdrie glanced up, a queer chill flowing through him. So engrossed had he been in his search that he had failed to hear the man enter. His carelessness angered him. It was Bob Singer.

"Yeah," Bowdrie said, "I've found something, all right."

Gingerly he lifted the pot with his left hand, turning it slowly. On one side was a clear imprint of a thumb, a thumbprint with a peculiar ropy scar across it.

"Yes, I've found something. This is the paint that was used to paint a horse to look like Roway's skewbald."

"Paint a hoss? You've got to be crazy!"

Several men had followed them into the barn and were listening.

"Somebody," Bowdrie said, "figured on stickin' Roway with this robbery. He painted a horse to look like Roway's."

"And left the paint can here?" Singer said. "It must have been young Bates himself."

"It wasn't young Bates. You see . . ."—Bowdrie looked at Singer—"I've known that horse was painted from the first. He stamped his feet and some paint fell off into the dust up in front of the Rest. Young Joel must've figured out the same thing. Either that horse was painted here or young Joel found that bucket of paint and brought it here to hide.

"The man who painted that horse followed him here and knifed him. He left him in the barn until there was nobody around, then carried him out here, because he did not want anybody nosin' around the barn."

"Hell," Singer scoffed, "that bandit is nowhere around Morales now. He got away and he's kept goin'."

"No," Chick said, the dimplelike scar under his cheekbone seeming to deepen, "that bandit never even left town."

"What?" Singer's tone was hoarse. "What d'you mean?"

"I mean, Singer," Bowdrie said, "that you were the man on that paint horse. You were the man who murdered Joel Bates. You've got a scar on the ball of your thumb, which I noticed earlier, and that thumbprint is on this can of paint!"

"Why, you . . . !"

Singer's hand clasped his gun butt. Bowdrie's gun boomed in the close confines of the barn, and Singer's gun slipped from nerveless fingers.

"Singer!" Plank gasped. "Who would have thought it was him? But who are the others? The other four?"

"Five," Bowdrie said. "Five!"

"Five?" Bates had come into the barn again. "You mean there was another man in on this?"

"Yeah." Bowdrie's eyes shifted from face to face and back. Lingering on Bates, then moving on to Kegley and Mig Barnes, who had just come in. "There was another. There was the man who planned the whole affair."

He walked to the door, and some of the others lifted Singer's body and carried it out.

Jackson Kegley looked over at Bowdrie. "Singer was supposed to be good with a gun."

There was no expression on Bowdrie's hawklike face. "It ain't the ones like Singer a man has to watch. It's the ones who will shoot you in the back. Like the man," he added, "who killed Lem Pullitt!"

"What d'you mean by that? Pullitt was shot—"

"Lem Pullitt was shot in the back, and not by one of the three in the bank."

It was long after dark when Bowdrie returned to the street. He had gone to his room in the Rest and had taken a brief nap. From boyhood he had slept when there was opportunity and eaten when he found time. He had taken time to shave and change his shirt, thinking all the while. The ways of dishonest men were never as clever as they assumed, and the solving of a crime was usually just a painstaking job of establishing motives and putting together odds and ends of information. Criminals suffered from two very serious faults. They believed everybody else was stupid, and the criminal himself was always optimistic as to his chances of success.

The idea that men stole because they were poor or hungry was nonsense. Men or women stole because they wanted more, and wanted it without working for it. They stole to have money to flash around, to spend on liquor, women, or clothes. They stole because they wanted more faster.

Walking into the Chuck Wagon, Bowdrie took a seal at the far end of the table where he could face the room. The killer of Pullitt was somewhere around, and he was the one who had the most to lose.

Bates was not in the Wagon, nor was Kegley, but Henry Plank was, and a number of punchers in off the range. One by one he singled out their faces, and there were one or two whom he recognized. As the thin, worn man who waited on the tables came to him to take his order, Bowdrie asked, "Who's the big man with the red beard? And the dark, heavy one with the black hair on his chest?"

"Red Hammill, who rides for Big Jim Bates. Ben Bowyer used to ride for Kegley, but he rides for Bates now. They ain't tenderfeet."

"No," Bowdrie agreed, "Hammill rode in the Lincoln County War, and Bowyer's from up in the Territory."

Rip Coker threaded his way through the tables to where Bowdrie sat. "Watch your step, Ranger. There's something cookin', and my guess is it's your scalp."

"Thanks. Where do you stand?"

"I liked Lem. He staked me to grub when I first come to town."

Without having any evidence, Bowdrie was almost positive Hammill and Bowyer had been involved in the holdup. Both men were listed as wanted in the Rangers' bible, both had been involved in such crimes before this. As wanted men they were subject to arrest in any event, but Bowdrie was concentrating on the present crime. Or crimes, for now another murder was involved.

There had been others. Was Coker one of them? He doubted it, because the man seemed sincere and also there had been obvious enmity between Coker and Singer, who had been involved.

Who was the man behind it? Who had planned and engineered the holdup? He believed he knew, but was he right?

Bates opened the door and stepped into the room. His eyes found Bowdrie and he crossed the room to him.

"I guess my bank will hold together for a while. I am selling some cattle to Kegley, and that will tide me over."

"You gettin' a good price?"

Bates winced. "Not really. He was planning to stock

blooded cattle, but he's buyin' mine instead. Sort of a favor."

Chick Bowdrie got up suddenly. "Coker," he whispered, "get Bates out of here, *fast!*"

He thought he had caught a signal from Hammill to Bowyer, and he was sure they planned to kill him tonight. There had been an appearance of planned movement in the way they came in, the seats they chose, the moves they made. He hoped his sudden move would force a change of plan or at least throw their present plans out of kilter.

"I'm hittin' the hay," he said to Coker, speaking loud enough to be heard. He started for the door.

He stepped through the swinging doors, turned toward the Rest, then circled out into the street beyond the light from the door and windows and flattened against the wall of the stage station.

Almost at once the doors spread and Red Hammill stepped out, followed by Bowyer. "Where'd he go?" Red spoke over his shoulder. "He sure ducked out of sight mighty quick!"

"Bates is still inside," Bowyer said, "an' Rip Coker is with him."

"It's that Ranger I want," Hammill said. "I think he knew me. Maybe you, too. Let's go up to the Rest."

They started for the Rest, walking fast. Bowdrie sprinted across to the blacksmith shop. Hammill turned sharply, too late to detect the movement.

"You hear somethin'?" he asked Bowyer. "Sounded like somebody runnin'!"

"Lookin' for me, Red?" Bowdrie asked.

Red Hammill was a man of action. His pistol flashed

and a slug buried itself in the water trough. Bowdrie
sprinted for the next building, and both men turned at
the sound.

Chick yelled at them, "Come on, you two! Let's step
into the street and finish this!"

"Like that, is it?" The voice came from close on his
right. *Mig Barnes!*

Bowdrie fired, heard a muffled curse, but it did not
sound like a wounded man.

A movement from behind him turned his head. Now
they had him boxed. But who was the other one? Was it
Roway?

He backed against the wall. The door was locked. On
tiptoes he made it to the edge of the building, holding to
the deepest shadow. He saw a dim shape rise up and the
gleam of a pistol barrel. Who the devil was *that*?

A new voice, muffled, spoke up. "You're close, Tex!
Give it to him!"

The shadow with the pistol raised up, the pistol lifting, and Bowdrie fired. "You're on the wrong side, mister!" he said, and ducked down the alley between the
buildings, circled the buildings on the run, and stepped
to the street just as Bowyer, easily recognized from his
build, started across it. Bowdrie's bullet knocked the
man to his knees. Red Hammill fired in reply, and a shot
burned close to Chick, who was flattened in a shallow
doorway.

He started to move, and his toe touched something.
A small chunk of wood. Picking it up, he tossed it
against the wall of the livery stable. It landed with a
thud, and three lances of flame darted. Instantly Chick
fired, heard a grunt, then the sound of a falling body. A

bullet stung his face with splinters and he dropped flat and wormed his way forward, then stopped, thumbed shells into his right-hand gun, and waited.

Tex was out of it, whoever he was. Bowyer had been hit, too. Chick thought he had hit Bowyer twice.

He waited, but there was no sound. He had an idea this was not to their taste, while street fighting was an old story to him. What he wished now was to know the origin of that muffled voice. There had been an effort to disguise the tone.

He was sure his guess was right. They intended to kill Bates, too. Maybe that was where . . .

He came to his feet and went into the saloon with a lunge. There was no shot.

The men in the room were flattened against the walls, apparently unaware of how little protection they offered. Bates, his red face gone pale, eyes wide, stood against the bar. Rip Coker stood in the corner not far away, a gun in his hand. Red Hammill stood just inside the back door and Mig Barnes was a dozen feet to the right of the door.

Why his dive into the room hadn't started the shooting, he could not guess, unless it was the alert Coker standing ready with a gun.

Hammill and Barnes were men to be reckoned with, but where was Roway?

The back door opened suddenly and Jackson Kegley came in, taking a quick glance around the room.

"Bates!" Bowdrie directed. "Walk to the front door and don't get in front of my gun. *Quick!*"

Hammill's hand started, then froze. Bates stumbled from the room, and Bowdrie's attention shifted to Kegley.

"Just the man we needed," Bowdrie said. "You were the one who killed Lem Pullitt. You stood in an upstairs bedroom of the Rancher's Rest and shot him when his back was to the window."

"That's a lie!"

"Why play games?" Mig Barnes said. "We got 'em dead to rights. Me, I want that long-jawed Coker myself."

"You can have him!" Coker said, and Mig Barnes went for his gun.

In an instant the room was laced with a deadly crossfire of shooting. Rip Coker opened up with both guns and Chick Bowdrie let Hammill have his first shot, knocking the big redhead back against the bar.

Kegley was working his way along the wall, trying to get behind Bowdrie. As Hammill pushed himself away from the bar, Bowdrie fired into him twice. Switching to Kegley, he fired; then his gun clicked on an empty chamber. He dropped the gun into a holster and opened up with the left-hand gun.

Kegley fired and Bowdrie felt the shock of the bullet, but he was going in fast. He swung his right fist and knocked the bigger man to the floor. He fell to his knees, then staggered up as Kegley lunged to his feet, covered with blood. Bowdrie fired again and saw the big man slide down the wall to the floor.

Bowdrie's knees were weak and he began to stagger, then fell over to the floor.

When he fought back to consciousness, Rip Coker was beside him. Rip had a red streak along the side of his face and there was blood on his shirt. Bates, Henry Plank, and Tom Roway were all there.

"We've been workin' it out just like I think you had it

figured," Henry said. "Kegley wanted a loan and got Bates to have the money in the bank. He killed Lem, just like you said.

"Kegley wanted to break Bates. He wanted the bank himself, and Bates's range as well. He planned to get Tom Roway in trouble so he could take over that ranch and run Bates's cattle on it.

"Mig Barnes apparently sold out to Kegley, but Lem Pullitt guessed what was in Kegley's mind, because he could see no reason Kegley would need a loan. Kegley was afraid Lem would talk Bates out of loaning him the money. Kegley hated Lem because Lem was not afraid of him and was suspicious of his motives."

"After you was out to my place," Roway said, "I got to thinkin'. I'd seen Barnes ride off by himself a time or two and found where he'd been meetin' Tex and Bowyer. I figured out what was goin' on, so I mounted up an' came on in."

Coker helped Bowdrie to his feet. "You're in bad shape, Bowdrie. You lost some blood and you'd best lay up for a couple of days."

"Coker," Bowdrie said, "you should be a Ranger. If ever a man was built for the job, you are!"

"I am a Ranger." Coker chuckled, pleased with his comment. "Just from another company. I was trailin' Red Hammill."

Chick Bowdrie lay back on the bed and listened to the retreating footsteps of Coker, Plank, and Bates. He stared up at the ceiling, alone again. Seemed he was alone most of the time, but that was the way it had always been for him, since he was a youngster.

Now, if he could just find a place like Tom Roway had . . .

SUNDOWN
TROY D. SMITH

Troy is a past winner of the Western Writers of America Spur Award for Best Paperback Novel for *Bound for the Promise-Land*. His newest novel is *Cross Road Blues*. His story "The Sellers" appeared in the anthology *Boot Hill*. While this story features a fictional Ranger, it also guest stars the Texas legend William "Bigfoot" Wallace. The story takes place during the early 1840s, not long after Wallace was a member of the Mier Expedition, which had been taken prisoner by the Mexicans—but that's another story.

Luke Temple remembered a time, when he was a small boy, that he had wished he could speak Spanish. It seemed like such a musical language, the way the vaqueros had spoken it. That little boy could never have dreamed up all the things that were going to happen to him over the next few years. He could never have guessed that at the age of twenty-two he would be able to speak that tongue almost perfectly, having learned the words over the sound of gunshots and dying men.

It was a little different now. Luke wished he could not speak the language at all, not a single word of it, so that he could not understand the shouts of the people of Monterrey. After ten years of fighting Santa Anna's armies, the Texas Rangers were at the general's back door hungry for revenge.

The Texans had learned long ago never to surrender to a Comanche or a Mexican, for neither group believed in honoring prisoners—at least that was the common understanding. The Rangers did not necessarily honor prisoners either, when those prisoners were Mexican or Comanche. Many of the men who rode beside Luke today had lost kinsmen at the Goliad massacre, when Santa Anna had ordered the execution of men who had surrendered in good faith. Others had kinsmen who had died at the Alamo, where no surrender was even asked for and the bodies were desecrated after they fell—among them eighteen-year-old Donald Temple, Luke's only brother. Some were survivors of the Mier expedition, in which captured Texans were forced to partake in a lottery to decide which would be executed and which would be sent into prison and forced labor.

Today it was definitely the Texans who would not be accepting prisoners.

There was still plenty of resistance—the Mexicans had set up sharpshooters on nearby roofs. Their ancient muskets were not sharp, and in fact could barely shoot, but there were enough of them to present a danger to the invaders. What was worse, at the end of the street the Mexicans had set up a couple of cannon, which were pounding at the Rangers with deadly effect.

"Foller me, boys!" a Ranger sergeant shouted. The man, who stood several inches over six feet, dashed across the rubble-strewn and into an adobe house. He waved a hatchet as he ran.

"Yeehaw!" yelled Luke's friend Frankie Johnson. "Ever'body foller Bigfoot Wallace!" A lead ball crashed into the side of Frankie's head and he pitched forward. The other Rangers jumped over him, some firing as they ran. Luke emptied his five-shot Colt repeater at the snipers. He ran inside then, not pausing to determine the success of his barrage.

"What good are we to anybody holed up in here?" one Ranger demanded.

"You'll see, boy," Bigfoot said with a grin. He was only a few years older than Luke, but was a Mier expedition survivor—the big trapper had seen so much fighting and dying that he seemed decades older than his comrades.

"Look an' learn, fellers," he said. Bigfoot smashed at the wall with his hatchet once, knocking a hunk of plaster loose. "Stand ready with them shootin' irons," he commanded. Then the big man stepped beside the scar in the wall and hacked at it some more.

Soon a gaping hole had been torn in the wall, and bullets were coming through it. "I reckon we've found some of our snipers," Luke said, as he and two others stepped up to the wall and returned the Mexican's fire. No more shooting came from the other room. Luke peered inside, squinting at the smoke. He was eventually able to see three bodies lying on the floor.

Bigfoot was still hacking—he did not stop until he had produced a hole big enough to step through. Once they were in the room, the sergeant started working on the next wall.

"The proper thing to do when you move into a new neighborhood," Bigfoot said, "is to go around an' meet all the neighbors."

"By God!" a Ranger said, laughing. "We're fixin' to work our way clean down the street and come out right on top of them cannon gunners!"

"That's the idea," Bigfoot said.

Again the Rangers fired through the hole until resistance ceased, then stepped inside. This time, however, a few Mexicans were hidden in the smoke waiting for them. One Texan was shot through the chest, and the others unloaded their pistols at the enemy. A scraping sound came from the corner behind them. Luke whirled around and saw two small figures. He raised the single-shot pistols which he held in reserve, but his arm was knocked aside by Bigfoot.

"We ain't Comanches, partner," Bigfoot told him. "Look."

The figures were children, neither more than seven or eight years old. Bigfoot picked them up in his big arms. Another, smaller child was behind them.

"Come on, Temple," Bigfoot said, after their comrades had broken through the next wall and moved on. "Let's take these young'uns a couple of doors down where it's safe."

Before Luke could speak, the big sergeant was stepping back through the first broken wall. Luke scooped up his own burden and followed. Before he passed through the hole, Luke noticed that Bigfoot had stopped short—three Mexican soldiers had walked into the room from the outside door. Bigfoot had not had time to set the children aside or draw his weapon—he could only stand there, facing the muskets.

"You boys hold off on shootin' me," he told the Mexicans. "Until I put down these young'uns."

Luke placed his own human burden onto the floor and took his pistols back out. "Duck!" he yelled, and Bigfoot dropped to the ground. Luke's guns boomed, and two soldiers fell. Bigfoot sprang from the floor and plunged his Bowie knife into the surviving Mexican with such force that the man was lifted several feet into the air.

"Obliged, Luke," Bigfoot said. "You young'uns stay put now, hear?"

Without a further word to each other, the two Texas Rangers climbed through the wall and rushed toward the distant gunfire.

Domingo Sánchez was not happy. None of the soldiers struggling to defend Monterrey were exactly *happy,* of course, but Domingo found it hard to imagine that any of them were quite so unhappy as him. No one likes being shot at, but it was not the bullets Domingo minded so much. He had been shot at plenty of times, since long before he had put on a uniform.

What Domingo Sánchez did not like was being shot at so damn *much.*

He had spent most of his twenty-three years as a

thief—he could hardly remember a time when things were given to him instead of dangled out of his reach as a test of his stealing ability. It was one especially challenging item—a locket dangling from the neck of the alcalde's wife—which had led him into his current predicament. A slight misstep at the critical moment, a stumble, and what had been planned as a smooth purloining motion turned into a very embarrassing gaffe. Neither the alcalde nor his wife—nor the assembled crowd—were especially amused. He had barely escaped the town with his neck intact, and a group of very stubborn *rurales* dogged his every step for days with the apparent intention of remedying that oversight.

Domingo had decided it was his patriotic duty to volunteer as a soldier. Besides, who would think to look for him there? And it had worked out quite well, for a while. Killing, robbing, and looting, and being paid by the government (although very meagerly) to do so—it was the life of a king.

Then the *guerreros* had started their little war, greedy for Mexican lands, and everything went to hell.

Today Domingo and a dozen of his fellow infantrymen stood amidst whizzing bullets in Monterey—serving as the last line of protection for a group of very unimaginative artillerymen.

"Madre," Domingo's comrade Carlos muttered. "The gringo soldiers are bad enough, but these damned Rangers are like devils from hell."

"Then they will feel at home when we send them there," Domingo said. Under his breath he added, "But I don't want to escort them all the way personally."

He fired his musket into the distant mass of

Americans. It was too smoky to know if he had hit anyone or not. He half turned in his efforts to reload quickly—and noticed something very peculiar about the wall behind them.

A very small hole had appeared in it. As he watched, the hole got larger—pieces of wall crumbling to the ground—and larger still, in the space of a couple of heartbeats. He saw the blade of an axe poke through, and then the wall collapsed outward.

"*Mierda*," Domingo said, and never had he meant it so much.

A giant of a man rushed though the cloud of dust raised by the tumbling masonry, another giant close behind him. It seemed a small army was on their heels. The first giant swooped down on a cannoneer, his madly swinging hatchet bashing in the unfortunate man's skull. The Rangers swarmed over them like angry bees.

Carlos rushed toward the enemy, his bayonet extended. His brains exploded about his head like a misty red halo.

Domingo Sánchez decided to retire from the military life. He spun on his heels and made a mad dash for an appealingly quiet alley. The lieutenant in command of the artillerymen stepped angrily in front of him.

"Where are you going, you coward!" the lieutenant said.

"I am retired," Domingo responded, and plunged his bayonet into the lieutenant's guts. Domingo then rammed a shoulder into the man, to knock him off his blade and out of his way. He had no time for idle conversation.

Domingo scurried into the alley. Half a dozen of his comrades quickly joined him—two were shot dead by the Rangers, but those Mexicans who chose to remain behind and fight occupied the gringos enough for Domingo and his companions to escape. They ducked from one alley to another, and soon ducked their way right through the rear of their own lines and into the countryside. Many of their fellow soldiers took note of their flight, and especially of Domingo Sánchez (who killed a couple more of his own officers when they tried to stop him.) Now *here,* some of those soldiers seemed to say to themselves, is a determined man with a clear goal: not being killed. Many of the soldiers decided that Domingo's goal was a worthwhile one, and decided to give it a try. They fell in behind the hurried thief.

Domingo did not spare them a backward glance for some time. When he finally did, a world of possibilities opened up for him. Here were several other recently retired military professionals. If they could manage to escape the *norteamericános,* there just might be some business potential there for an enterprising young man like himself. He began to make mental calculations even as he ran, and to come up with a plan to ensure that he could get the other soldiers to follow him in more than just the literal sense—and to keep them intact until he could make good use of them.

Domingo Sánchez was good at thinking on his feet.

Luke Temple paused a moment to catch his breath. Two dead Mexican artillerymen lay at his feet. Things were starting to die down—with the cannons out of commission, it was now only a matter of mopping up. The

fight was rapidly going out of the enemy, and several
had high-tailed it into the brush outside of town.

The sharp crack of a nearby musket, and the sight of
the seemingly invulnerable Bigfoot Wallace crumpling
to the ground beside him, made Temple realize that he
had relaxed too soon. The Mexican infantryman,
enveloped in a haze of gun smoke, tried to duck back
behind the rubble which had previously concealed
him—Temple's reflexes were too fast. The Walker Colt
bucked in Temple's hand and the Mexican was hurled
back against the crumbling wall, the front of his uniform a red ruin.

"Shit," Bigfoot mumbled.

Luke knelt beside his friend. "How bad is it, partner?"

"Shit."

Bigfoot's leg was bleeding. Luke probed the wound,
and his friend gasped.

"I don't think the bone is broke," Luke said. He tore a
strip of cloth from a Mexican corpse to use as a bandage.

"Well, I *thought* that was all of them," Luke said as he
tied the wrapping tight.

"Dern if that don't smart a mite," Bigfoot said. "I hate
gettin' shot by Mexicans."

"They don't seem to like bein' shot by us, much,
neither."

One of the younger Rangers, Olson, approached
them. "What do we do now, Sarge?"

"I aim to set here and bleed, and maybe cuss a little,"
Bigfoot responded.

"Maybe we ought to check in with the regular army
boys, see what we're supposed to do next," said another
Ranger, a stout redheaded man named Richards.

Bigfoot looked up at Richards, his face wrinkled up like he had caught some strange bug crawling in his breakfast.

"What y'uns is going to do," Bigfoot said, "is chase down them'uns that got away before they get too far. Looks like things is winding down here, except for the occasional potshot. I'll set here and watch for snipers to get up enough nerve to stick their heads up."

"Why bother with a bunch of deserters, anyway, Bigfoot?" Richard said. "Let 'em go."

"We come down here to kill Mexicans, by God, and I reckon that's what we'll do. You keep a sharp eye out for tall ones. If'n you get one, fetch me back his britches. That sum bitch with his blunderbuss has plum ruint mine."

"You heard the man," Luke said. "Let's get back to our horses and head out."

"There ain't but six of us, if you don't count Bigfoot," Richards said. "There looked to be over a dozen of them, maybe more." Richards was starting to get on Temple's nerves. He had never seemed like a timid man before. Luke suspected he was trying to find excuses to stay behind and take what little loot could be found, which Luke did not find endearing.

"Six mounted Rangers with Colts are more than a match for twenty or thirty scared Mexicans with muskets," Luke said. "No more arguments. Let's go."

Luke paused beside his wounded friend. "You want us to leave one man behind with you, just to be on the safe side?"

Bigfoot flicked his eyes toward Richards—he knew what Luke was up to, and who he would get stuck with.

"I'll manage," he said. "I had these britches made special. I'm mad enough right now I could eat a couple of Mexicans if I ran out of bullets."

Luke nodded and strode away. Bigfoot Wallace sat and loaded his spare revolver as the other Rangers disappeared.

As much as he disliked Richards, Luke had begun to think that he might have a point about hunting down stragglers. It hardly seemed like a sporting thing to do—the Mexicans had lost fair and square, after all, and then taken themselves out of the game. What if they didn't put up a fight when the Rangers found them? What if they just threw down their guns—if they hadn't already done so—and ran faster? Were the Rangers supposed to just run them down? Luke knew he would not be able to do such a thing, and doubted if Bigfoot would either if faced with the prospect.

As it turned out, he had little reason to worry in that regard.

The Rangers had been riding along at a decent clip, confident they would overtake their quarry at any moment. Richards was the first one to fall—a bullet passed through his neck and he toppled out of the saddle. Luke reined in his mount, trying to get a clear handle on what was going on, and two more men fell beside him.

The deserters were on a ridge above them. The Rangers had expected the Mexicans to still be running blindly into the brush, thinking of nothing but their own survival, when instead they had set up a nice little ambush and turned the tables on their pursuers. Luke cursed his own foolishness.

One of the fallen Rangers was only injured—blood streamed from his shoulder. Young Olson leaned down and helped the man mount up behind him.

"Ride!" Luke yelled at his surviving comrades. "Get out now!"

A bullet thunked into the flesh of Luke's horse. The animal screamed and reared. Luke held tight to the poor beast's mane, but another bullet crashed into its chest and it collapsed like a wet sack. He barely managed to throw himself clear and avoid being crushed.

Olson and his passenger were both shot multiple times. There was little hope for them. The only Ranger left besides Luke was a grizzled veteran named Bertram. Bertram had spurred his mount for all he was worth and thundered back toward Monterrey—he was leaned forward in the saddle, dust billowing in his wake. Luke was starting to believe the other man would actually make an escape. Even better, while the Mexicans concentrated their fire on Bertram, Luke had breathing room to run for cover. He grabbed his rifle from its boot and sprinted away. There was little cover to be had—he managed to throw himself into a shallow scrub-lined culvert. It would not afford him much protection, but perhaps it would enable him to make his death a costly one for the enemy.

Luke had briefly entertained the hope that he might be able to hold them off long enough for Bertram to return with help, but that hope was dashed. Just before the other Ranger got out of range, one of the musket balls whizzing around him flew home. Bertram pitched headlong out of the saddle and lay unmoving in the dust.

"Well, hell," Luke said. The Mexican guns fell silent. They had apparently realized that there was still one Texas Ranger unaccounted for, and were no doubt even now trying to figure out his location. Luke figured it would be no more than half a minute before a dozen guns were firing onto his position. He scrabbled around, hoping to find some sort of additional cover—and noticed what at first seemed like only a depression in the rocks. When he ran his hand along it, though, he realized it was more than that. It was a recess, just large enough that with some effort he was able to squeeze his body into it. He pulled a piece of brush behind him—if he was lucky it would shield him from the enemy's eyes. Luke squirmed his way deeper into the nook. He expected to meet resistance immediately, but to his surprise he was able to keep pushing himself backward for a long while.

Domingo Sánchez was enjoying his retirement. The sight of those Texas Rangers lying lifeless in the distance made life seem even sweeter. Every celebration, of course, has its spoilsport.

"Where is the other *guerrero?*" one of the deserters said.

Domingo counted the bodies. Five men, three horses. He had indeed counted six men on their approach—they had lost track of one of them in the excitement.

"*Mierda,*" Domingo said. "Where *is* the other *guerrero?*"

"He must be in that brush down there, where the ground dips," another soldier said. Most of the men who made up their little party were still strangers to

Domingo; he had only served closely with a handful of them.

A total of nineteen *soldados* had joined Domingo in his escape. Of that number, six had refused to double back with them to set up their ambush and had instead scattered, hoping to find their way to their respective homes. Domingo was left with thirteen men who were willing to listen to his advice; soon they would realize that they were actually taking his orders, but by then they would not mind so much. Domingo himself, the fourteenth man, kept them from being unlucky. In more ways than one. This victory over the Rangers— the hated *diablos tejanos*—would assure them of that. Domingo was already laying plans for the things he could accomplish with his own band of armed freebooters. Those plans were all lacking in nationalistic interests.

"Si," Domingo acknowledged. "That is the only place he could be." He scanned the terrain around them once more. The ridge, the plain, and besides that only a large rock which loomed above all the rest. This rock was a good distance away to the west, though, and a large clearing separated it from the site where the Rangers fell. It would have taken a man a good ten or fifteen minutes to run across that clearing, and the *soldados* had only been distracted by the final escaping Ranger for a minute or two at the most. The missing gringo could not be there.

One of Domingo's new acquaintances followed his gaze. "Puesta de Sol."

"*Qué?*"

"Puesta de Sol," the man repeated. *Sundown.* "I am

from here—we call that rock Sundown, because when the sun sinks behind the thing it seems to glow with the sunlight. It is too steep to climb without a rope; he could not be there."

"Of course not," Domingo said. He jerked his head back toward the culvert. "Let's put twenty or thirty musket balls in that spot over there. Then we can go down and drag what is left of him out of the brush."

Fourteen muskets belched flame and sent lead hurtling at Luke Temple's hiding place. A minute later they did it again.

"*Mierda*," Domingo said yet again.

He poked at the brush with the toe of his boot. There was nothing beneath it. Domingo sighed in frustration.

He and his *compañeros* had ventured down from their protective cover on the ridge—very hesitantly at first, even though they knew that nothing could remain alive in the gully. They had been emboldened by the fact that there was no stirring there at all at their approach, let alone any gunfire. Now they were finding out why. There was no one *in* the gully.

"He has to be somewhere, though," Domingo said under his breath. "I hate those damn Rangers."

One of the *soldados* toppled over, blood spurting from his chest, and there was a distant boom. Domingo's head snapped around at the ridge they had just come from—no one was there. A moment later several other shots rang out. Domingo realized they were coming from the sheer rock which he had been told was inaccessible. These new shots were apparently coming from a revolver, for the bullets fell short of the gully—

except one, which smacked into the skull of a deserter who had been lingering closer to the ridge.

A couple of men dropped to their knees and raised their muskets to fire at the rock. "Not now!" Domingo barked. "Get back to the ridge and take cover before he has time to reload!"

Domingo himself sprinted back toward their previous location. One of the kneeling men joined him, as did most of their amigos, but the second man fired toward the rock anyhow. A couple of seconds later a musket ball plowed into his belly and he rolled over. Domingo did not spare the idiot a second glance; he kept running.

One of the wounded man's friends did glance back at him, and more. This *soldado* ran back and helped the injured fool to his feet—he half-dragged him toward the ridge.

As Domingo scrabbled his way up the ridge a minute or so later, he heard the rifle boom once more. The loyal Good Samaritan who had gone back for his fellow paused briefly in his tracks as his head exploded. Then he fell. He let go of his burden then, and the gutshot man slid back down the ridge aways. No one went back for him this time, despite his pleas. Domingo briefly considered putting him out of his misery, but hated to waste the powder.

The remaining Mexicans lay on their bellies on top of the ridge. There was no more firing from the rock.

Domingo scanned the faces of his men. "You," he said, pointing at the one who claimed to be from the region. "I thought you said that rock was too steep to climb."

"It is!"

"Perhaps the *guerrero* grew wings and flew up there. Is that possible, do you think? Do Rangers have wings tucked under their ponchos?"

"I—I don't know."

"*Idiota.*" Domingo spat. "He got up there somehow when we weren't looking."

Domingo raised his head to get a better look at the crag his companion had called Puesta de Sol. The rifle rang out again, and a bullet scarred the rocks near Domingo's head. He promptly hugged the ground.

"*Mierda,*" he said. He had got sand in his mouth.

Luke reloaded the rifle and waited patiently for more of his enemies to get impatient and lift their heads. He wished they were not out of range of his Colt—he could lay down a nice fire on them indeed if they were closer.

He had thought himself a goner when he first squeezed into the cranny. It had proven to be more than a cranny, however—it opened into a very narrow cave, and the cave had led him straight to the crag. It might be impossible to climb from the outside, but from the inside it was easy. Luke wondered if it were all pure luck, or if some people had carved out a secret entrance to the imposing rock in an earlier era. It made for a wonderful fortress; he doubted if it could have occurred naturally. What really mattered was that it had saved his skin. He had been nervous when that Mexican had started poking around at the brush with his foot. If left alone, he might have figured out that all was not what it seemed. It was a good thing Luke had gotten into a position to fire on them and distract them by then.

"Hey, Ranger!"

Luke had climbed up the rocks on the inside of the stone fortress and discovered that a very spacious cave existed near its top. A small hole in the side of the crag, perhaps four feet wide and equally tall, served as a sort of window. It was perfect for a sharpshooter to hold off his enemies—although the people who first used it were probably armed with bows instead of guns.

He peered over the lip of the window. The Mexican was calling to him again, but would still not raise up.

"Hey, Ranger!" he repeated.

"Hey, Mexican!"

"You nice and cozy up there, Ranger?"

"Cozier than you!"

"We will see! You will get thirsty soon!"

He had a point there.

"You may be right," Luke called out. "Then again, there'll be a whole passel of U.S. troops out looking for me before long. Not just a handful this time. Then I'll not be thirsty no more, and you'll be dead."

"Maybe so," Domingo answered.

"I know so. Looks like we have a Mexican standoff. Pardon the expression."

"Come on down here and we'll talk about it, amigo! I bet we can work something out!"

"You come on up here!"

"I don't know how to get up there."

"Climb!"

The Mexican laughed. "If we start climbing that cliff, I think you'll end our little trip real quick! *Gracias*, but we'll just stay right here!"

"Suit yourself."

"*Mierda!*" the Mexican yelled, but without much feeling.

Just before dusk, Luke saw them leaving. He considered taking a shot or two at them, but saw little point in it. They would only dig back in and the standoff would continue. It was best to let them go.

What worried him was their number. He thought he had counted twenty to begin with, down at the gully, and he knew he had killed four at least—but in the dim light he could not get a clear count of the number leaving. It *looked* about right, but he could not be sure. Luke decided to play it safe for a while, just in case. He stayed at the window, trying to keep one eye on the ridge and the other on the entrance into the cave—but it was a moonless night, and soon he could see nothing at all. He dozed lightly though the night, his revolver clasped tight in his hand.

The morning sun finally came out, Luke's throat still pleasantly uncut. He watched the ridge until midmorning, and still saw no sign of activity. Finally he decided it was safe to come down.

Luke pulled himself out of the recess in the gully, squirming on his belly and then raising himself to his knees.

"*Hola,* amigo," the Mexican said. His musket was pointed at Luke's head, and the reins of Bertram's horse were wrapped around one of his hands. "I had a feeling you'd come this way. When I poked my head up and no one shot at me, I knew you were on your way down. Looks like our standoff is over, no?"

"Reckon so," Luke said. "Shit."

"Indeed."

Luke tensed, wondering if he could get to his feet and cross the distance between them without being shot. He knew the answer.

The Mexican chuckled. "Domingo Sánchez, at your service, amigo. And I was lying. Our standoff is not quite over after all. On my way down here I saw those soldiers you spoke of—they should be here in about fifteen minutes or so. Unless they hear the sound of me blowing your brains out, in which case they would get in a big hurry and it would be more like five. This would not be in my best interests."

Luke said nothing.

Domingo smiled. "So it is up to you, gringo. Unbuckle that gunbelt and toss it over to me quickly. If you do, I will mount up and ride away, and we will finish this standoff some other time. If you don't, I will have to shoot you, and we will both lose."

Luke nodded and slowly moved his hands to the belt buckle. "You sure waited out here a long time, just to let me go," he said.

"Oh, I don't care if I kill you or not. I just wanted to know how you got in and out of that crag over there. I knew this gully had to have some secret that might come in handy for me someday."

Luke tossed the gun at Domingo's feet. There was defiance in his face. "You could go ahead and shoot me anyway," he said.

"I could have shot you before. I can't shoot all of those other gringos, though, and I am in a hurry. Adios!"

Domingo jumped into the saddle and galloped off, taking Luke's Walker Colt with him.

"I'll get my damn gun back!" Luke yelled. Domingo looked back and laughed, and was gone.

Luke started walking toward his approaching countrymen. All in all, it had not been the best couple of days of his life. He would have other chances, though. He'd make sure of it.

"Shit," Luke said without much feeling, and walked on.

THE PLUM CREEK FIGHT
DUSTY RICHARDS

❧

Dusty Richards is the author of over thirty novels, most recently *The Natural* and *Trail to Fort Smith,* a Ralph Compton Traildrive novel. Here Dusty tells his fictionalized version of the factual Battle of Plum Creek.

The hot August wind in my face, I pushed the dun horse harder. There were more bloodthirsty Comanche bucks on the warpath in South Texas than a man could count. Ever since that scared-half-to-death kid from Goliad had shown me the sea of pony tracks they'd made, my best senses told me lots of innocent folks would die in their wrathful swath through the countryside if something wasn't done to put everyone on their guard.

Filled with purpose, I drove off the steep hillside headed for the Farnsworths' place, grateful for the sure-footed dun between my knees. At the base of the hill, I leaped him over a split-rail fence and charged for the house.

"Ben McCulloch," Mida Farnsworth shouted. The girl of sixteen or so came on the run holding up her dress tail. "Whatever is wrong?"

"Comanches," I said, stripping out the latigos with hardly time for talk or explanation. "I'm taking one of your fresh horses."

"Help yourself. How many of them are there?" she asked, paling under her suntanned face.

"Hundreds of them. I need your brothers to ride and tell everyone to get to Goliad. Maybe we can hold them off there."

"But—but—"

"Go ring that bell and get them in here right now," I said and gave her a not-so-gentle shove to untrack her. Wasn't that I didn't like Mida—but I wanted her and everyone else in Gonzales County alive when this thing was over.

She swallowed hard, rolled her lower lip in under her even white teeth, then ran for the belfry set on four tall posts. The strong afternoon breeze swept the knotted hemp back and forth. With no time to talk, I led the hard-breathing dun to the corral and turned him in. A stream of sweat ran off his lathered shoulders and trembling flank, then down his legs. I hoped he wasn't windbroke, but there was no time for regret.

The bell clanged and clanged as she tugged on it with both hands. The alarm was sounded. Besides the Farnsworths, others in the country would hear it and know something was wrong. Taking a reata off a post, I shook it loose to capture another mount. Two swings over my head and the loop shot out from my hand for the target. When the circle settled around a big roman-nosed blue roan's throat, I jerked my slack. A stout horse, he might not have all the speed of my dun, but he was big and should be up to the task ahead.

My pads and saddle over on the roan's back, I led him out of the corral and headed for Mida.

"Can I stop now?" she asked, out of breath, still pulling hard on the rope.

"Hold him." I gave her the reins and took the bell rope in my hands. Jerking it harder, I set it to pealing with an urgency that marked the situation. Sometimes it took a while for the sound to penetrate the Texas Hill Country. People would stop working and hear the faint noise. The most important thing was they heard it and knew that things weren't right.

"I could get you something to eat," she offered as the nervous roan circled her.

"Not now."

"Who's leading them?" she asked.

"Only one I could figure that could get that many bucks on the warpath is Buffalo Hump."

"How will they ever stop them?"

"I ain't sure, but there ain't no one else to stop them but us."

"You mean the volunteers?" Her blue eyes opened wide and she gave an impatient jerk on the reins to settle the upset roan, who tried to pull her away from the noisy bell.

"Ain't another soul here but us. Texas has no army."

"But hundreds of Comanches against a handful of volunteers. Ben, you'll all be slaughtered."

"Maybe, but we'll take lots of them red devils with us."

"Oh my Gawd, Ben." Tears began to run down her cheeks and she lashed out at the impatient horse as she tried to hold him. "Whoa, stupid."

I quit ringing the bell and reached past her for the reins. In control, I set my flat boot heels in the dust and brought the roan around with my strength.

"Tell them brothers of yours that we're meeting at Goliad. They need to get word to everyone they can. They miss anyone, they're liable to be killed."

"Where're you going?"

"To scout them Comanches. Tell everyone when I figure out which way they're coming back, I'll send word and I'll need every rifle and pistol in this country ready to shoot."

"Benjamin McCulloch, you damn well be careful. I don't want to go to no funeral of yourns." She chewed on her lower lip.

I nodded my head that I'd heard the attractive tomboy's concern. She'd make a good catch for a guy looking for a wife. She ran the whole Farnsworth household ever since her mother died the year before— perhaps for even longer than that. Aggie had been sick for several years. Besides, I admired Mida's spunk.

"You figuring"—she wiped her wet eyes on her sleeve—"they'll come here and attack us?"

"They were headed south in an all-fired hurry. But they have to come back. Their wives, families, and lodges are all up north. That's when I worry about the safety of things around here. Tell your brothers they need to warn everyone. Have one of them load you up and take you and your little brother to Goliad."

"I will, Ben. You take care."

My left foot in the stirrup, I swung a leg over with an "I will."

Any more words were cut off when the roan bogged his head into the dust. I left the ranch yard in long, ground-clearing bucks aboard the big gelding. My spurs jabbed his hide and I cross-whipped him with the long reins to break his train of thought about tossing me off.

When he reached the wagon road, I had sawed his head up and he was running sideways. Must have picked the craziest horse in their string. I whipped him southward—no time for me to go back and change now.

In the next hour, I discovered a thin stream of black smoke that streaked the azure sky in the south. *Thompson's place.* The roan's hooves pounded the dry dust and he grunted deep in his throat like a hog, but he could run and had plenty of bottom. The next thirty minutes passed like an ant crawling a mile. When I burst into the open country, I knew what I'd suspected since I first saw the streak—too damn late.

Engulfed in flames, the shake roof on the main house was caving in. Haystacks were on fire and I reached for the flap over my five-shot Colt revolver. If there were any redskins left there, I aimed to make them pay for this with their lives.

Three dead lay on the ground, their naked bodies floured in dirt. Black spots marked their faces or torso where bullets or spears had penetrated them. The family dogs with smashed-in heads or lance wounds lay about, silenced by the red invaders. A shudder went through my shoulders. I didn't want to have to look at the remains of the women and children—two brothers and their families lived at this place above Calico Creek.

Dropping heavily from the saddle, the acrid smoke from the house fire hurting my nose, I led the hard-breathing roan by the reins with one hand and carried the .36-caliber in my other—in case.

Behind the house, I discovered the mutilated body of Ira Thompson's wife, Bertha. The grim sight made the butterflies in my guts turn into wildcats. Not ten feet away was a scalped boy perhaps five years old. They called him Chub. The next thirty minutes were the longest in my life. I wrapped the bodies up in what cloth I could find, dragged them inside an unscathed shed for later burial, and barred the door. Neither of the brothers were among the dead—either they'd been away and had not known about the impending danger or the Comanches dragged them off to torture. Either way, it wasn't easy. Two mutilated women, three bloody children's bodies, and more unaccounted for. I caught the roan; since the Comanches had taken all the horses, there was no fresh mount for me at this disaster. They'd made pincushions out of the women's milk cows and ransacked the place before setting it afire, taking only the choice items they wanted and scattering the rest.

At sundown, I was still hot on their main trail. At this point I began to realize—besides all the side raids that were close by their route—the main body of warriors was headed straight for Victoria. Comanches usually hit and run—making small raids on outlying ranches and farms. Never before had they taken on a town or village, but I knew that this time with such a large force, they'd strike a town. No way I could ever get there ahead of them red devils. I could only hope those poor folks had some warning. Still I needed to know the direction they had taken and when they were coming back. I felt deeply convinced that Buffalo Hump's marauders had to return north sooner or later.

An hour later, an armed rider guarding a crossroads hailed me. "Captain Tanner insists that all men join his company to make war on them red devils," the young man said.

"Where's he at?" I asked, looking around.

"Camp's up this road a couple miles. You can find it." The youth in his late teens pointed to the east. "I've got to stay here on guard or I'd show you."

I nodded and sent the roan on the wagon tracks that led east. Maybe this captain had enough men to make a good attack against them. The notion of a real force of fighting men raised my spirits as I short-loped in the twilight.

"Halt, who goes there?"

"Texas militia member," I said, reining up the roan.

"Whose outfit?"

"Gonzales County." Every second I sat there on my winded horse, I grew more impatient with the one in the road pointing a rifle at me. I damn sure wasn't a Comanche or I'd already have cut his throat and scalped him.

"How the hell do I know who you are? Get down off that horse."

"If you don't step aside, you'll never learn nothing but what a casket looks like from the inside." I booted the roan on in the growing twilight.

"Where do you come off? I'm the damn guard here. I ought to gut-shoot you!"

"You better watch for the Comanches. They'll kill you and answer your dumb questions later."

In camp, I reined up beside the first figure I saw in the firelight. They had enough big blazes going to tell all the Comanches in Texas where they were at, but that wasn't my affair.

"Captain Tanner. Where can I find him?"

The man rolled his head from side to side trying to focus on me and I noticed he had a crock jug in his hand. Then I smelled the fumes—whiskey.

"Down there." He pointed with his crock and then he offered it to me.

"No, thanks, I've got pressing business with Tanner."

I found the man with several others; all of them were dressed in business suits, sitting around a rough-hewn table that still smelled of pitch. They were playing cards and drinking hard liquor.

"Captain Tanner?"

A tall man with beard and mustache rose. "Sir, I am Captain Tanner. Commander of this army. What may I do for you, sir?"

"I'm in bad need of a good horse. I've been scouting the main band all day and my horse is about done in."

"Who are you?"

"Ben McCulloch, Gonzales County Volunteers, sir."

"Who is your commander?"

"Me, sir. Captain Talbot died. They made me commander."

"And your rank?"

"Private, I guess, We don't go much on rank. We do

lots of scouting and rangering and try to keep them red devils away from here."

"You're a mere private and you come here expecting me to give you a valuable horse for your own usage?"

"Sir, we need to stop them when they come back."

Tanner threw his head back and gave a great belly laugh. The others joined in. "Oh, you are mad, Private McCullum, was it?

"Why, we'll be lucky if they don't raid the whole state clear back to Louisiana. Wait, where are you going? Come back here. You are disobeying a military order of a superior officer!"

The cold chills ran up my face. My anger boiled at this bunch of laggards. Innocent folks were dying and all they could do was sit around, gamble, and get soused. In a flash, I bounded into the saddle and asked for one more burst of speed from the roan. Bless his heart, he gave me that surge and we left Tanner's camp of drunks and cowards. I vowed as I rode the gelding as hard as he could manage—I'd show them how my men would give them Comanches what for.

At dawn, outside of Victoria, an older rancher generously traded me his fresh horse for the roan after learning my purpose. He'd heard about the trouble and was coming to check on his kinfolks. When I explained my business, we switched saddles in the road.

"I reckon from all the smoke in the sky, I'm too late anyway. Good luck, McCulloch."

The death and destruction I discovered in Victoria was more of the same brutality I'd found earlier at the Thompsons'. Dead bodies, scalped and dismembered, littered the streets, some victims hung half out of windows of partially burned residences. If I ever imagined how hell looked, it was the way I found Victoria that morning.

Billy Jim Rawlings rode up and we recognized each other covered in road dirt and without a meal in twenty-four hours amid the corpses and shifting bitter smoke. We hugged each other and fought back tears. Words couldn't describe the horrendous sights around us.

I quickly told him of my plans to ambush them, win or lose, and see if we couldn't make them pay for their senseless marauding.

Billy Jim agreed. "They've got a couple thousand horses now, so the dust should be telltale." Then he looked hard at me. "You really need to go back and get the militia ready. I'll scout them and ride up there when they start that way."

"We need a few more to scout them than one man," I said, concerned about something happening to a single lookout. "Then if someone gets afoot or hurt, I'll still have word in time to shift the forces around up there."

Billy Jim agreed with a grim bob of his head. "Have you ever seen how many there are of them?"

"No, I've only seen the pony tracks and what they did here and in other places."

"Let me tell you, they about ran over me. I laid in a thicket for them to go by, thinking it was my last day, and they took hours to just ride by me."

With a quick nod, I agreed, but still if my volunteers had the element of surprise, Comanches weren't soldiers. They fought fierce, but never stayed and battled against any show of force—in the face of which they usually choose to retreat. This could be the big advantage of a surprise attack on them.

"We need to find a few more scouts. If the Comanches ride back the same way as they came down here, then my volunteers will make them pay for all this killing."

"That would be too good to be true." Billy Jim gave me a grim nod.

I agreed. But their lodges were somewhere northwest, so they'd go back that way somehow.

"Ain't that Liberty Jones?" Billy Jim shouted to a man coming up on a speckled gray horse.

"Liberty? What you doing here?" I asked the familiar man in buckskin with a rifle across his lap.

"Come to see what I could do about these heathen red niggers. They killed some folks of mine back up the way. Been tracking this bunch for a while." He spat tobacco off to the side. "They sure must be a passel of 'em."

We agreed. Billy Jim started in on my plan and the older man nodded. "I'll help do anything to send them devils to hell where they belong."

By mid-morning, the August sun beat down on us and my belly, despite the upset of all this around us, began to pain some for food.

"You ate anything, Liberty?"

"Yes." He turned and flung his arm in the direction he came from. "There's some women cooking a few blocks from here and feeding everyone. Come on, I'll show you. Dick Johnson's up there. We find him, he'd make you a good ranger, too."

Those four women maintained a lard kettle full of boiling beef stew and handed out steaming bowls and spoons to all takers. Bleary-eyed folks sat around on the ground eating. Most had tearstains on their cheeks like the cooks did, but they weren't crying for themselves— it was the ones hurt, maimed, and dead that wrung out their tears.

Liberty found Dick and brought the short stockman over to talk with us. He agreed to join my scouts. Each man was to take a different focus on the main war party, but once they started north, the scouts were to send word of the mass direction so I could set up my defenses for an ambush.

After the meal, I shook their hands. That's all state militia members were paid for ranger duty on the frontier, aside from the Colt revolver they had issued us. The legislature promised us horse feed and sustenance and pay, but even the horse feed never showed up, Texas was too broke. Why, the Lone Star dollar was worth only five cents American. Didn't matter—we were Texans and we'd show them Comanches. For all them folks that needlessly died, we'd do it.

On the long ride home, I avoided Captain Tanner and his drunken bunch. Made it straight to Goliad, but rode two horses into the ground, a fact I'd later regret, but there was little else I could do at the time.

My militiamen and many other volunteers met me on the courthouse lawn. We broke out the lead and gunpowder and loaded everything we had in wagons, so we'd be ready.

I stood in the back of one of the rigs to tell them the plan. "There is a good chance they'll ride right through the way they came. If they do, then my scouts will tell us and we can cut them to ribbons at the Plum Creek

Crossing. I want some men to haul some logs out there and build some low walls on the rise on both sides that we can hide behind and shoot at them from. There is one thing." I held my hand up for their silence. "You must bring that material in from the north and not disturb anything that they can see on their road or they'll get spooked."

"We can handle it, Captain," someone shouted. The yell went up, "We can do her!"

When I finished, I felt satisfied the plan was going forward. Getting down off the rig, I saw Mida standing at the edge of the crowd.

"They're calling you captain now, Ben," Mida said, her face beaming, the littlest Farnsworth hanging on to her hand.

"They can call me whatever they want. Just so we stop them."

"You had any sleep at all?"

"I'll be fine."

"Ben, come sleep under our wagon for few hours. You'll need some rest to lead those men in a battle."

"You better do what she says," Goliad mayor Rupport Conklin said. "We'll get them defenses up. You go get some rest."

Mida's middle brother Earl took my spent horse and said he'd have a fresh one for me when I got up from my nap. Nothing else that I could do but follow her and little Jody to the wagon.

I hit the pallet like a dead man and despite the buzzing flies was soon deep asleep.

*   *   *

"Dick Johnson's here to see you," Mida said, shaking me.

If she hadn't held me down, I'd have bolted up and struck the center pole under the wagon with my head. My heart went to pounding about how them Comanches were already on their way back.

My eyelids felt stuck together with glue, but when I got them open, I discovered it was night. "What is it?"

"Billy Jim said he thinks they'll come back the same route." Dick began his story when I crawled out from under the rig. "They tore up Linville on the Gulf, and the only way any folks escaped was in boats. They've got enough horses—you can see their dust for miles—and they've got them loaded down with all that stuff they've stolen. Besides that, you won't know them, because they're dressed in everything they found. I saw one drunk Injun wearing a woman's corset for a hat."

"Guess they've found plenty of liquor?" I asked, hoping their drinking party lasted this far north.

"They've got plenty. But they've also got guns and ammunition."

I agreed.

"Liberty will be here at sunup and tell us if they're still on course."

"When do you think they'll get here?"

"Tomorrow at midday, I figure."

"You did good. Thanks."

"I ain't leaving. I'm fighting with you."

"Sorry, I'd sure appreciate your help."

"More men have been coming in all night to join you," Mida said, handing me a cup of steaming coffee. "You'll have lots of militia to go with you and help."

At dawn I inspected the log buttresses; they looked good. If the Comanches rode into this trap, they would be cut down by our cross fire—provided nothing spooked them short of it.

Liberty arrived and I rode over to talk to him. In his opinion, their route looked the same.

"You got a dozen men you can spare with revolvers?" Liberty asked.

"Might have. Why?" I listened close.

"If we strike the rear guard with a small force before they reach here, we might panic them right into your gun sights."

"That's also taking some firepower away from my men up on the creek." The plan worried me.

"But if they thought all of Texas was after them, they might just ride on like lightning had struck them in the butt and you'd get what you can of them charging by."

I had to agree; his idea would be a safer bet for my small militia even with the new volunteers swelling the ranks. Panic the Comanches and then cut them down when they fled through the creek. That would leave me eighty men, forty to each side. Men both young and old who could sure enough aim and hit something when they squeezed the trigger.

"I'll let you have eight. Any more and my men on the barricades would be too thin."

"I'll take eight. When I see they're close enough to you, we'll come whooping and screaming, shooting our guns off and try to make them bolt into your ambush."

I agreed. In the south, already I could see the veil of dust in the sky from the thousands of horses they drove, loaded down with their spoils. My butterflies went to

churning—I didn't need an Alamo on Plum Creek.
There were lots of men with families come to fight, not
the same as the militia members, who were mostly single boys like myself.

Filled with concern, I rode the bay that they'd found
for me wide of the Comanches' route to get over to the
west side. A youth quickly took my horse back into the
woods and out of sight.

When I started up the line, the men rose and saluted. I
felt awkward about it, but returned their address. Everyone
knew their job. A natural leader, Dick Johnson, was com-
manding the forces for me on the east. Before I left over
there, Liberty was getting recruits for his raiding party.

I told the men on the west side the plan and they
agreed. Kegs of powder were open and ready. Pails of
water to cool the gun barrels if they had time. Everyone
had a fresh-looking edge—even the young boy who
brought me a cup of coffee.

Taking the cup, I frowned at him. Because of the too-
big cap I couldn't tell much, but when I saw the blue
eyes I knew he was no boy.

"Mida," I hissed. "What're you doing here?"

"Hush, the others don't know. I came to reload your
weapons. I know how, my brothers showed me."

"You can't—"

"I can't go back now. See their dust. Accept me?"

I closed my eyes. Trapped, what next? "All right, but
keep your head down."

"I am not the only woman here."

In defeat, I nodded that I'd heard her.

Flies buzzed on and time crept by. A boiling sun was
at its highest point. The thousands of hooves pounding

the ground were becoming audible. Men peeked over
the ramparts hoping to be the first to see them.

"Get your heads down," I ordered. Surprise was our
greatest asset and I wanted them red devils to stare
down the gun barrel of death when they first saw us.

I heard screaming far off, like distant crows, and then
shots. Liberty had struck them in the rear. I looked to the
sky for help. We'd sure need lots of God's providence.

"Hold your fire," I said to pass up and down the line.

The wait was not long. In minutes, Comanches
began to rush from the south. I blinked my eyes in disbelief. The lead one was dressed in a red silk fancy
gown. You ever seen a man-eating buck, warpaint on his
dirty face, wearing an evening gown? The sight of him
must have shook me.

"Fire!"

The barrage of bullets wilted the ranks of the hard-
riding Comanches. A cloud of gray smoke soon engulfed
both sides. My eyes teared as I watched the confused
Injuns going right and left to get by us. No fight in
them—only trying to save their red asses.

With her back to the log wall, Mida sat on the ground
and very handily reloaded my pistol each time. While
she did that, I used the cap and ball rifle and reloaded it
myself. The gun smoke grew thick enough to cut with a
butter knife and we both coughed on the fumes and dust
churned up by the desperate Comanches. But both sides
of our men were taking a heavy toll on our enemy. The
field between us lay full of bodies of bucks and their
fallen ponies.

Then the shooting stopped. I didn't know how many
hundred Injuns had rode by us and got away. When the

shooting let up, I saw Liberty on horseback coming on the run toward me.

"It worked, McCulloch. They've abandoned all the horses and we have them." He reined his horse up short.

"Good news. But if we've got all that, then we ain't done with them yet." Buffalo Hump wouldn't ever stand for that. No way.

Liberty agreed and gave me his horse so I could go over and check on the other side.

"How are your men, Dick?" I shouted when I rode up.

"Ain't got a scratch on us."

"Good, but make sure that everyone stays put. Since we've got the horses and loot, they'll be right back. Can't take any chances."

"We'll be ready," Dick said.

I turned the pony and rode back to my side.

"Anyone get hurt over here?" I dismounted at the log rampart and looked at the bleary-eyed bunch standing behind it, leaning on their rifles and waiting on the word. I handed Liberty back his reins.

"Anyone hurt over here?"

"No one's hurt here, Captain." Then a big roar went up. But I felt convinced it was too soon to count the win—the battle wasn't over.

"No drinking yet. Everyone stay behind those walls. Liberty says we have all the stolen horses and the loot that they took, so they'll sure come back and try us. Everyone down behind those walls!"

Buzzards circled. In late afternoon, I sent Liberty out with a small group to ranger the area north. If Buffalo Hump was coming back, I wanted the outfit to be ready.

Day slipped into night. With sweaty hands dried on our pants, we waited. Mida fed me beef jerky and the other women kept the hot coffee flowing. The skin crawled on the back of my neck at any different sound. When would they come back?

At dawn, a scout rode in and reported that a large party of men were riding out of the south.

"Who would they be?" Mida asked, trailing at my heels.

I looked into her dirt-floured pretty face and smiled. "I hope to hell they're Texans."

Colonel Jim Buckley arrived on a white horse with a couple of hundred haggard volunteers behind him. They looked caved in but determined.

"You the man in charge here?" Buckley asked.

I saluted him. "Yes, sir. Glad to see so many men with you. We routed them red heathens yesterday, but I figured they'll come back since we have all their stolen goods and horses."

"All of it? You mean you have all the loot back?"

"Can't say all, but all they left us anyway."

"This your outfit?" Buckley asked, looking at his own officers gathered around him on horseback, all shaking their heads in disbelief. He turned back to face me. His blue eyes narrowed. "You led this handful of men you have here against those hundreds of Comanches and beat them?"

"We made it rough enough they left all that stuff."

"How many men did you lose?"

"None." I shrugged. What did he expect?

"Captain McCulloch," Mida said, stepping forward to

stand at my side, "you might take and show the colonel all those horses you've captured."

"Women are here, too?" Buckley blinked his eyes in disbelief at the sight of her.

"Oh, yes, sir, Colonel," Mida said with a smile. "It's a Texas tradition. We fight beside our men. Right, Ben?"

I could only nod in agreement.

NOTE: The Texas Rangers were first formed as local militia on the frontier with outfits like McCulloch's. They didn't even capitalize the word *Rangers* until after the Civil War. The Linville Raid/Plum Creek Fight was taken from actual historical events of August 1847. Years later, Ben McCulloch became a Civil War general. He was killed by sniper fire at the Battle of Elkhorn Tavern—or as it's called today, the Battle of Pea Ridge. Many consider the loss of him and his leadership on that field to be what cost the Confederacy the fight that day.

TIME OF THE GUN-WOLVES

JAMES REASONER

———❦———

James Reasoner is one of the most prolific authors of his time, having written more than 140 novels in multiple genres, as well as a bushel of short stories. The only reason he hasn't received more recognition is that many of his novels were written under pseudonyms. However, his ten-volume Civil War series, which concluded with the book *Appomattox,* should earn him some of the respect and recognition he deserves. His book *Draw* is a nonfiction account of some of the most famous gunfights in history. Here he writes about one Ranger—half Comanche—who tries to make amends for the past while riding for the famous "Rip" Ford and Old Company.

Of all the men I met while riding with the Texas Rangers as company surgeon, the one with perhaps the most interesting background was our scout, Roque Maugricio. Half Mexican, half Comanche, he had been carried off by the savages during a raid when he was but a young boy and was raised by them, ultimately becoming one of their war chiefs before leaving the tribe. During the time I knew him, he dressed in white men's clothing—homespun shirt, whipcord trousers, cowhide vest, high-topped boots, and broad-brimmed black hat—and carried a white man's weapons—a brace of Walker Colts, a pair of muzzle-loading rifles, and a heavy-bladed Bowie knife. He spoke English without a trace of an accent other than a faint Texas drawl. He was equally adept in the Mexican and Indian tongues. No one in the border country was better at reading sign, and no one was a more cool-headed fighter in times of trouble. None of the men who rode with him held any part of his heritage against him. In short, Roque Maugricio was one of the most highly valued members of the Old Company, that group of Rangers, young in years but old in frontier wisdom, led by Captain John S. "Rip" Ford.

So it should come as no surprise that when danger threatened Roque, the rest of the Rangers were ready to "go to war" on his behalf.

But I find myself getting ahead of the story.

The blue waves of the Gulf lapped gently against the piers across the street from the tavern in Corpus Christi where several of the Rangers had repaired for a drink. The company had ridden into Corpus from our permanent camp at the ruins of the abandoned rancho, San

Antonio Viejo, in order to replenish supplies. We had been patrolling the South Texas brush country along the Nueces River heavily over the past few weeks, that spring of 1851, and were short on just about everything.

I had already picked up some medical supplies and put them in the wagon driven by our company sergeant, David Level. Probably I would have stayed with the wagon until we were ready to return to camp had not Doc Sullivan come along with several other members of the company and dragooned me into joining them.

Though I was the company surgeon, it was Ranger D. C. Sullivan who was known by the name "Doc." It seemed to fit him better. He was slender, with hair so fair as to be almost white and prominent eyebrows of the same shade. His face nearly always wore a ready grin. He was the prankster of our outfit, ever ready for a joke of some sort, usually at someone else's expense. Whenever the humor was turned on him, however, he bore it exceedingly well and laughed just as hard. His hands were big, and he could use them to draw and fire a revolver as fast as anyone I've ever seen.

"Come along and have a drink with us, you old saw-bones," Sullivan said to me as he took my arm and tugged me away from the wagon. "Might be a long time 'fore we get back to town."

"I'm really not much of a drinking man," I began, but Sullivan interrupted me.

"Damned if I don't know it. Don't you know that a fella's got to have a certain amount of whiskey to keep his gut cleaned out proper? Hell, I'm surprised at you, bein' a medical man and all. Fella'd think you never had no learnin'."

Realizing it would be a waste of time to argue with him, I went along. But I told myself I would have only one drink. It would not do to have Captain Ford find the company surgeon in his cups.

Roque Maugricio was already at the tavern when we arrived, leaning on the bar and sipping a mug of beer. It was a measure of how highly thought of he was that he was allowed to drink openly, since of course he was half Comanche. No one seemed to take that into consideration, however. As some of those who fought alongside him put it, Roque Maugricio was a "white" man, no matter what the color of his skin.

Unfortunately, as we were soon to see, not everyone felt that way.

Roque was friendly enough but tended to keep to himself. He smiled when his comrades slapped him on the back but didn't join in the general hilarity. In fact, he was about to leave when two men came into the tavern and braced him.

"Where you goin', you damn red nigger?" one of them demanded.

The loud, offensive words put an immediate damper on the festivities. Doc Sullivan and I and the other Rangers turned to look at the newcomers. Both men wore buckskins and wide-brimmed hats and carried guns on their hips. I didn't actually recognize them, but to my eyes, they were typical border hardcases, smugglers and outlaws, more than likely.

Roque said in measured tones, "I was just leaving."

"Well, we say you ain't goin' anywhere."

"That's right," the other man said. "We got a score to settle with you."

Roque said, "I never saw you two before in my life."

"Maybe not," the first man said, "but we know you. You're that greaser Injun, and we're here to get justice for Alvin Callahan."

Roque shook his head. "I don't know any Alvin Callahan."

From the bar, Doc Sullivan called, "Need a hand, Roque?"

The fact that there were several Rangers lined up along the bar made the two strangers glance nervously in our direction, but they seemed determined to go through with this confrontation anyway. And they began to look more confident again as Roque said, "No thanks, Doc, I can handle this." He took another step toward the two men. "Like I told you, I don't know you or Alvin Callahan, and I'm leaving."

"Callahan was killed at Mirabella," one of the men said. "Remember that?"

I saw the shock in Roque's eyes. His face tightened. He remembered Mirabella, all right, that was certain.

"There's five thousand dollars on your head, redskin, and we aim to collect." The words came out of one man in a rush, and then he grabbed for the gun on his hip.

Roque Maugricio's Walker Colts whispered from leather first. And then they shouted.

Both men managed to draw their guns and fire, but their shots were overwhelmed by the roar of Roque's Colts. He thumbed off two shots from each weapon, the heavy bullets driving into the bodies of the would-be assassins and throwing them backward. Each of them landed with a crash on the sawdust-littered floor into which their revolvers had discharged. Though Doc

Sullivan was the fastest man I knew, Roque Maugricio was right behind him when it came to gun speed.

Sullivan and the other Rangers had drawn their weapons as well, but they weren't needed. The two men on the floor were dead. Sullivan stared wide-eyed at them and demanded, "Roque, what in blue blazes was *that* all about?"

Roque holstered one gun, began reloading the exploded rounds in the other. Without looking up from the grim task, he answered Sullivan's question. "That was the past come to call," he said.

When Captain Ford heard about the shooting, he summoned his scout to explain. I accompanied Roque to the hotel, where the captain met him in one of the back rooms.

Captain John Salmon Ford was tall and slender, with white hair, a closely trimmed white beard, and the most piercing eyes of any man I ever knew. It was said he could look right through a man, especially an evildoer. Doc Sullivan, who had a penchant for nicknames that the captain shared, had dubbed him "Rip," for a pair of reasons. One had to do with the captain's record keeping and his habit of marking "R.I.P." on reports concerning the deaths of Rangers or other upstanding citizens. The other was that when it came to trouble, Captain Ford "ripped" right through it, according to Sullivan. He had been a doctor, newspaperman, and politician before being awarded a captaincy in the Rangers, and he was the finest natural commander of fighting men in Texas since the days of Sam Houston.

"Now, what's all this about?" he said as he sat at a table and turned that intense gaze of his on Roque.

The scout shrugged. "Couple of yahoos drew on me, Cap'n. Figured I'd better shoot 'em."

Ford clenched a fist and banged it on the table. "Damn it, Roque, don't get all closemouthed on me. *Why* did those bastards want to kill you?"

"From what they said, I reckon there's a bounty on my head."

The captain sat back, openmouthed. "A bounty," he repeated.

"Yes, sir. Five thousand dollars."

Ford let out a whistle. He looked at me for confirmation, and I said, "Yes, sir, that's what one of the, ah, dead gentlemen mentioned before the hostilities commenced."

"Well, I'll swan," Captain Ford said, shaking his head as he did so. "Who would be foolish enough to put a bounty on the head of a Texas Ranger?"

"It's not because I'm a Ranger. It's because I'm part Comanche." Roque hesitated, and I saw he did not want to talk about this. The captain's steady regard forced him to go on, however. "You ever hear of a place called Mirabella, Cap'n?"

"A little village down on the Rio, on the Texas side, isn't it?"

Roque nodded. "That's right. There are a few ranches nearby, but that's all. About ten years ago, not long after the settlement was founded, the Comanch' raided it. Burned down about half the town."

"I don't recall that," Ford said.

"I do. I was there." Roque's face was as hard as stone. "I led the war party that attacked Mirabella."

The captain and I couldn't help but stare at him. We had ridden with Roque Maugricio, fought side by side with him on dozens of occasions. More than once, his expertise as a scout had saved the entire company from disaster. So we tended to forget that there had been a time in his life when he had fought on the other side of the conflict.

"Well," Captain Ford said after a moment, "that was a long time ago."

"Some people have long memories," Roque said. "I don't know who Alvin Callahan was, but according to those two bounty hunters, he died at Mirabella, and my guess is that someone who cared about him put the bounty on me."

Ford leaned forward in his chair. "I won't stand for a Ranger being hunted like a common criminal," he declared.

"In the eyes of some men, that's what I am. Nothing but a murderin' redskin."

"By God, a man can change! In the past few years, you've served Texas faithfully, Roque, often at great risk to your own life. You've earned a second chance if anyone ever has."

"I would have liked to think so," Roque said.

Ford shoved his chair back and stood up. "We'll ride over to Mirabella, the whole company of us, and—"

"No, Cap'n."

The quietly spoken negative took the captain by surprise. Rip Ford was not accustomed to being told no by anyone, let alone by one of the men who rode for him. Roque Maugricio had always possessed a proud, independent streak in his personality, though, so his declaration did not come as much of a shock to me.

"I'm requesting a leave of absence," Roque went on. "I'll go to Mirabella and see if I can straighten all this out."

"You ride in there alone and there'll be a bull's-eye on your back," Ford cautioned. "Besides, you're a member of the Old Company. This is Ranger business."

Roque shook his head. "No, Cap'n, it's personal. I won't drag the rest of the boys into it." He took a deep breath. "I'll resign from the Rangers first, before I let that happen."

I knew what such a decision must have cost him. The Rangers were as close to a home and family as the scout had. He had spent most of his life trapped between the two worlds of red man and white, fitting into neither, until joining the Rangers. For him to even contemplate resigning was almost beyond belief.

"Damn it, don't do that," Captain Ford growled. "If it means that much to you, I reckon you can go. You'd better be mighty careful, though. You're the best scout I've ever had and am likely to have. If anything happens to you, I won't be a happy man."

"I just want to try to set things right, Cap'n. As soon as I've done that, I'll ride on back to San Antonio Viejo."

"We'll be waiting for you," Ford said as he shook hands with Roque. "*Vaya con Dios,* my friend."

"He done *what?*" Doc Sullivan said, even though I knew he had heard me quite well.

"Roque has ridden to Mirabella," I said again. "He believes he can find whoever has placed the bounty on his head and get it lifted."

"He's lost his fool mind," Sullivan said. "He won't do anything 'cept get hisself killed."

"Well, that seems the most likely outcome to me, too," I admitted, "but he was insistent, and evidently Captain Ford didn't feel that he had the right to deny Roque permission to leave."

We were on our way back to San Antonio Viejo, riding behind the wagon carrying our supplies. Captain Ford and several other Rangers were out in front of the wagon, while Doc Sullivan and I and a few others had dropped back. Everyone was alert. While the Comanches seldom ventured this close to Corpus Christi, it wasn't unheard of for them to raid in the area. Nor was it likely that anything except the largest war party would attack a group of heavily armed Rangers, but it was impossible to predict what notions the savages might get in their heads. Watchfulness was ingrained in the Rangers.

"Remember that fight over on the Nueces 'bout six months ago?" Sullivan said. "One of Carne Muerte's braves had a bead on me and would've dropped me, sure as shootin', if Roque hadn't got him first. Way I see it, ol' Roque saved my life that day. Weren't the first time, neither. That's why I got to do it."

"What are you getting at, Doc?"

Sullivan squinted over at me from the corners of his eyes. "If I tell you, are you gonna run to the cap'n and start squawkin'?"

I managed to look offended as I said, "Have you ever known me to betray a confidence?"

"Nope, but I know you and the cap'n are close."

"I may not approve of your actions," I said, "but as long as they don't endanger the rest of the company, I won't say anything to Captain Ford."

"Good," Sullivan grunted. "'Cause I'm goin' after

Roque and lend him a hand. I know how to get to that Mirabella place. Thought I'd ride out tonight, after we get back to camp." He looked directly at me. "Now, you gonna keep your word?"

"Of course," I said. "For one thing, I intend to go with you."

Sullivan's pale eyebrows lifted. "You?" he said. "You'd go agin the cap'n's orders?"

"It's been only two months since Roque Maugricio saved *my* life down in the desert between here and Brownsville, remember? If he hadn't found me, I would have died of thirst in that wasteland."

Sullivan rubbed his jaw and grinned. "Yeah, I recollect you gettin' lost. Ol' Roque saved your bacon, all right. But you're a sawbones, not a fightin' man."

I patted the stock of the rifle that stuck up from the boot on the side of my saddle. "I can handle a weapon if necessary," I assured him. "And I ride every bit as good as you."

"You're a fair hand with a horse, that's a fact. Not as good as me, of course, but I ain't goin' to waste my breath arguin' with you about it. Still, you're the company surgeon. What if there's trouble and you're needed at camp?"

"You know the captain doesn't plan any patrols for at least a week. The chances that the company will be attacked while in camp are quite small. My services shouldn't be required at all."

"Maybe not," Sullivan allowed. "Well, I guess if you got your mind made up, there ain't nothin' I can do to stop you." He grinned as he added, "Besides, the cap'n thinks mighty high of you. When he finds out we done gone after Roque, maybe he won't be as likely to throw me to the wolves if you're part of it, too."

"We can only hope," I said.

Mirabella was about halfway between Brownsville and Laredo. Sullivan and I rode cross-country toward the border that night after slipping away from camp. Morning found us far out in the brush country. The landscape was flat and covered with mesquite for the most part, broken up by stretches of sand and the occasional creek. The country was not well suited for agriculture, but it supported the hardy, longhorned cattle that roamed freely over it. In those days there were no fences, of course; the ranchers ran their stock on open range, with only their brands to mark them. Most of the men who tended the cattle were Mexican vaqueros; the Americans who worked on the ranches sometimes called themselves "buckaroos," a corruption of the Mexican word.

It was a vast, lonely land, and if we were to encounter a group of Comanche raiders, our only hope would be to outdistance them. Our mounts were strong and well rested, so we thought we would have a good chance to escape trouble if it came our way.

But as it turned out, instead of trouble coming after us, we were the ones who rode up on it.

The first indication that something was amiss was the sudden popping of gunfire somewhere ahead of us. One shot, perhaps even two, could be dismissed as someone killing a snake. Several shots might be required to bring down one of the wild, dangerous pigs that roamed the brush country. But a veritable fusillade such as the one that came to our ears that morning could mean only one thing: somewhere nearby, men were trying to kill each other.

Doc Sullivan and I galloped our horses toward the sound of the shots. The frequency of the reports lessened slightly, but the battle continued. We came into view of several men riding in circles around a dark shape on the ground. They were shooting at it, clouds of smoke puffing into the air with each blast.

Sullivan reined in and pulled a spyglass from his saddlebags. He put it to his eye, squinted through it for a moment, and then exclaimed, "That's Roque, by God! His horse is down, and he's hunkerin' behind it for cover!"

Once Sullivan had said that, I could make out some of the details with the naked eye, such as the shape of the horse, which apparently was dead. I saw smoke coming from behind the animal's corpse, too, and knew that Roque was putting up a fight. I would not have expected any less from the scout. The men attacking him looked to be white, probably the same sort of ruffians as the two who had foolishly accosted him at the tavern in Corpus Christi. The odds were even higher against Roque this time. There were four of the attackers.

Doc Sullivan let out a whoop, jammed the reins between his teeth, drew both of his pistols, and kicked his horse into a run. He raced toward the mounted men, holding his fire until he was within range for the Walker Colts.

The attackers were not so patient. They opened fire as soon as they became aware that they were under assault from an unexpected quarter.

I drew my rifle and galloped after Sullivan, guiding my mount with my knees. I knew better than to try to draw a bead on any of the men from horseback. The odds against making an accurate shot under such conditions were astronomical, at least for someone with my level of skill with firearms. Sullivan was a different story. When he finally began to blaze away, two of the men pitched from their saddles immediately.

I hauled back on the reins and dropped from the saddle, hitting the ground even before my horse stopped running. After stumbling forward a step, I caught my balance and brought the rifle to my shoulder. I pulled back the hammer and sighted on one of the remaining attackers. I drew a deep breath, steadied the sights, and fired.

I had taken an oath to preserve life, but this was, after all, Texas. Sometimes a life has to be ended in order to save other lives. So I felt a strange mixture of elation and sadness when I saw the man who was my target topple from the back of his mount. The fourth man, who appeared to have been wounded by Sullivan's fire, whirled his horse around and raced away at top speed, abandoning the fight while he still drew breath.

By the time I remounted and rode on ahead, Sullivan had reached Roque's side. Though Roque's horse was dead, the scout moved around like he was unharmed. Together he and Sullivan checked the bodies of the fallen men.

"This one ain't dead," Sullivan called as he knelt beside the man I had shot. He grinned up at me. "You just winged him."

It was an accurate description. The man's right arm had been broken by the bullet. I bound up the wound and then splinted the arm, ignoring the curses rained upon my head as I did so.

Roque drew his Bowie knife and knelt on the man's other side. "After all the trouble the doctor went to patching you up, it'd be a damn shame to have to kill you now," he said as he rested the edge of the blade against the man's throat. A tiny trickle of blood appeared. "Why'd you jump me?"

The man was pale and nervous, as well he should have been, but he still possessed a core of defiance. "For the money, of course," he said. "Don't you know there's a bounty on your head, Injun?"

"Who put it there?" Roque asked.

"Cass Callahan. Owns the Diamond C, not far from Mirabella."

"Why?"

"Because you killed his pa, ten years ago! Filthy Comanch'—"

The man stopped as Roque pressed harder with the knife.

"Better be careful," Sullivan said. "You'll slice his head clean off."

"No," Roque said. "Not until I'm ready." His dark eyes bored down into the man. "So Callahan sent out word that he wanted me dead, did he?"

"That's right." The bounty hunter licked his lips. "There's men ridin' in from all over. Callahan figured you might come after him when you found out what's goin' on, so he told everybody to come to Mirabella. If you ride in there, Maugricio, you'll find thirty or forty rifles pointin' at you. They'll all be tryin' to kill you first and claim the money."

A rare look of concern appeared on Sullivan's face. "Thirty or forty guns? Dang, Roque, that's more'n I figured on."

"You and the doctor can return to camp," Roque said flatly. "I didn't ask you to come along. You know I didn't want anybody else getting mixed up in this."

"You better turn around, too," Sullivan said. "The sawbones told me ol' Rip offered to take the whole company over there to Mirabella. You better take him up on it."

Roque shook his head. "No, this is my problem, my past. I'll handle it . . . alone."

"Well . . . not hardly alone. If you're gonna be stubborn about it, I reckon we'll just have to go along to see that things are done legal and proper-like."

Roque finally took the knife away from the wounded man's throat. The man closed his eyes and breathed a sigh of relief. Roque stood up and said, "No. I don't want the two of you with me."

"You ain't got no choice in the matter. We're your friends, and we're goin'." Sullivan looked at me. "Ain't that right?"

I knew that if Roque rode into Mirabella alone, he would have no chance. He would probably be dead within moments. But if he were to be accompanied by two men who were known to be Texas Rangers, the bounty hunters might hesitate before cutting him down in cold blood.

"What is it, exactly, that you intend to do?" I asked him, ignoring for the moment Sullivan's question.

"I want to talk to this Cass Callahan. I don't reckon there's much chance he'll listen to reason, but I've got to try. I want to make him see that things have changed since the days I rode with the Comanches."

"There is a chance that you *are* responsible for the death of the man's father," I pointed out.

Roque's face was as hard and bleak as stone. "A good chance, I'd say. And I'm as sorry for that as for everything else I did back in those days. I've been trying to atone for all of it, for years now. But I reckon some things can't ever be forgiven . . . or forgotten." He drew a breath. "Leastways, if Callahan is bound and determined to settle the score, he and I can have it out, man to man. There's no need to bring a bunch of bounty hunters into it."

"It'll probably come to that," Sullivan said. "I don't figure he'll be the forgivin' sort."

"Then so be it." Roque looked down at the wounded man. "Get him on a horse and send him on his way. I'll see if I can catch one of those other horses to replace the one they killed."

The shape the wounded man was in, he represented no immediate threat. We sent him riding off toward Corpus Christi. As Sullivan watched him go, he said, "That fella will circle around and try to get to Mirabella before us, I reckon, so he can warn Callahan that we're comin'."

Roque swung up into the saddle of the horse he had caught and nodded in agreement with Sullivan. "That's what I figure, too, Doc, but it doesn't really matter. The one who got away will take care of that."

"And you don't mind, do you? You want Callahan to know you're comin'."

"Callahan already felt like I would come after him, unless those first men he sent after me got lucky enough to kill me. He *wants* a showdown. I'm just giving him one, that's all."

Sullivan picked up the reins and clucked to his mount. "Well, let's go. It's still a long ride to where we're goin'."

As we rode, Roque told us about how the four men had lain in wait for him and ambushed him as he rode toward Mirabella. "They were hidden in the brush. My horse must've caught wind of their horses, because he shied a little. Reckon that saved my life. Horse caught the first volley, rather than me being blown out of the saddle by it."

"You're lucky you were able to stand them off until we got there."

Roque nodded. "Lucky for me, maybe, but not for you boys. You'd have been better off if I was dead when you got there. Then maybe you would've turned around and gone back to camp."

"Turn around, hell!" Sullivan exclaimed. "We're Rangers, son. We'd have ridden right on to Mirabella and cleaned out that rat's nest. Callahan's got to learn he can't put a bounty on a Ranger, no matter what the hombre might've been or done a long time ago."

"You're a good friend, Doc." Roque looked at me. "Both of you are. Damn fools, of course, to get tangled up in this mess with me."

"Ain't arguin' about that," Sullivan said with a grin.

We didn't run into any more bushwhackers or even see anyone else until we reached Mirabella that evening. The settlement perched on the north bank of the Rio

Grande. It had one main street and a couple of cross streets. The second-largest building in town was the general store that served the ranches in the area. The largest was the lone saloon.

We made sure we were all wearing our badges in plain sight. They were handmade emblems, stars in circles cut from Mexican pesos. No matter what happened, no matter whether we lived or died, the men who waited for us would not be able to claim truthfully that they were unaware we were Rangers.

Roque angled his horse toward the store. It and the saloon were the only buildings where lights burned. The rest of the settlement was oddly dark. Many frontier folk "went to bed with the chickens," but it seemed to me that there should have been *some* lights showing in Mirabella. It was as if, save for the store and the saloon, the town was deserted.

We swung down from our saddles and tied our mounts at the rail in front of the store's long, raised porch. Roque led the way up the steps. We went to the door, opened it, and walked inside. Our footsteps seemed to echo from the high ceiling.

One man stood behind the counter at the rear of the long room filled with shelves full of merchandise. He wore an apron over his rough clothing and had his hands underneath the counter. "Howdy, gents," he called to us as we came toward him. "Something I can do for you?"

"Where is ever'body?" Sullivan asked. "'Cept for this place and the saloon, the whole blamed town looks empty."

"Lots of men over at the saloon," the storekeeper said. He licked his lips. "You boys are Rangers?"

"I'm Roque Maugricio," Roque said. "Name mean anything to you?"

The man licked his lips again. He had a long, sandy mustache, and his face was burned the color of old saddle leather. He said, "I heard of you," and then his hands jerked up quickly and swung a shotgun from under the counter.

Roque was ready for him. The right-hand Colt came out and up and flame exploded from the muzzle. The man with the shotgun was thrown back by the bullet striking him. His back rammed the shelves behind him, causing them to collapse and dump goods on top of him as he fell. The shotgun clattered to the floor, unfired.

"I figured he was waiting for us," Roque said as the echoes of the shot faded. "No storekeeper spends enough time outside to be burned that dark."

A soft groan drew our attention. Doc Sullivan drew his guns and investigated, opening the door to a small room in the rear, where he found an elderly man who had been struck over the head and tied up.

We brought the man into the main room of the store, freed him from his bonds, and helped him sit on a cracker barrel. I examined the lump on his head and informed him that in my professional opinion, he would be all right except for a headache.

"Figured as much," the old man said. "This noggin o' mine is pretty hard. Fella like to bent his gun barrel when he walloped me with it, I reckon."

"Who are you?" Sullivan asked.

"Stanley Edmonds. I own this store."

Roque inclined his head toward the dead man behind the counter. "And who was he?"

"Hell, I don't know his name. He was just one o' those snake-blooded killers Cass Callahan's brought in to murder some fella." Edmonds's eyes lit on our badges. "A Ranger, I hear tell."

"I'm the one they're after," Roque confirmed.

"Well, then, I'm sorry for you, young fella, because there's a whole mob o' them hardcases over to the saloon. Ain't no way even three Rangers can handle them."

"We'll see about that," Sullivan said.

"Where are the townspeople?" Roque asked.

"Pulled out, headed up to Laredo. When the mayor and the rest of the folks in town got wind of what Callahan was plannin' to do, they tried to talk him out of it, but he wouldn't listen to reason. He was bound'n determined to settle what he figured was a blood debt with the fella he blames for his pa's death. Seemed to most folks, though, that what he was really doin' was declarin' war on the Texas Rangers, and they thought that was a damn fool thing to do. They was afraid the whole town'd get shot up, so they left until it's all over."

"Except for you," Roque said.

"I got a damn sizable investment in this store," Edmonds said. "I figured to stay and guard it. But then, one o' Callahan's gun-wolves came ridin' into town earlier and said you was on your way, and one o' the other fellas got the bright idea of pretendin' this was his store. He figured you might come in here before you went to the saloon, and he'd get first crack at you that way." Edmonds laughed harshly. "He was right, I reckon, but the only bounty he collected was in lead."

Sullivan rubbed his jaw. "The fellas over in the saloon

must've heard that shot. How come they ain't rushed over here to see what happened?"

I answered that one. "They know that if Roque had been killed, the man who did it would have come forth to claim his reward. Therefore, they know that Roque was victorious, and they're waiting for him to come to the saloon."

"It'll be forty to one if you go in there, son," Edmonds said to Roque.

Sullivan drew himself up and said, "Forty to three, you mean."

"Only thirteen and a third to one," I added.

Edmonds looked around at us and shook his head.

"What about Callahan?" Roque said. "What sort of man is he?"

"What do you mean, what sort is he? He's a vengeful son of a bitch, is what he is! Who else would bring in a bunch of killers from all over the Southwest, just to settle a score with one man?"

"He won't listen to reason? He won't accept an apology?"

Edmonds stared. "Hell, no! Things've gone too far for that." He frowned, though, and after a moment continued, "Thing of it is, in every other way, Cass ain't a bad fella. Not a bad fella at all. Always deals fair in business, and he treats the folks who work for him mighty decent-like. Some of the vaqueros who work out on the Diamond C got their whole families with 'em, and Cass sees that they're took care of. Raised up a pretty good boy, too, name of Dan."

"Did you live here when the Comanches raided the town, ten years ago?"

"Sure did. I'm one o' the founders of Mirabella, I guess you could say. I knew the whole bunch. Cass was a young man then, but full-growed, with a wife and a young'un about eight years old. That'd be Dan. Alvin always planned to turn the ranch over to Cass, but when Alvin was killed, Cass had to go ahead and take over then. He did fine, but I reckon he never got over his pa dyin' that way. Then a year or so later, Cass's wife passed on sudden-like, and he got even more bitter. He couldn't do nothin' about that—can't take revenge on a fever that comes outta nowhere and strikes somebody down—but he started figurin' on how someday he'd even the score for what happened to his pa. When he heard that the Comanch' war chief who led that raid was a half-breed who'd gone over and joined up with the Rangers . . . well, I reckon you know the rest of it after that."

"Thank you," Roque said quietly. "I appreciate you telling me about the man."

"Knowin' that don't change anything," Edmonds pointed out. "Callahan still wants you dead, son. Ain't nothin' you can do to change that. You and your friends might be able to get on your horses and ride out of town before they can stop you, though."

"If I run away, I'll be looking over my shoulder for Callahan's hired killers for the rest of my life," Roque said. "I've tried to leave my past behind me. I won't invite it to follow me around with a gun."

"I don't know of a thing I can say, then, that'll help you."

Roque patted the old man on the shoulder. "Better lie low for a while," he advised.

"Oh, I will, don't you worry about that. Soon's I drag out the corpse o' that hydrophobia skunk you plugged."

We turned toward the door. Roque said over his shoulder, "If you'd just blow out the lamp, too, so they can't see us against the light when we step out . . ."

"Sure thing, son," Edmonds said.

One more thing occurred to me. I asked, "You said one man rode back into town earlier, after ambushing Roque?"

"That's right."

"Did he have a splint on a broken right arm?"

"Nope. He'd been creased a time or two, I think, but no broken bones that I saw."

"What's it matter?" Sullivan asked me.

"I was just curious. It seems the man I wounded must have gone on to Corpus Christi as we suggested, rather than doubling back."

Sullivan was right; it didn't matter. If there was gunplay, as there was almost sure to be, I couldn't be worried about such things as whether or not I'd be facing a man I had already wounded.

Edmonds blew out the lamp, plunging the store into darkness. Roque and Sullivan and I moved to the front of the building. Roque opened the door. If anyone were watching from the saloon across the street, as seemed likely, they had probably noted the movement of the door, even with the light out.

"We'll go out low, and in a hurry," Roque said. "There's a water trough to the left. You two get behind it. I'll head for that rain barrel at the corner."

"You reckon they'll open up on us just like that?" Sullivan asked.

"Don't know, but there's a chance they will."

Sullivan nodded and looked at me. "You ready?"

My hands were sweating slightly as they clutched the rifle. But I managed to say, "I'm ready."

"Let's go," Roque said.

We left the store as swiftly as possible. Roque went first, followed by Sullivan and then myself. As Roque had predicted, the men in the saloon opened fire as we darted through the shadows. Glass crashed in the front window of the store as bullets shattered it. I threw myself off the porch and landed hard on my belly as I stretched out on the ground behind the water trough. More bullets thudded into the thick adobe sides of the trough, which was about six feet long. Doc Sullivan lay immediately to my left. "Keep your head down," he warned.

I didn't waste the breath it would have required to tell him that I had no intention of lifting my head.

The men in the saloon continued the barrage for what seemed like hours but was surely only minutes. When I looked along the street, I could see the rain barrel where Roque had intended to take shelter, but from where I was I could not see if he was safe or not. Finally, the shooting died away, and I heard a man in the saloon shouting, "Hold your fire! Hold your fire!"

Sullivan lifted his head slightly. "Hey, over there!" he called. "You jugheads know you're shootin' at the Texas Rangers?"

The spokesman for the gunmen ignored that question. He shouted, "Maugricio! You hear me, Maugricio?"

"I hear you." Roque's voice was strong, and I felt relieved at the sound of it.

"You're the only one I want, Maugricio," the man said, which seemed to confirm his identity as Cass Callahan. "The other two can get on their horses and ride away."

That was not exactly possible at the moment, considering the fact that our mounts had panicked when the shooting started, jerked their reins loose from the hitch rail, and bolted up the street, but I knew what Callahan meant.

So did Doc Sullivan. He said heatedly, "Go to hell, Callahan! You shoot at one Ranger, you shoot at all of us!"

"This is none of your affair," Callahan warned.

"You won't be thinkin' that when Cap'n Rip Ford and the rest of the Old Company ride in here and string up the lot of you for murder!"

That gave them pause, make no mistake about it. Captain Ford's fame had spread throughout the border country, and no one doubted that he was capable of extracting rough justice when the spirit moved him. Even from a distance, I heard concerned muttering from the other men in the saloon.

But Callahan had been nursing his hatred for too long. It had grown to consume him. He shouted, "Ten thousand! Ten thousand dollars to the man who kills Roque Maugricio!"

That commenced the ball once more. A deafening thunder arose as the men in the saloon opened fire.

They would have kept it up all night, or until their ammunition ran out, whichever came first, if they had not been distracted. At first I didn't see what caused the shooting to taper off and then stop completely, but when I heard the horrified shouts and curses, my curiosity got the better of me and I had to disregard Sullivan's warning and lift my head. Beside me, he was doing the same thing, and as he saw what was in the street, he choked out an exclamation.

"My God, what'd they do to that poor fella!"

The man was tied onto the back of his horse. He swayed slightly as the animal plodded along the dusty street. Dark streaks of blood were etched on the horse's flanks, but the blood came from the rider, not the mount. He had been scalped and mutilated and was nude so that the hideous injuries could be plainly seen.

I never would have recognized him had it not been for the splint I had fashioned and strapped to his right arm earlier in the day. It was still in place.

I thought surely the man was dead. But to my horror, as the horse finally came to a stop between the saloon and the store, a grotesque, bubbling groan came from the wretch. His mouth moved, but nothing comprehensible emerged. I realized then that the ones who had tortured him had also ripped out his tongue.

No matter. The mere sight of what had been done to him was enough to tell us who was responsible.

"Carne Muerte," Sullivan breathed.

Dead Meat. The fiercest Comanche war chief from one end of the Rio Grande to the other. The Old Company had crossed swords with him, so to speak, on several occasions in the past. In each of those battles, the Rangers had dealt out more damage than they received, but still, Carne Muerte had slipped away each time, only to return and bedevil us again.

Someone in the saloon yelled, "Lonzo! My God, look what they done to Lonzo!"

"Callahan!" Roque called sharply. "Callahan, listen to me!"

After a moment of silence, Callahan said grudgingly, "Go on, Maugricio."

"That's the work of Carne Muerte. He's sent us a calling card, and that can mean only one thing: he's going to attack the town, probably in a matter of minutes."

"You don't know that," Callahan said.

"Yeah, I do," Roque insisted. "You've got a lot of men here. We can fight off the Comanches . . . but not if we're busy trying to kill each other."

"It's a damn lie!" Callahan said. "How do we know *you're* not responsible for what happened to Lonzo, you filthy savage?"

"I ride with the Rangers. You know we wouldn't do this."

"He's right, Cass," another man said inside the saloon. "Maugricio's half Comanch'. He'd know Carne Muerte's handiwork, and he'd know what it means."

"No!" I heard the rage in Callahan's voice. He didn't want to give up the dream of vengeance he had nurtured for so long. He didn't even want to postpone it. "It's a trick, I tell you!"

The tortured man groaned again.

"Damn it, somebody's got to put him out of his misery!" And with that, a man rushed from the saloon with a pistol in his hand and raised the weapon as he approached the horse, obviously intent on putting a bullet through Lonzo's brain.

With a whisper of sound, followed by a deadly thud, an arrow came out of the night and struck the man, piercing his chest. He screamed, dropped the gun, and clawed at the shaft as he fell to his knees and then pitched to the side, dead.

With that, there could no longer be any doubt. The battle was on.

As rifles began to crackle and arrows hissed through the air, Doc Sullivan came up on his knees and shot Lonzo through the head, putting an end to the man's suffering. Then Sullivan twisted and began firing down the street with both guns, aiming at the figures that flitted through the shadows.

Some people say an Indian will not attack at night, but in truth, an Indian will fight when it best suits his purposes to do so, day or night. In this case, the darkness was friendly to Carne Muerte and his band of warriors, because it had allowed them to sneak all the way into town unobserved, so that they were among us before we knew it. Hearing a rush of footsteps, I rolled over and saw a Comanche charging toward the water trough where Sullivan and I lay. The rifle in his hands bloomed fire, but the hastily aimed bullet splashed into the water. I thrust my rifle at him and pulled the trigger. Flame leaped from the barrel, and the Comanche was so close that it almost touched his chest. He flipped backward as if he had run into a wall.

I started reloading as the roar of gunfire continued all around me. When I looked up, I saw an Indian running toward the saloon, brandishing a torch. Sullivan snapped a shot at him and knocked him off his feet. The torch sailed through the air but landed in the street, falling short of the saloon.

My rifle was ready again. I raised myself to my knees and drew a bead on some movement I spotted on the roof of the saloon. Knowing that no one in that position could be up to any good, I fired, and a second later was rewarded by the sight of a limp, war-painted figure toppling off the roof to plunge into the street. The Comanche warrior landed, in fact, on the still-blazing torch, and when he didn't move, I knew he was dead. His body extinguished the torch, but not before the flesh burned enough to put a stink in the air.

I dropped to the ground and began to reload again. Beside me, Sullivan let out a whoop of pure battle joy as he finished emptying his Colts. He crouched and began reloading as well.

"Seen Roque?" he asked me, raising his voice over the roar of guns.

"No." I glanced toward the rain barrel but still couldn't tell if Roque was there or not.

He wasn't. I knew that because in the next heartbeat, he came rushing along the porch, guns blazing as he fired into a knot of warriors charging us. Roque dropped to a knee at the end of the water trough. An arrow tugged at the sleeve of his shirt as it went past him. He triggered again and sent the Comanche who had fired the arrow spinning off his feet.

I heard the crackle of flames and looked toward the saloon. The Indians had managed to set it on fire somehow, after all. The windows glowed a garish red as the flames showed through them. Men came boiling through the door, slapping the batwings aside as they were forced to flee the inferno. Some of them fell victim to the bullets and arrows of the Comanches, but most of the defenders managed to reach other cover. Killers they might be, but they were also tough, battle-hardened men, swift with their guns and swift on their feet when they had to be.

By attacking Mirabella on this particular night, Carne Muerte had perhaps bitten off more than he could chew, as the old saying goes.

One of the men from the saloon tried to dash across the street. He made it only halfway before he tumbled off his feet. Whether he had been wounded or had simply tripped, I didn't know. But he seemed stunned by his fall, and as one of the Comanches rushed toward him, I assumed that his misfortune was about to prove fatal.

Roque Maugricio surged up out of his crouch and aimed his pistols toward the onrushing warrior. Both hammers fell on empty chambers. I heard Roque curse as he flung the revolvers aside and then grabbed his Bowie knife from its sheath. He charged into the street to intercept the Comanche and protect the fallen man.

Roque may have been a hair slower with his six-guns than Doc Sullivan, but nowhere in the border country of Texas was there a deadlier fighter with a knife. Cold steel responded to the scout as if it were part of his own arm, hooked into the nerves and muscles of his body. Firelight flickered on the broad blade as it thrust and slashed. The Comanche was armed with a knife, too, and the blades rang like bells as they came together. Though the struggle raged up and down the street around them, these two men might as well have been alone in some primeval world as they did battle to see who would live and who would die. It was a thrilling combat, and I found myself forgetting to breathe as I watched it unfold. Once I lifted my rifle to my shoulder, thinking to shoot the Indian, but I realized that in the uncertain light, as fast as the men were moving in their high-stakes dance, I stood just as good a chance of hitting Roque. I lowered the weapon.

I heard Roque grunt in pain as the Comanche's knife cut him, low on the left side. The warrior bore in, trying to press his momentary advantage. Roque slashed backhanded at him and forced the man to leap away or be cut deeply. The scout went on the offensive then, his blade moving so swiftly I could scarcely follow it. The Comanche counterattacked, slowing Roque's charge and then turning it back, forcing Roque to retreat.

For one of the few occasions during the time we rode together, I saw Roque Maugricio do something less than graceful. His clumsiness was no doubt caused by his wound. Still, I was shocked to see him trip over the leg of the man he was trying to save. I let out an involuntary cry of alarm as Roque toppled backward and the Comanche rushed in to deliver the coup de grace.

Roque's foot shot up, caught the Indian in the stomach, and sent him flying through the air above Roque and the fallen man. The Comanche landed well, however, rolling over and coming up ready to attack once again. But Roque was on him in an instant, thrusting his blade past the man's guard and into his chest. They were face-to-face, only inches separating them. The Comanche struck at Roque's back with his knife, tearing vest and shirt and gashing the skin, but Roque's blow had been a mortal one and already the warrior was losing strength. Roque ripped his Bowie free, and I swear I heard the blade rasp on bone as it came loose from the Comanche's body. Roque shoved the dying man away and reeled to his feet, blood dripping from the knife in his hand. He reached down with his other hand and helped the fallen man to his feet.

So enthralled had I been by the life-and-death struggle unfolding before my eyes, I had not taken notice that the shooting had diminished. I heard a different sort of thunder then, the pounding of hoofbeats, and Doc Sullivan pounded me on the back and let out a whoop of exultation. "It's the Rangers!" he cried. "It's Old Rip!"

True enough. A sizable contingent of the Old Company, led by Captain Ford, had swept into Mirabella and was in the process of putting the Comanches to rout. I wondered if Carne Muerte would get away, or if this time he would fall in battle. I was willing to wager that somehow he would give the Rangers the slip.

The fight didn't last long. The Rangers chased the remaining Comanches across the Rio Grande as the survivors of the raid limped out from their cover. The saloon still burned, but the buildings on either side of it were constructed of adobe, and it seemed unlikely the fire would spread to them. Roque stood in the middle of the street with the man he had saved, and as Doc Sullivan and I approached, we heard him ask, "Are you all right, son?"

Before the man could answer, another man rushed up to them. "Dan!" he shouted. "Oh, my God, Dan!" He threw his arms around the young man on whose behalf Roque had interceded.

"Reckon that'd be Cass Callahan," Sullivan drawled.

I had never seen the man before, but as I looked at his hard-planed face in the firelight and then studied the features of the young man he embraced, I saw the family resemblance. I was convinced they were indeed the Callahans, father and son.

"I'm all right, Pa," the younger man said. "I'm all right, really, thanks to this fella."

Cass Callahan turned slowly toward his son's savior. "Maugricio?"

"Yeah," Roque said. His left arm was pressed tightly to his side where the Comanche's knife had cut him. The bloodstain didn't appear to be dangerously large. I was confident Roque would be all right if I could give him some medical attention.

"Still want to pay ten thousand bucks for Roque's head, Callahan?" Sullivan asked harshly.

Slowly, Callahan shook his head. The man appeared somewhat numbed by everything that had happened. He stared at Roque for a moment and then said, "You took my father from me, and I'll always hate you for that, Maugricio. But you gave my son back to me. I got to call it square."

Roque nodded. "Fair enough. And for what it's worth . . . I'm sorry about what happened ten years ago. I'd change it if I could, but I reckon nobody can do that."

Callahan returned the nod and started to turn away, but Doc Sullivan said, "You better make sure all those gunnies know there ain't no more bounty to be had around here, mister. Anybody else comes after Roque, the Rangers'll be comin' to call on you again."

"No bounty," Callahan repeated. "I'll make sure they all know."

He started to lead his son away, but Dan Callahan balked. He turned back and held out his hand to Roque. "Thank you."

Roque wiped the blood from his knife on his trousers and then shoved the blade back in its sheath. He shook Dan's hand. "You're welcome," he said.

The Rangers rode back into town then, having splashed across the Rio Grande a short distance to make sure the Comanches were going to continue their flight. Captain Ford trotted his favorite mount, Old Higgins, up to Roque, Sullivan, and myself. He reined in and leaned forward in the saddle.

"I figured I'd find you boys here," he said with a stern frown. "Did you really think I'd let my best scout and my company surgeon go gallivanting off into trouble and not come after them?"

"Hey, Cap'n!" Sullivan exclaimed. He jerked a thumb at Roque and me. "You mean to say you was all worried about them two, but not about me?"

"I can always find another damn fool," the captain growled, but I could tell he was trying not to let a grin creep onto his weathered face.

Roque picked up the guns he had thrown aside and holstered them. "Let's get back to camp," he said. "One thing about Texas, there'll always be another chore for the Rangers."

REQUIEM FOR LOST SOULS

RANDY LEE EICKHOFF

—✦—

Dr. Randy Lee Eickhoff, a former professor of classics, is the award-winning translator of *The Ulster Cycle* and Homer's *Odyssey*. He spends his time between his home in El Paso, Texas, and Dublin, Ireland. He is the author of *The Fourth Horseman* and *Bowie*. He has twice been nominated for the Pulitzer Prize. His newest book is *The Fourth Horseman*. Here he tells the touching story of the penance paid by a Ranger who was a survivor of the Alamo.

> *Hell hath no limits nor is circumscribed,*
> *In one self place, where we are is Hell.*
> —Marlowe

1

He is old, and nightmares invade most of his sleep. Tonight is no exception as he awakens early in the morning beside the ash-covered embers of his campfire, trembling from the familiar nightmare. The ground in West Texas is covered with frost, and he shivers as he rolls from his blankets and checks his saddle horse and packhorse, ground-staked nearby, and his old Colt Navy revolver that he had converted to cartridges. The scarred walnut handle fits his hand, and the barrel is shiny from use.

He coughs and spits night phlegm from his throat and blows the ashes off his campfire. He puts small mesquite twigs on the embers and waits patiently until a small fire begins again before placing the coffeepot, still half full from his meager supper the night before, on the edge of the fire. He shrugs into his vest with the Texas Ranger badge pinned on the left breast and rises, going to his pack and removing two nosebags with the last of the oats he'd packed in Pecos before setting out across the Big Empty toward San Elizario. He slips one nosebag over the packhorse's head, then crosses to his old saddle horse, talking softly.

"Morning, Jim. How'd your night go?"

The sorrel nudges him, hoping for a lump of sugar, but the sugar ran out the day before, and Ranger Bill Walton apologizes as he slips the bag of oats over Jim's head.

"Meager rations, Jim," he says. "But we should be in San Elizario in late afternoon. I'll make it up to you then."

Jim grumbles as he begins munching the oats with worn teeth. Walton stands for a moment beside the sorrel, rubbing the night cold from him.

"I dreamed again last night," he says conversationally. "The same old one. Wish it would go away, but don't expect it to."

Years ago there would have been a trace of bitterness to his words, but the years have resigned him to the nightmare of when William B. Travis had called him to his room in the Alamo two days before Santa Ana sent Mexican soldiers over the Alamo's walls and slaughtered the garrison. Now a day doesn't pass when he doesn't remember that late-night meeting when the garrison was quiet as exhausted men slept the day's battle away at their posts along the ramparts of the Alamo walls.

"Bill," Travis said, "I need someone to carry a last message to Houston for help." He lit a cigar and poured two small glasses of brandy, handing one to Walton. "But I'm not ordering you to go. You know the danger as well as any man here."

Walton nodded thoughtfully as he drank his brandy. Santa Ana's lines surrounded the mission, and getting through would be little short of a miracle. He'd have to go over the wall when the moon set and crawl through the lines, hoping he would be able to steal a horse at the rear of the Mexican army. Then his troubles would really begin as he tried to make his way to Houston's headquarters somewhere near the Trinity River. He knew his chances were slim, and no one even knew where Houston had encamped.

"How long you figure I got?" Walton asked.

Travis shook his head. Food was running low as well as ammunition. The last charge had thinned the Alamo's ranks noticeably. The chapel was filled with wounded men, and those who were still able to fight were so exhausted that he wondered if they would be able to repel another attack at all. He looked closely at Walton, noticing the tired circles under the pale blue eyes, the fatigue lines etched deeply in his face.

"Not much," he admitted. "In fact, I don't know if we'll be able to last a week. You may be making the run for nothing."

"Well," Walton said, "a slim chance is better than none, I reckon." He finished his brandy and gently placed the glass back on the crude table. "You got the message written?"

Travis shook his head. "I don't want Santa Ana to know anything in case you get caught. You know what to tell Houston when you find him." He hesitated, his eyes burning as he stared at Walton. "I don't have to tell you not to get caught."

Walton shrugged, knowing what Travis was saying and what he could expect if he was taken alive by Santa Ana's men.

"I reckon the best thing, then, is not to get caught," he said. He took a deep breath. "Well, I'd better get ready. The moon'll be going down soon."

"Good luck," Travis said solemnly. He shook hands with Walton.

"I'm going to need it," Walton said. Then he grinned and left, making his way across the Alamo's yard. He collected a small sack of pemmican and a leather bag filled with water. He checked his rifle and took a horn of powder and a small bag of shot. He took a deep breath, wiping his hands down his stained butternut shirt, then left, climbing the north wall. He made his way to the corner shrouded by darkness and carefully studied the ground between the Alamo and the Mexican lines. He took another deep breath and slipped over the wall, landing softly on the balls of his feet. Keeping to the shadows, he slipped across the corpse-strewn ground to the Mexican lines. He came to a small drainage ditch and dropped flat, crawling carefully along it, working his way deeper and deeper through the army until at last, he came to the cavalry's horses picketed on the bare prairie. He picked a deep-chested bay, still saddled, and led it behind the tents before leaping onto its back and galloping away. A sentry fired a shot at him and then he was in the clear, galloping west to lead pursuit away before swinging back to the north to find Houston.

Five days later, he rode wearily into Houston's camp and discovered he was three days late—the Alamo had fallen, its defenders slaughtered, and although Houston did not condemn him for not staying at the Alamo, there were others who spoke scornfully to him for leaving before the final battle. His word meant nothing and was considered a coward's excuse. The following years had been marked with brawls and contempt that followed him even when he joined the Texas Rangers and was given the lowliest of assignments in the most remote areas.

He sits on his blankets by the fire, sipping his morning coffee, reflecting stoically on what had become a life spent in loneliness as he stares into the flames and sees the past reflected in the dancing shadows. Black as a wolf's mouth and as vicious, but he resists the darkness and settles, instead, into the familiar melancholy where he exists day by day.

He sighs and takes a paper from his shirt pocket and unfolds it, reading:

> You will proceed directly to San Elizario to take charge of a prisoner and escort him back to Austin to stand trial for murder. You will travel by the most direct route. This letter will serve as your warrant and draw for expenses.
>
> CAPT. WILLIAM MACNALLY
> TEXAS RANGERS

Terse and succinct and, he knows, the usual assignment for him. Normally, a U.S. marshal would be assigned to bring a prisoner back, but he has had a career of prisoner transport and other assignments of this mien meant to belittle him and force him to resign. But he has long been resolved to such work, and the letter, other than being orders, has little meaning to him now.

Funny, he thinks while refolding the paper, how a man comes to accept most anything that keeps coming his way despite doing everything a man can do to make things right. If only those Comanches hadn't delayed my ride to Houston, things might have been different. But, he sighs, you play the cards as they are dealt to you and there's no use crying over a bad hand.

He rises and makes ready to leave his camp, covering

his small fire and loading his pack and saddling his horse. Within the hour, he sets off across the mesquite-dotted desert, heading toward the distant Sierra Blanco mountains. He huddles deep inside his heavy coat as an early-morning wind comes down from the north. He smells the cold, and a wry smile crosses his thin lips beneath his heavy salt-and-pepper mustache. The return trip will be made through winter cold, and although spending Christmas escorting a prisoner is not an assignment he would have chosen, he is content with the solitude that the trip will provide for the two of them. Besides, he reasons, it's better to be busy during the season instead of sitting in a saloon somewhere, drowning his thoughts in whiskey or spending the days in Rosa's whorehouse.

2

He rides into San Elizario in the dead of night, weary and covered with trail dust. He guides Jim over to the jail and dismounts stiffly, looping the reins loosely over the hitching rail. He places his hands upon his hips and arches his back, feeling the cramped muscles loosen. He is as tired as a mining camp whore, but he mounts the steps and enters the jail, slipping off his heavy coat and draping it over his left arm.

The sheriff sits behind a scarred walnut desk, his brow furrowed in concentration as he writes. He looks up, notices the Ranger badge pinned to Walton's vest, and drops the pencil stub upon the desk.

"Got a telegram from MacNally saying you was on the way. Wasn't expecting you until morning," he says. He motions to a stained blue-bottom coffeepot on the potbellied stove. "Help yourself."

Walton nods and takes a tin cup from a warming hook on the side of the stove and pours a cup of coffee. He blows gently across the surface of the coffee, cooling it, then sips cautiously. He sighs as the warmth begins to spread through him.

"Saw no reason to draw the trip out. 'Sides, there's a norther coming down, and I'd just as soon get a good start before it hits."

"Uh-huh," the sheriff says. "Most folks would rather stay in town and ride out the storm 'fore starting back."

"Ain't most folks," Walton says.

"Yeah, so I hear," the sheriff grunts, rearranging his bulk in the captain's chair. "The last of the old wolves. I heard about you."

"What did you hear?" Walton asks, fixing the sheriff with a hard stare. He takes a small sip of coffee.

The sheriff drops his eyes to the top of his desk. "'Spect it's nothing more than what others hear. Don't put much stock in what other folks say. I like to make my own mind up about a man."

"Admirable," Walton says. He nods toward the back. "I'll want to leave at early light. Best that way. Keep the man's friends from causing any problem."

"All right. You looking for a place to stay, the hotel's across the street. I got them to save a room for you. Meals are pretty good, too."

"Appreciate it," Walton says, finishing the coffee. He slaps the dregs out into a wastebasket and hangs the cup back on the warming hook. "I could use a good night's sleep. Won't get much on the way back, watching the prisoner and all. Can you get someone to take care of my horses and have another one ready by false light?"

The sheriff nods. "Easy enough. We only got the one prisoner 'cept a couple of drunks sleeping off season's greetings. I'll have someone take your animals down to the stable and settle them in. You want a drink to warm you?"

"No. Don't like riding with a bad head. Time to drink's when I'm back."

"Suit yourself," the sheriff says indifferently, but Walton sees the relief in his eyes that he doesn't have to spend any time with him in the saloon. He nods and crosses to the door, slipping his coat back over his shoulders. He leaves and steps down to his saddle horse and unties his saddle-bags and takes his Henry rifle from its saddleboot. He rubs his hand up and down Jim's thick mane.

"Get what rest you can, old boy," he says. "We leave early in the morning."

Jim turns his head and gives Walton a nudge with his nose. Walton pats him and walks away, crossing the dirt street to the hotel.

3

He awakens in his room, forgetting for a moment that he is in San Elizario. Then he remembers and sighs, swinging his feet over the edge of the bed and rising. He crosses to the mirror hanging above the washstand and peers into it, noticing the deep circles under his eyes and running his hand over the stubble on his chin. He shaves carefully, then dresses in a fresh warm shirt and pants, knowing it's unlikely that he'll get a chance to change until he's back in Pecos before heading down to Austin with his prisoner.

Purple light streaks the street as he steps out of the hotel and makes his way across to the jail. Jim is tied to the rail along with his packhorse and a walleyed mule. He checks the pack and the saddles, then takes hand-cuffs out of his saddlebags before tying them behind Jim's saddle. He slides the Henry back into the saddle-boot and mounts the stairs, entering the jail. The sheriff is waiting for him.

"Sleep well?" the sheriff asks, rising from behind his desk.

Walton shrugs. "Thanks for getting the horses and mule ready. You want my chit for receipt of the mule?"

The sheriff shakes his head. "Not needed. I used MacNally's telegram for a receipt. I had the jailer pack coffee and beans and some hardtack for you along with some jerky. That enough?"

"Good enough for the trail," he says. "I'll send a telegram telling you when I get to Pecos so you know the first leg of the trip has gone okay."

"Good enough," he says. He picks a paper from a pile on the desk and hands it to Walton. "If you sign for the prisoner, I'll get him out and ready."

Walton hands him the handcuffs and says, "Cuff his hands in front of him. I don't want him falling off the mule."

"Your choice," the sheriff says, taking the cuffs and disappearing into the back of the jail.

Walton scans the paper and scrawls his signature across the bottom, then takes the Navy Colt from its holster and checks the loads. He slips the Navy back into his holster as the sheriff reappears with the prisoner, a Negro, slight of build with a scruff of a beard around his chin. He's dressed warmly and looks to have been well fed, although his eyes are wide and expressionless in his face as he stares at Walton.

Walton returns the stare. "You Sam?" The Negro nods. "I'm Ranger Bill Walton. I'll be taking you back to Austin to stand trial for murder. You understand that?" The Negro nods again. "Good. I only got one rule for you to remember: you run and I'll shoot you. You cause problems, I'll cuff your hands behind you and leg-iron you and tie you onto the mule you'll be riding. Otherwise, everything will go nice and easy. You understand that?"

Sam nods again, remaining silent.

"Long as we understand each other," Walton says. He looks at the sheriff. "Wasting light. Might as well get on with it."

"I say you're a man of few words," the sheriff says. He prods Sam toward the door.

"Talking ain't gettin' the ridin' done," Walton says.

4

The sun shines briefly; then leaden clouds heavy with rain and snow begin to roll ponderously down from the north as Walton and his prisoner ride toward the Sierra

Blanca mountains across the high desert dotted with mesquite and greasewood. They ride silently, Sam's long legs dangling down beneath the mule's belly, his hands handcuffed in front of him. He wears black worsted pants and coat and a white shirt long overdue for a laundry. Yet there is a dignified quiet about him, his face impassive, and he rides with his head up instead of slumped in the saddle as do other prisoners. Walton is grateful for the silence, as many prisoners begin to whine and complain their innocence from the minute they clear the towns where they have been held in jail.

Walton rides easily in the saddle upon his sorrel, his eyes constantly sweeping the country around him. Apaches and Comanches have been known to ambush parties this close to towns. Just a couple of years ago, Vitorro, leading a band of renegade Apaches, had way-laid a small troop of Rangers in the foothills of the Sierra Blanca until being driven away by withering fire from the Rangers' Winchesters. And Vitorro is a madman, taking great delight in torturing any prisoners, Americans or Mexicans, that he can capture. Automatically, Walton reaches down and loosens the Henry in its saddleboot and fingers the cartridges in a belt around his waist.

But it is the weather that worries Walton the most. He doesn't want to be caught in the open if the clouds coming down are the forerunners of a blue norther that would force them to hole up in the open to ride out the storm. At least in the mountains shelter can be found. Four years ago, a man and his wife and two children had been caught in a blue norther for three days and froze to death only miles from shelter and he had found them, the husband and wife huddled around their children in a vain attempt to slip their body warmth into the children to keep them from freezing. When they were discovered two days after the storm had passed, the Mexican wolves had already been at them, gnawing what flesh they could from their bodies.

He shivers and huddles deeper into his warm coat and casts a critical eye at his prisoner, wondering if the Negro is dressed warmly enough for this weather. As if sensing Walton's contemplation, Sam turns in his saddle and looks back, questioning, and Walton makes his decision.

"I think it'd be better if we hole up in those mountains somewheres until this storm blows itself out," Walton says, pointing toward the Sierra Blanca. "There's a cave a bit off the trail, and we still got time to gather some wood for a fire. No sense in pushing on for the sake of saving some miles and being caught. You give that mule a kick to get it moving a little faster. Weather don't wait on no man."

Sam nods and turns his attention back to the trail, kicking the mule into a trot. He bounces all over the saddle when he rides, like a pumpkin-roller on a plowhorse, his workshoes clapping against the sides of the mule.

They just make it to the pass over the Sierra Blanca, when a stiff wind comes barreling down across the desert, bringing with it cold rain mixed with bits of ice. Jim grumbles and shakes his mane. Walton pats his neck reassuringly and takes the lead, climbing off the trail and following a narrow game trail a half mile until he comes to a shallow cave large enough to hold the horses in the back.

He dismounts stiffly and stands aside watchfully as Sam slides awkwardly from his saddle. He pulls the collar of his coat tight against his neck and looks impassively at Walton.

"We'd better gather wood quickly," Walton says. "But you stay where I can see you. Remember what I said."

"I'll remember," Sam says softly. "I ain't going to cause you no trouble."

"See that you don't," Walton says gruffly and gestures outside the cave.

The two move down the side of the mountain and gather as much dried wood as they can find. They make three trips each back into the cave, neatly stacking the wood to one side. Then Walton builds a small fire before stripping the tack and pack from their animals. He tosses blankets to Sam and says, "You build yourself a pallet next to the fire while I get some coffee on. We could use something warm inside."

"I can do the coffee if you want," Sam says. "I worked as a cook back in Austin."

"All right," Walton says. "You'll find what you want in the pack. There's a frying pan in there as well."

Walton spreads his blankets on the other side of the fire away from Sam and sits, his Henry in his hand, checking the action. Sam watches him out of the corner of his eye as he scurries around, laying his pallet and setting out coffee and beginning supper.

"It's gonna be kinda lean. You don't have much to work with," he comments.

"Wasn't expecting no fancy eating-house fare," Walton says. "But it'll keep us warm and filled while we wait here."

Sam nods.

"You're a quiet man, for a nigger," Walton says. "I don't mean nothing personal. It's just that usually prisoners talk my ear off about how everything is a mistake with them."

"I figure you wouldn't believe anything I said anyways," Sam says. "So there's no use me saying anything. Far as you and other white folks are concerned, a black man is guilty just because a white man says he is. Always been that way; always be that way."

"You been accused of murder."

"I've been found guilty of murder."

"You ain't had a trial yet," Walton says.

Sam remains silent, but he looks up, his eyes steady on Walton's eyes. A tiny smile flickers around his lips, then he turns his attention back to cooking.

"A trial is just another way of saying a black man's guilty," he says.

"Man's supposed to be innocent until he's proven guilty," Walton says.

Sam shrugs. "'Spose that works for white men, but there's a different law for black folk. When the last time you see a black man turn loose by the courts?"

Walton frowns, studying Sam. The wind begins to howl around the mouth of the cave, and the horses move uneasily. He rises and goes to them, soothing them, and begins to rub them down with their saddle blankets.

"Well, you might as well tell me your story," Walton says.

"Didn't think you wanted to hear," Sam answers.

"We ain't got much else to do in this here cave while it's storming outside. Talking will help pass the time between us."

Sam studies him carefully, then shrugs. "All right. You want to hear, I'll tell you. I was a cook for Cullen Wakefield. You hear of him?"

Walton nods. Cullen Wakefield is one of the richest men in Austin with a fancy house and servants off Guadalupe near the capitol. Senators and representatives seek his advice, and it is well known that the governor considers him his best friend.

"Yeah, I've heard of him," Walton says. "He swings a big loop down in Austin."

"That's true," Sam says. "And he got a beautiful wife that makes other men hunger for her."

"I've heard about Sarah Wakefield, too," Walton says drily. "She was Sarah Caufield before Wakefield married her."

"She was a singer up in Saint Looey," Sam says. "I was cookin' for Mister Wakefield 'fore he brought her back as his wife. But I could tell that there was more to Missus Wakefield than others thought. She had a wanderin' eye and that make Mister Wakefield angry, some of her antics does. She wasn't the showpiece he wanted her to be. She about twenty years younger than him, and old men and young women don' mix well together. Like castor oil and water."

"I've heard that, too," Walton says, remembering the stories that floated quietly in and out of the saloons about how Wakefield's wife liked to entertain when her husband was out of town.

"Well, one day last September—the fourteenth, I recall—Mister Wakefield come home and find her with another man. He chased the man out of the house, and then he and Missus Wakefield get to shoutin' upstairs in

her room. I can hear it way down in the kitchen. I hear
the words, and they ain't words that a married couple
say betwixt themselves. Mean words. Then I hear her
laugh and there ain't nothing nice about the way she
laughs. Then I hear a scream and it scare five years out
of me. I go running up and see Mister Wakefield come
out of her room with blood all over him. He look at me
and goes running down the stairs and slams out the
door. I go into her room and find her cut to pieces and
Mister Wakefield's fancy knife he claims his granddaddy
got from Jim Bowie himself lying on the floor. There
ain't nothing I can do for Missus Wakefield, cut as bad
as she was, and I wondering what to do when I hear the
door slam open downstairs and voices shoutin' about
where that nigger and get a rope."

He shrugs. "Don't take much for me to know that
Mister Wakefield had some men with him and that I
gonna be the one to hang for what happened to Missus
Wakefield. So I drop out the back window and run
away. Figured that be the best thing for me to do."

"But you got caught," Walton says, returning to the fire.

Sam nods. "I ain't no killer. I a cook. That's all. But I
hear as I come out this way 'bout how I 'sposed to have
raped and killed her and Mister Wakefield he come
home to find her body and me with blood all over me
and such." He looks up at Walton. "But there never any
blood on me. These the clothes I was wearing and you
see no blood on them. But I a nigger and ain't no white
man gonna believe that. You don't."

"No, I don't see no blood on you, but that don't make
your story true," Walton says. "It's just like the other stories I hear from prisoners I take back to trial."

Another tiny smile flickers around Sam's lips.

"It the only story I got. And it the truth." He pauses and sits back on his heels. His brow furrows as he considers Walton. "You think I don't know what happens to a black man accused of such by a white man like Mister Wakefield? You think I stupid enough to forget that?" He shakes his head. "Don't matter. I ain't. And no nigger in a house in Austin gonna forget that. They know." His shoulders slump dejectedly. "And all niggers know that ain't nowhere they can go where they be safe. Once the bad name's put on them, they don't ever live that down."

Walton flinches. He rises and crosses to the mouth of the cave to study the storm. Sam's last words fit him as well. No one lived down a bad name once it came on them. A loneliness comes upon him, and he crosses his arms against the cold coming in through the mouth of the cave. He shivers and turns and looks back at Sam, fixing supper. The small fire blazes, and shadows dance on the walls of the cave. He stares at the shadows, seeing puppet masters making puppets dance jerkily on thin strings. He watches as one of the figures separates itself from another and moves toward the fire only to double up as if a great pain lances across its stomach. Shadow after shadow tries to cross from the walls to the fire only to be drawn back again by the puppet masters.

He shakes his head and looks back at Sam, feeling himself drawn into the darkness of the prisoner's eyes.

"You ever hear about me?" he asks impulsively.

Sam looks away, concentrating on the skillet he's laid on the fire.

"I mean, you hear any stories about me?"

Slowly Sam nods. "Yes, I hear stories. In Texas, a man hears all stories come time. Ain't nothin' kept away." He raises his head and looks at Walton. "I hear all about you, Mister Walton. I hear what you done and what you ain't supposed to have done, but it don't matter none what you ain't supposed to have done, 'cause no one believe you."

Bitterness sweeps over Walton.

"They ain't true."

Sam shakes his head. "Don't matter none, do it? No one believe what you say. No man ever believe what you say, do they?"

"I ain't like you!"

Sam shrugs.

"Damn it, I ain't like you!"

Sam silently takes the skillet off the fire and scrapes the dinner out onto two tin plates. He sets one across the fire on Walton's blankets, then takes the other and goes to his pallet and sits, crossing his legs. Methodically, he begins to eat.

"Ain't nothin' I do about that neither," he says.

"You believe them stories?" Walton asks, going to his blankets.

"Make no difference what I believe, do it?"

"No. Guess it don't," Walton says. He takes a bite of the food, but has no appetite and places the plate next to his leg. Sam notices.

"Best you eat 'fore it get cold," he says. "Otherwise, you get a mouthful of grease."

But Walton ignores him and hunkers down, staring out at the storm mounting its fury against the cave mouth, feeling the familiar blackness begin to settle over him.

5

They stay in the cave for two days while the storm rages outside. They speak about the lives that they once knew and what they have become, and the shadows continue to dance on the walls, coming toward the light, then moving back again to the walls where they jerk helplessly to the strings held by the puppet masters.

The storm moves away by the noon of the third day and Walton rises, stretches the night kinks from his back, and moves toward the horses to ready them for travel. Sam cleans the coffeepot and plates, and rolls the blankets tightly and ties them onto the packhorse.

"You in the cave!"

Walton stiffens and picks up his Henry, moving cautiously to the mouth of the cave. He peers out and a bullet whangs off the rock near his head. He ducks back inside and levers a round into the Henry. He glances at Sam.

"Get down!" he says.

Obediently, Sam drops to the floor and lays flat.

Walton inches closer to the mouth of the cave and risks a quick glance. Men with Winchesters have scattered themselves among the boulders at the foot of the incline. A man in a white hat and dressed in a mackinaw with a fur collar stands next to one rock.

"Hold your fire! I'm a Texas Ranger taking a prisoner back to Austin!" he yells.

"We know who you are!" the man yells. His words echo off the stones of the cliff above the cave.

"That be Mister Wakefield," Sam says. He laughs, but

no humor comes with the laughter. "I don't think you gonna take this nigger back, Mister Walton."

Walton ignores him. "I'm ordering you all to fall back and put up your guns!" he shouts.

Laughter comes hard upon his words, and bullets ricochet off the stones and whine around the walls of the cave. The mule grunts and sags to the ground and slowly lays on its side.

"Give up your prisoner and we'll let you go!" Wakefield shouts.

"Can't do that. I have my orders!" Walton shouts back and ducks as bullets whine around him again.

"I don't think they gonna listen to you," Sam says calmly. "Fact, I don't think they gonna let you go neither. They don't want witnesses."

Walton slips near the edge and fires down at the men as quickly as he can work the lever on the Henry. A bullet answers him, whines off the wall, and he feels it slam into his lower back. He grunts from the impact but feels no pain. The pain will come later.

"I'm hit," he says.

Sam crawls forward and cautiously lifts himself to examine the wound. He crawls back and grabs a blanket, ripping strips from it. He crawls back to Walton.

"It bad," he says. "But you raise up a little and I can wrap it."

Walton backs away from the edge and eases up, gasping from a sudden pain that cuts through him like a razor. Sam wraps the blanket strips around him, pulling them tight, ignoring Walton's pain. He knots the ends together firmly and pats him on the shoulder.

"You won't be riding," he says. He moves back and

rubs his hand over his head, sighing. "Well, look to me like we done for."

Walton takes a deep breath. The pain intensifies, and he lets the breath out slowly and begins to breathe shallowly. He feels the cold moving up him and sighs.

"Reckon you're right," he says. "But maybe you're wrong."

He looks back at the horses and notices the mule. A wry grin tugs at his lips. He takes the handcuff key out of his pocket and unlocks Sam's handcuffs, then unbuckles his gun belt and hands it to him.

Sam frowns as he takes the gun belt and looks questioningly at Walton.

"Go on," Walton says. "Put it on. You're gonna need it 'fore this is over."

Wordlessly, Sam buckles the pistol around his waist.

"Now," Walton says, "it's gonna get dark quick around here and there ain't gonna be no moon. Not with this sky. When it gets dark, I want you to take Old Jim and the packhorse and make your way up around that game trail. Move slowly and stay as quiet as you can. Then when you get over the top, you ride hell-bent-for-leather away from here. Understand?"

"You letting me go?" Sam asks.

"Uh-huh," Walton grunts. The Henry feels slippery in his hands. "I was you, I'd make a big swing to the east and then make your way up north into the Oklahoma territory. I hear about some black folks who have built their own settlements up there. One's called Paradise, but I can't remember the others. Don't matter. They're there. You can lose yourself in them easy enough. Build a new life."

"Why you doing this?" Sam asks.

Walton nods toward the mouth of the cave. "Figure what you said was true. Otherwise, why would Wakefield and his boys be out there? They knew you was arrested and that I was bringing you back. Don't take a wise man to figure out why they down there shooting up here at us when I told them I was a Ranger."

He glances back at the horses.

"I figure you got enough food to get you up there, you eat sparingly. You get up over the Red River and you can swap the packhorse for what all you need." He smiles, feeling light-headed. "That's about the best I can do for you, Sam."

"It enough," Sam says solemnly. He stretches out his hand and Walton takes it, shaking it firmly.

"You get yourself ready now. This ain't no sure thing. But after you clear away a bit, I'm gonna let them know that someone's still here. I'll keep them down there until I figure you're well away."

6

They wait silently, patiently, Walton firing an occasional shot down at the men to let them know that they were still there. Then, night comes rapidly over the Sierra Blancos and Walton turns to Sam.

"It's time," he says. "There's no moon. Dark as the bottom of a well."

Sam rises and crosses low back to the horses and leads them out by the reins. He pauses and looks down at Walton.

"I ain't never forget this," he says.

"Neither will I," Walton answers. "Go on, now. Get while you can."

Sam pauses, looking out into the dark. "Just remembered. This is Christmas."

Then he disappears out the cave. Walton hears the horses moving quietly up the game trail leading over the mountain. He counts slowly and when he reaches a hundred, he crawls to the edge of the cave, takes a deep breath, and fires as rapidly as he can down into the blackness. A yelp answers a shot and he grins. He knows that they'll be coming for him at first light. For a second, he sees Travis again in his mind and the dusty room in the Alamo. Then bullets begin to whine around him, ricocheting off the dim shadows on the walls of the cave.

ONE AND FOUR
ROBERT J. RANDISI

———◆———

The author of more than three hundred western novels, Bob Randisi's most recent book is *The Reluctant Pinkerton*. He is also the author and creator, as J. R. Roberts, of the long-running series "The Gunsmith." Here is a tale of the capture of the badman who was number one on the Texas Rangers' fugitive list, John Wesley Hardin. Randisi's other anthologies of westerns are *Tin Star, White Hats, Black Hats,* and *Boot Hill.*

He is also the author of *The Widowmaker: Invitation to a Hanging,* book one in a series.

1

October 11, 1878
Giddings, Texas

Texas Ranger Sergeant John B. Armstrong knew that Wild Bill Longley's main complaint about his hanging was that his sentence was so much more severe than that of another legendary Texas outlaw, John Wesley Hardin, who only months earlier had been sentenced to twenty-five years in prison for similar crimes. Armstrong—the man who had apprehended Hardin—knew for a fact that Hardin was considered to be the number one Texas badman by everyone involved in law enforcement, and he too wondered at the comparative leniency of Hardin's sentence.

But there was nothing that could be done about it at the moment. Longley was scant moments away from having his neck stretched. His claims of a conspiracy had garnered him no pity from any quarter, and in fact, the hangman himself showed him none, for when the trapdoor opened beneath his feet, Longley's neck did not snap, as it was supposed to. Instead, the hangman pulled up on the rope and the crowd—including Armstrong—watched Wild Bill Longley kick his way to an ugly death by strangulation.

Hardin and Longley were two of what was considered

the "Big Four" of Texas badmen, the others being King Fisher and Ben Thompson. All four men had in fact reached legendary status in Texas and were considered by some to be "heroes." Of course, none of those who considered them as such were counted among the Texas Rangers.

Armstrong was attending the hanging because he was the Ranger who had tracked down and apprehended Wild Bill Longley. Likewise, he had also arrested John Wesley Hardin. Of course, when it came to Hardin he'd had some help, which was why he too thought that Longley's sentence to hang was not at all in line with Hardin's life sentence.

After Longley was pronounced dead, Armstrong repaired to the nearest saloon, got himself a beer, avoided the crowds of men who were celebrating the hanging, and found himself a back table where he could drink in peace. He wondered what his partner in the John Wesley Hardin apprehension would think of all this.

John Riley Duncan preferred to be called "Jack." An ex-policeman, at the time Armstrong met him he was generally considered to be the finest private detective in Texas.

The occasion of their meeting was Duncan's being appointed a Special Ranger by Governor Richard Hubbard, assigned to assist Sergeant Armstrong in the capture or killing of John Wesley Hardin. The governor made it quite plain to both men that he did not care which.

That night in Dallas they hatched their plan.

*   *   *

"You might be recognized in Gonzales County as a Ranger," Duncan said, "but I won't."

Gonzales County was the home of Wes Hardin's in-laws, the Bowens. His brother-in-law, Brown Bowen, was also on the run with a $500 bounty on his head.

"One of us has to go to Gonzales County and worm his way into the good graces of Wes's father-in-law, Neil Bowen."

"And how do you intend to do that?" Armstrong asked.

"By posing as a potential buyer for the Bowen store," Duncan said.

"Why would Neil Bowen bother givin' you the time of day, Jack?' Armstrong asked.

Duncan chuckled and said, "'Cause I'm gonna have a price on my head, myself."

2

Duncan went to Gonzales County under the guise of a man named Williams, a merchant who was also wanted by the law. It did not take long for him to make the acquaintance of Neil Bowen in a saloon, and quickly the two got to talking about the many things they had in common.

They discussed their mutual contempt for the law, and the fact that they were both merchants. In fact, Duncan/Williams went so far as to tell Bowen he was looking to buy a nice little store.

"Mind if I come and have a look at yours tomorrow?" he asked Bowen.

"Come ahead," Bowen said, and that's what Duncan did.

He showed up at Bowen's store the next day and the day after, admiring it, and several days after that before finally making an offer to buy. It was during one of these visits to the store that Duncan was able to intercept a piece of Bowen's mail. It was from Jane Hardin, Bowen's daughter and Wes Hardin's wife. She sent her love to her father. The name on the return address was J. H. Swain. One of the Hardin aliases Duncan and Armstrong were given was "John Swain," and this was close enough.

The return address was Pollard, Alabama. Duncan now had all he needed for Armstrong and him to go down south to pick up Hardin. Now he had to get out of town without arousing suspicion, so that no one would send a warning to John Wesley Hardin.

He went to the telegraph office and sent a wire to Armstrong saying, "Come and get your horse."

The next day Sergeant John Armstrong came riding into Gonzalez County with a guard and a wagon. He stopped in at the sheriff's office to announce his intentions.

"You got a fella named Williams in town," he said. "I've come to pick him up."

"He's a stranger," Sheriff Will Tully said. "Been hangin' around with Neil Bowen. In fact, I think he had ol' Neil an offer on his store. You'll probably find him over there right now."

"He isn't going to get a chance to close that deal," Armstrong promised. "Point me toward Bowen's store and I'll pick up my man."

The sheriff stepped outside his office and pointed the way.

"Sure you don't want any help?" he asked.

"This was just a courtesy call, Sheriff," Armstrong said. "I can handle it."

"Suit yerself."

Armstrong stepped down from the boardwalk and started walking toward Bowen's store.

Williams/Duncan saw Armstrong walk in and prepared himself for their act.

Neil Bowen saw the man with the Ranger's star enter his store and he shouted, "Out! We don't serve no Rangers here."

"You Williams?" Armstrong asked Duncan, ignoring Bowen.

"That's right," Duncan said.

"I got a warrant for your arrest, Williams," Armstrong said. "You're comin' with me."

"Like hell I am!"

"Don't go for your gun!" Bowen shouted. "Don't give him an excuse ta kill you. That's what they wanna do to my boy and to my son-in-law."

"Son-in-law?" Duncan said, contriving to look confused.

"John Wesley Hardin."

"Jesus," Duncan said, "you're kin to Wes Hardin?"

"He's married to my daughter."

Armstrong drew his gun and pointed it at Duncan.

"Don't make me kill you, Williams," he said. "Come peaceably."

"Do like he says, Williams," Bowen said. "This here's Sergeant Armstrong, the man who brought in Bill Longley."

"Well," Duncan said, "least I'm bein' taken in by somebody famous."

Duncan gave up his gun and Armstrong clapped irons on him and walked him out to the wagon. Trussed up like a prisoner, Armstrong and his guard drove "Williams" to the town of Cuero.

Once they were in Cuero, Armstrong released Duncan and they both boarded a train to Austin, where they obtained extradition papers for the names John Wesley Hardin and John Swain.

Armstrong and Duncan discussed their next moves on a train to Montgomery, Alabama.

3

"Why can't we both go to Pollard?" Armstrong complained. "I don't like bein' left out."

"The same reason you couldn't come with me the first time, John," Duncan said. "You're a Ranger."

"So are you, Jack!"

"A temporary one," Duncan said. "Nobody is gonna recognize me as one. They will recognize you."

Armstrong looked out at the countryside they were passing. "You're gonna wear a disguise."

"Yes."

"Then put one on me."

"John—"

"Damn it, Jack!" Armstrong said. "It's like you said. I'm the real Ranger here."

"Yes, you are, Sergeant," Duncan said, "and I'm the detective. I'll do my job and locate Hardin and then you can go in and do yours by apprehending him. That's how it's supposed to work." Duncan punched Armstrong on the arm to soften the impact of his words. "Come on, John. You know this already."

"Yeah, yeah," Armstrong said, "I know."

"Gimme a break," Duncan said. "You brought Longley in by yourself. Let me have my moment and help bring in Hardin."

Armstrong didn't bother correcting Duncan. If the detective wanted to believe that he'd brought in Wild Bill Longley completely on his own, who was he to disappoint him?

When they got to Montgomery, they got a hotel room and Armstrong watched while Duncan turned himself into a transient by use of some old clothes and theatrical makeup. When the man was done, he turned and presented himself to the Ranger for his approval.

"What do you think?"

"Not your typical Ranger uniform," Armstrong said. "I'd never recognize you."

"Well," Duncan said, "I'm not so much tryin' to go unrecognized as I am just tryin' to blend in and not be noticed."

"Believe me," Armstrong said, "I think you did it."

*   *   *

Duncan spent two weeks in Pollard while Armstrong stayed in a hotel in Montgomery and waited. Armstrong was sitting on the porch of the hotel when Duncan returned, still in his disguise. Duncan dismounted and joined Armstrong, sitting next to him.

"Thought maybe you forgot to come back," the Ranger said.

"Took me a while to get somebody to talk to me."

"And?"

"Hardin's in Florida with some friends," the detective said. "Pensacola, gambling."

"What friends?"

"Shep Hardy, Jim Mann, and Neil Campbell."

"Are they wanted?"

"I was gonna ask you that."

"Not that I know of."

"What about our warrants?"

"I'll wire for them today," Armstrong said. "When is Hardin comin' back?"

"I don't know," Duncan said. "We can go down there and get 'im, can't we?"

"We need our Texas warrants in order for us to have any authority," Armstrong explained.

"Isn't there some way around that?" Duncan asked.

Armstrong thought a minute.

"If we had some local authorities with us, that would give us the backing we need," he finally said.

"A sheriff?"

"The sheriff from here and from Pensacola," Armstrong said. "And maybe the warrants will arrive by the time we get him."

"But where?" Duncan said. "Where do you want to take him?"

"Let's get the locals in on this and then we can decide," Armstrong said.

"Okay," Duncan said, standing up. "Let's do it now."

Armstrong looked the filthy detective up and down and asked, "You want to take a bath first?"

4

The odd thing was that while the Montgomery, Alabama, authorities wanted nothing to do with the apprehension, the Pensacola, Florida, people agreed to meet with Armstrong and Duncan in Alabama. When they all met at the train station, Armstrong was surprised to find not only Sheriff William Hutchinson, but a Pensacola judge, as well as William D. Chipley, the superintendent on the Pensacola railroad.

They shook hands all around and repaired to the dining room of the hotel where Armstrong and Duncan were staying. It was then and there that Armstrong informed the men that the John Swain they were after was in fact John Wesley Hardin.

"Do you have warrants for Hardin?" Chipley asked.

Armstrong, surprised that the question came from the superintendent and not the sheriff, said, "They're on the way."

The sheriff didn't say a word, nor did the judge. They both looked at Chipley, who apparently carried a lot of weight in Florida.

"You'll have all the help you need if you take Hardin on the train when he boards to return here."

"Agreed," Armstrong said.

"And there's one more thing."

"What's that?"

"I want another man arrested."

"Who?" the Ranger asked.

"Brown Bowen."

"Is he in Pensacola?" Duncan asked.

"No," Armstrong said, "I've seen him around here. What about the locals here?" he asked Chipley. "They don't want to help."

"They'll help with Bowen."

Armstrong and Duncan knew that Bowen was related to Hardin, of course, so there was no problem with arresting him. He wasn't the desperado Hardin was, but he was still wanted.

But Armstrong was curious.

"If I may ask," he said, "why do you want Bowen arrested?"

Chipley, a well-dressed but portly man in his fifties, sat up straight and said, "The ruffian threatened me in my own train terminal last month, and for no reason."

"Threatened you?" Duncan asked.

"We had an . . . altercation and he threatened to kill me. I want him removed from the vicinity."

Armstrong looked at the judge and the sheriff.

"You go along with all this?"

"Whatever Mr. Chipley wants," the judge said. He was a white-haired man in his sixties, and was clearly subservient to the railroad super.

The lawman, however, was clearly happy about the

whole thing. He was in his forties and had been wearing a badge for over twenty years. He loved standing behind the tin, but he hated the politics of the job.

"I have my orders to assist you in any way," he said to Armstrong. "Frankly, I'm more than pleased that this fella Swain has turned out to be Wes Hardin. At least I know I'll actually be doin' my job."

And not just kowtowing to a politician, Armstrong added to himself.

"All right, then," the Ranger said. "We take Hardin and whoever's with him when they board the train."

"How will we know when that is going to be?" Duncan asked.

"I'll take care of that," the sheriff said. "I'll pass the word when I get it. All you'll have to do is take the train from here to Pensacola and wait there."

"How many deputies you got, Sheriff?" Armstrong asked.

"As many as I need."

"One," Armstrong said.

"What?"

"We don't want any passengers getting hurt, and we don't want anybody overreacting to a crowd of lawmen," he said. "I think four of us should be able to handle the situation."

"I appreciate the concern for my passengers, Ranger," Chipley said. "What about Bowen?"

"We can pick him up tomorrow," Armstrong said, "with no problem, if you're right about the locals cooperating."

"I'll see to it," Chipley said.

"All right, then," Armstrong said, "that's settled."

"And now, what about dinner?" Chipley asked. "I'm buying."

No one refused.

5

Pensacola, Florida

John Wesley Hardin approached the train with his friends Jim Mann, Shep Hardy, and Neil Campbell. His gambling trip had gone well, and his pockets were full of money. The same could not be said of his friends, whose pockets were empty.

"Goddamn Wes," Jim Mann said. "Luckiest gambler I ever seen."

"Luckier than you," Hardin said, "in everything."

"Even got him a purty wife waitin' for him in Pollard," Neil Campbell said.

"Lucky Wes," Shep Hardy said.

The four men boarded the train together, entered a passenger car, and took their seats—Hardin, Campbell, and Hardy on one side, Jim Mann in an empty seat across the aisle.

"They're on the train," Sheriff Hutchinson said as he entered the waiting room of the train station.

Sitting with John Armstrong and Jack Duncan were Hutchinson's deputies, A. J. Perdue and Martin Sullivan. The sheriff had decided that five against four was better odds for them—especially since one of the four was

John Wesley Hardin. This was also a fact he had not advised his deputies of yet.

"Somethin' you boys should know before we get on the train," he said to them.

"What's that, boss?" Perdue asked.

"This fella Swain we're gonna take today?" the sheriff said. "His real name's John Wesley Hardin."

Sullivan's eyes widened. "That's Wes Hardin on that train?"

"That's him," Armstrong said.

"Do we want him dead," Perdue asked, "or alive?"

Duncan and Hutchinson looked to Armstrong for the answer to that question.

"Any way we can get him," the Ranger said.

"Let's go then," Hutchinson said. "Me and my men will board from the front."

That left the back for Armstrong and Duncan.

As they left the station and moved onto the platform, Duncan asked Armstrong, "Do we have our warrants?"

"Not yet," the Ranger said. "Hopefully, they'll be waitin' for us in Pollard when we get there."

"And if not?" Duncan asked.

"Not our fault," Armstrong said. "Once we've got him, we've got him."

"Let the courts sort it out," Duncan said.

"Damn right," Armstrong said. "We're Rangers, not goddamned lawyers or judges."

Together, they moved toward the back of the train.

Hardin was still enjoying the bulge the money made in his pocket when he saw the three men enter the railroad car. There was no mistaking the shiny badges on their shirts. He didn't panic, though, because he wasn't wanted in Florida.

Then he turned his head and saw two more men enter the car from behind. On the chest of one of them was the circle-in-the-star badge of a Texas Ranger, and he knew the jig was up.

Hutchinson shouted, "Lawmen! Put up your hands."

The other passengers on the car looked around in confusion, wondering who the lawmen were talking to.

Hardin started to get to his feet, drawing his gun. He didn't usually wear suspenders, but his belt had snapped the day before, so he was wearing a pair now. In his haste his gun got tangled, and that was all the time Hutchinson and Perdue needed to reach him.

Hutchinson, seeing that Hardin's gun had gotten entangled in his suspenders, decided not to fire. Instead, he tackled Hardin and they both went tumbling into the aisle.

Hardy and Campbell were just as confused as the other passengers on the car. Perdue pointed his gun at them and said, "Hands up."

They obeyed.

Armstrong saw Hutchinson rolling around in the aisle with Wes Hardin. Duncan, behind him, was shielded from the action and didn't see what was going on.

Armstrong rushed forward, drew his gun, and as the two men on the ground rolled over so that Hardin was on top, the Ranger brought his gun butt down on Hardin's head, ending the struggle. With Hardy and Campbell under the barrel of Deputy Perdue's gun, the conflict seemed to be over . . . but not quite.

*   *   *

Jim Mann was not wanted for anything, neither was he guilty of anything, except going to Pensacola to gamble with his three friends. However, in the midst of all the commotion, he panicked. He stood up, drew his gun, and pulled the trigger. His shots went wild, and Duncan shouted, "Look out!"

Armstrong turned just as Mann pointed his gun at him. The young man's first two shots may have gone wild, but the Ranger could see that the third shot was going to fly straight and true . . . at him! He reversed his gun in his hand, but knew he would be too late.

Duncan was a detective, not a gunman. His gun had not been drawn as he entered the car, and as he drew it now he was also sure he would be too late to save Armstrong.

However, at the other end of the car Deputy Marty Sullivan, no more than a spectator at this point, already had his gun in his hand. He pointed and fired. The bullet struck Jim Mann in the temple, spraying the young man's brains and blood over the man and woman seated behind him. This, however, was the only damage done to any innocent passengers—that is, except for the previously innocent Jim Mann.

Armstrong had John Wesley Hardin in the Travis County jail in Austin within the week. As he finished his drink and came back to the present in Giddings, Texas, he recalled the legal battle over the lack of warrants, a paperwork muddle he still didn't understand to this day. In the end a judge had discounted that, found

Hardin guilty of murder, and sentenced him to twenty-five years to life. Although Hardin was known to have killed twenty-seven men, his conviction was only for one, the killing of a lawman. In a twist of irony, Brown Bowen, who had been arrested as part of the bargain with William Chipley, was later hanged in Gonzales County for murder. And today Wild Bill Longley suffered the same fate.

Jack Duncan went back to his life as Texas's best private detective.

Armstrong—who was forever in the debt of Deputy Sullivan for saving his life—went back to his pursuit of the most notorious outlaws in the state of Texas.

Of the big four, Hardin had been number one, and Longley number four. Armstrong took out his fugitive list, a personal copy of which was carried by all Rangers. With a pencil he drew a line through the names of Hardin and Longley, and wrote next to the names "incarcerated" and "hanged."

That took care of one and four.

Many names were left in the book, but the most notable were King Fisher and Ben Thompson, numbers two and three. Armstrong would also be around when those two gents met their fates . . . but that was another story.

GHOST COLTS
PETER BRANDVOLD

———◆———

Pete Brandvold has come a long way in a short time. He is currently considered one of the bright new stars of the western genre, with two series being published by Berkley, the Marshall series and the Devil series. Like Ed Gorman's story later in this collection, this one has a decidedly eerie quality to it.

The Ranger halted his paint between two high red-granite ridges cloaked in the gray muslin of winter storm clouds. Hunkered low over the horse's neck, he held the collar of his patched buckskin coat closed and squinted against the wind-driven sleet and snow.

Ahead, a handful of shabby buildings rose from the swaying chaparral tufting the canyon. Three stood tall, with false fronts, two facing the third across the trail.

The Ranger took a deep breath. Piñon and cedar smoke laced the wind.

The Ranger—a big red-haired man with a red goatee and a broad-brimmed Stetson with a snakeskin band—turned to look at the chestnut mare he was trailing on a lead line. His prisoner lay belly down across the chestnut's saddle, handcuffed hands tied to his feet. The man's sandy hair whipped this way and that, as did the tied ends of the bloody bandage wrapped around his head.

"It's more than you deserve, Renfrow," the Ranger said beneath the wind, "but I'm about to find you a bed. I want you well rested for the judge."

The prisoner gave no response beyond lifting his head slightly, then letting it rest once again against the horse's belly.

The Ranger lightly spurred his horse forward, jerking the chestnut along behind him. A minute later, he reined up at the hitchrack before a sprawling gray building with the windows on both sides of the door lit from within. A sign swaying beneath the awning read YSLETA MERCANTILE/SALOON in large faded-green letters to which several clumps of snow stuck. Another, smaller sign to the right said simply ROOMS.

The Ranger lifted his gaze above the sign, blinking against the stinging sleet and wind-driven sand. It was only three or four in the afternoon, but the gunmetal clouds hovered low, making it look like twilight.

The Ranger dismounted with a weary sigh, quickly tied the reins of both horses to the rack, and mounted the three wobbly wooden steps to the boardwalk. The

chinging sound of his spurs was drowned by the wind
and the signs squawking overhead.

He glanced in the window right of the door, then
stepped inside the building, causing the bell over the
door to ring.

He paused and looked around with the caution of a
lawman in unfamiliar territory. A dozen or so round
tables were scattered about the long, narrow room
before him, to the right of a mahogany bar. At two
tables sat six men drinking whiskey or beer and playing
cards. One was a well-groomed young cavalryman in
crisp, gold-buttoned blues.

Behind the bar stood a young, pretty woman wearing
a man's checked shirt. Her features slack with boredom,
she was drying glasses with desultory swipes of a towel.
Her thick, wavy hair hung down her back in a ponytail.

The air smelled richly of burning piñon and of wet
leather, liquor, and tobacco. The card players had positioned themselves near the black bullet-shaped stove in
the room's right-center; the stove ticked and sighed. The
Ranger felt its welcoming heat, like a soothing blanket.

"Come in and shut the door, Ranger," said a pigeon-
chested bandy-legged oldster with heavy-lidded eyes
and thin gray hair. He was playing cribbage with a
brawny bull of a shaggy-headed man, with a heavy nose
thrusting high between dark eyes, a buffalo robe thrown
over the back of his chair. The two sat separate from the
other four. "You're lettin' all the heat out."

The Ranger closed the door, let his hand fall away
from the butt of the Peacemaker .45 on his right hip,
and turned to the young woman who'd looked up from
her work when he'd entered. "Miss, you run this place?"

"Don't I look like it?" She offered the others a faint conspiratorial smile. Several glanced up and chuckled, as though it were a joke between them. To the Ranger, she said, "Name your poison."

"Later," the Ranger said. "I'd like to get a room for an injured prisoner I have outside. The rest of his gang—eight men—could be behind us. I think I shook 'em off my trail last night." He drew a deep, tired breath. "Like I said, my prisoner's injured. In this weather, I don't think he'd make it back to San Antone alive, and I *need* him alive."

The young woman's face remained expressionless as she glanced at the card players.

"Wake up and buck the tiger," one of them said to another. The Ranger wondered if they'd heard him. The blonde set aside her glass and towel and returned her eyes to the Ranger.

"I wouldn't turn a man away in this weather," she said. She turned to a small jar containing several keys on the bar behind her. "Fetch your prisoner, Ranger. I'll open room three for you. Second door on the left at the top of the stairs."

The Ranger slid another curious glance to the card players, engrossed in their game, as though they'd forgotten he was here. Finally he went out and came back a few minutes later, his prisoner draped over his shoulder. The prisoner groaned, his gloved hands sweeping the floor as the Ranger kicked the door closed, then wove a course through the tables, heading for the stairs just beyond the bar.

The card players looked up from their pasteboards to regard the Ranger dully, as though he were crossing the room with a mere potato sack.

The half-conscious prisoner was nearly as big as the Ranger, and the lawman crouched beneath the weight, wincing as he grabbed the newel post, hiked his load higher on his shoulder, and mounted the stairs.

He stepped aside when a towheaded boy of about twelve appeared at the top of the stairs. The boy brushed past the Ranger on his way down, his high-topped miner's boots hammering the scarred planks. The youngster gave the Ranger a timid glance but said nothing. The Ranger continued to the top of the stairs, walked a few feet down the smoky hall in which most of the heat from below had collected, and turned into the second door, open on the left.

The young woman was there, kneeling beside a small sheet-iron stove and balling a yellowed newspaper in her hands. She glanced at the Ranger's load and arched a brow.

"What happened to him?"

"Had a little heart-to-heart with my rifle butt," the Ranger grunted under the weight.

"Go ahead and lay him on the bed," the woman said. "It's one of the few I keep made up. Don't get many travelers through here these days, since the gold pinched out and the stage line rerouted."

When the Ranger had deposited his load, the prisoner falling onto the bed with another groan, the Ranger said, "Much obliged to you, miss. I hope I haven't brought trouble."

The woman struck a match and held it to the pile of paper and pine bark she'd arranged inside the stove. "I doubt you could bring any more trouble than we could handle," she said tonelessly as the flame grew. "Between Injuns and outlaws, there isn't much we haven't seen."

She stood and extended her hand. "I'm Ann Coleman, owner and manager of the Ysleta Mercantile and Saloon, though the mercantile part burned down two years ago and we saw no point in rebuilding." She offered another soft, bland smile, her blue eyes pretty but oblique, her lips thin and straight. "You can call me Ann."

The Ranger shook her hand, which was small but strong, the palms lightly callused—the hands of a woman who knew her way around a barn and feedlot as well as a kitchen. "I'm Tim B. Armstrong, ma'am. Special Troops, Texas Rangers." He smiled and pinched his hat brim. "As soon as I've got this man secured to the bed here, I'd like to stable my horses, if that's possible. I saw a barn across the road . . ."

"There is, indeed," Ann Coleman said, "but your horses are already taken care of. I sent my son to bed them down with fresh hay and oats."

"I saw the boy," Armstrong said. "I didn't realize he was your son."

She'd knelt before the stove again and was adding kindling to the growing fire. The corners of her mouth stiffened slightly as she read Armstrong's mind. "Everyone thinks Michael's my younger brother." She grabbed another piñon stick from the apple crate that served as a kindling box, and added it to the fire, which was already nudging the chill from the room.

She lowered her head for a better look inside the stove. "We drop 'em young out here, I reckon."

"I didn't mean to be forward, ma'am."

"I didn't take you to be, Mr. Armstrong. We're just jawing. I don't often have many people to talk to . . . besides Dad, that is. My father's the gray-headed old reprobate you saw downstairs." She poked one more kindling stick into the stove, closed the door, then stood and slapped her hands against her thighs. "I'll fetch more wood. When I saw the storm coming, I covered a whole cord with a tarp."

Armstrong was removing his prisoner's high-heeled riding boots. "I can do that, ma'am."

"I don't have much to do around here anymore," she countered from the door. "You and the men downstairs are the first customers I've had in a month of Sundays, and this weather doesn't help."

She nodded to indicate the snow slanting and ticking against the room's single window. Then she turned through the door and walked away down the hall.

The Ranger handcuffed his prisoner's wrists and ankles to the tarnished brass bed frame, then cast a glance outside, seeing little but the weather-obscured barn across the trail and the tiny white javelins of snow and sleet driven by the keening wind. He ran another glance over his unconscious prisoner, then walked from the room, leaving the door open for the woman.

Downstairs, Ann's father was pouring drinks at the bar while three of the four others played cards. The big bearded man—round-faced, barrel-chested, and wearing a big bowie knife in a sheath around his waist—stood warming his backside at the stove. A thin cheroot smoked between his teeth.

The other men regarded the Ranger with only passing interest as he crossed the room to the window between the door and the bar. Peering out, he looked up and down what had apparently been the town's main road. Now, with most of the town died off, its buildings either dismantled or in ruin, the street was just a trail between the saloon and the yellow 'dobe post office and the wooden livery barn.

When the wind shifted he caught a fleeting glimpse of the red sandstone ridge behind the disheveled buildings.

Satisfied Renfrow's gang hadn't caught up to him, Armstrong shrugged out of his wet, foul-smelling buckskin. He shook the beaded moisture off, then draped the coat over the back of a chair near the window. He tossed his hat on the table, angled the chair so that it sat sideways, affording him a view to the east, and slumped down with a weary sigh.

The old man delivered drinks to the card players. When he'd handed a beer mug to the big man by the stove, he turned to Armstrong. "You look like you could use a toddy, Ranger."

Armstrong lifted a shoulder and ran his hands through his thick red hair combed straight back from a sharp widow's peak. "A whiskey might cut the chill. 'Specially if it was backed up by a beer."

"Comin' up," the old man said.

He limped off behind the bar and stepped out from behind it a minute later, carrying a filled shot glass in one gnarled hand and a beer schooner in the other. When he'd set the shot and the beer on the table before Armstrong, the Ranger leaned back and reached into a pocket of his wet denims.

The old man shook his head. "On the house. We appreciate you Rangers standin' up to them curly wolves. Seems like every time you turn around, we got Mex or American bandits collarin' stolen beef, runnin' down stagecoaches, or robbin' banks. They'll shoot a lawman on sight, no questions asked."

"I wish we were makin' more headway against 'em," Armstrong said. "There's plenty more where the lobo upstairs came from."

The old man put his gnarled hands on a chair back. "Outta what hole'd you smoke the snake upstairs?" He lifted his chin, indicating the second story above the room's pressed tin ceiling.

"A roadhouse near Eagle Pass. Him and his gang was stompin' with their tails up last night, havin' too much fun to post guards."

The big bearded man, now sitting on a hide couch near the door that led into the mercantile, said, "Bole Renfrow. I'd recognize ole Hatchet Face anywhere. Leads an arm of King Fisher's band." His gaze settled on Armstrong with interest. "You take him down alone, Ranger?"

Armstrong nodded. "He was on the back stoop, tendin' nature. I didn't realize another man was out there till me and Renfrow were ridin' away. The man gave a yell to alert the others, and Renfrow came up with a hideout gun. That's when I introduced him to my rifle butt."

Just then, footsteps sounded on the stairs. All heads turned as Ann came down, vagrant strands of blond hair wisping about her cheeks.

"Your prisoner's fast asleep, Ranger," she said, her

eyes finding Armstrong's. His stomach tightened, her gaze reminding him of another young woman in his past. Swinging her gaze around to the others, she said, "I'll bring out a pot of soup in a few minutes."

Brushing tree bark and sawdust from her shirt, she strolled past the bar and disappeared through the swinging door behind it.

"Shoulda shot the son of a bitch," said one of the four men playing cards, taking up the conversation where it had left off before Ann had appeared. He was a tall, slim man with a pitted beak nose and sweeping salt-and-pepper mustaches. He wore a calico shirt, suspenders, bull-hide chaps, and large-roweled spurs.

"That's Chess Burgenreich," said the old man. "He used to ranch out that way till Fisher's gang cleaned him out, shot several of his cowboys, and ran his herd clear to the Sierra Madres."

"Shoot 'em all twice," Burgenreich grunted around the twisted quirley protruding from his mustache. He studied his cards and said, "Lieutenant, I'll see your nickel, and I'll raise you a dime."

The old man said to Armstrong, "The man to Chess's right is Jake Magoon out of Corpus Christi . . ."

"And headin' back that way," Magoon said, flicking his blue eyes at the window behind Armstrong. "As soon as this weather clears." Magoon was dressed in the fawn-colored vest, trousers, and claw-hammer coat of the professional gambler. He had the pallor of one who spent most of the daylight hours in smoky gambling dens and bucket shops.

"The feller across from Magoon is Jeb DeRosso," the

oldster continued. "He hunts buffalo with Big Bill Morgan, over there on the sofa."

"Jeb answers to One-Eye," Morgan growled over his beer mug, one high-topped boot resting on a knee.

When DeRosso looked at Armstrong, the Ranger saw that the buffalo hunter's left eye appeared perpetually swollen and milky, spoiling an otherwise handsome face.

"The Kiowa brave woulda fixed my other'n for me if'n Big Bill hadn't jumped in and thrown the hot tar on his powwow." The hider held up his rawhide necklace, trimmed with what looked like two shrunken marbles and dried potato skins but could only have been the Kiowa's eyeballs and ears. "That brave's now stumblin' around blind and deaf in the next world." DeRosso wheezed, snorted, and returned his attention to the fan of cards in his hand.

The soldier sitting to DeRosso's right looked over at Armstrong. He was a tall, well-groomed redhead with a cavalry mustache and piercing blue eyes. He couldn't have been much over twenty-five. "Lieutenant George Paine at your service, Ranger," he said with a noble air. "I was on my way to Fort Bowie when the clouds blew in."

Lifting a long thin cigar to his lips, he tossed a nickel into the pot. "Let's keep the bets low, eh, fellows? My trust fund disappeared with my old man's shipping business."

"I'm Lowell Hart," the old man said to Armstrong, pulling out a chair from the Ranger's table and sitting down heavily. "Couldn't tell it by lookin' at me, but I'm Ann's father." He poked a finger at the ceiling.

"She told me," the Ranger said. He turned his head

from the window, where he'd been keeping one eye on the trail, and extended his trunk-like arm across the table. "Tim B. Armstrong, Special State Troops, Texas Rangers."

"McNelly's Viking," the oldster said with an admiring smile.

"Been called worse."

"I've heard of you. Tough area you're workin'."

"I'd heard you folks were burned out." Armstrong glanced around the room and grinned. "Reckon I got some bad information."

"Several ranches been burned hereabouts. That's what you musta heard."

"Who was it? Coon Davis? Tiburon from across the border?"

"The snake you got upstairs," Hart said, lifting his chin at the ceiling again. "Him and his gang been raisin' hob ever since Munson and Prewitt swore out affidavits against 'em in Austin. Been ridin' roughshod, killin', rapin', burnin', and collarin' beef to sell in Mexico."

"They get themselves a herd together and disappear south of the Rio Grande for a few weeks at a time," said Big Bill Morgan. "Then they're back, killin' and burnin'. They won't stop till they've stolen every cow between the Jackrabbit and Duck Creek, and killed every man who spoke against 'em."

The Ranger sipped his beer and wiped the foam from his mustache and spade beard with the back of his wrist. "What about Munson and Prewitt?"

"Hanged outside their ranch houses and roasted over mesquite fires." That was the rancher, Burgenreich. He spoke without turning in his chair, lazily pondering his cards, a cigarette smoldering in the ashtray near his elbow.

"You alone out here, Ranger?" Hart asked darkly, slowly rolling a cigarette from a hide sack he'd set on the table.

Armstrong nodded and cast another wary glance eastward out the window. "My company split up outside Tepehuanes." His upper lip curled without humor. "Reckon the other Rangers lost the trail."

He reached into his coat pocket and produced his own hide makings sack. He set it on the table, dragged out the soggy papers, and cursed under his breath. Hart tossed his own sack to Armstrong, who nodded his thanks.

He was rolling a smoke when the door opened suddenly, the bell chiming. It caught Armstrong by surprise, and he had his Peacemaker half out of his holster when he saw the towheaded boy turn and close the door behind him.

Michael doffed his sleet- and snow-dusted cap, slapped it against his thigh, and turned to Armstrong, who settled the six-shooter back down in its holster. "Your horses are bedded down, Ranger. Watered, grained, and curried."

"Much obliged, boy." Armstrong was about to flip the boy some coins. As he walked past the Ranger's table, Michael shook his head. "We don't take money from Rangers in these parts, Ranger." He hung his patched denim coat on a peg behind the bar and disappeared into the kitchen.

"Good boy," the Ranger said, reaching across and setting two twenty-cent pieces on the table before Hart. "Give those to him later, will you?"

The old man nodded and deposited the coins in a

shirt pocket. "He's had a tough time of it, but he's turnin' out all right."

The old man had invited the question, so Armstrong snapped a match to life and lit his quirley, saying, "No pa?"

Hart shook his head. "Killed in the mine behind this place, when Michael was two years old. We came out here together from Missouri—Ben, Ann, Michael, and me. We were lookin' for El Dorado." He glanced ironically around the saloon. "Well, here we are!"

The Ranger's blood warmed as he remembered another boy and another woman, the remains of whom he'd found in the yard of his one-cow ranch operation in the rich bottomlands flanking Corazon Creek. The boy had been shot in the belly and left to die while his mother was savaged in the tall grass near the spring house, before the Mexican bandits had shot her in the left temple and taken the horses.

His wife, Mary. His son, Paul.

He ran a hand down his broad, weathered face, rubbing the memory from his mind, and turned his dark gaze to Lowell Hart.

"You boys armed? If Renfrow's roughs picked up my trail, you're gonna want to be."

Armstrong shifted his gaze from Hart to the others. The other men returned his look, then glanced at each other bemusedly. Hart got up, walked around behind the bar, then returned with a black leather cartridge belt coiled around two holsters housing pearl-handled pistols. Hart set the double rig on the table and grinned.

"Won those two beauties off'n Magoon," he said, showing a half-set of tobacco-stained teeth and jerking his thumb over his left shoulder. "Last time he come through on his way to the riverboats at Yuma." Hart snickered. "He set down four kings and a trey and was ready to scoop the pot into his saddlebags, when I spread out four aces and a six!" Hart slapped the table and guffawed.

Armstrong glanced at Magoon, who turned toward Hart with arched eyebrows. "You're a real student of the picture cards, Mr. Hart."

The old man was delighted. "Well, I called *your* bluff!"

"One of these trips, I'm going to win those pretties back," the gambler growled.

"Oh, I'd never be fool enough to throw these ladies in the pot, Mr. Magoon." The oldster unsheathed one of the Colts. In both hands, he turned the silver-plated, hand-engraved pistol to the wan light pushing through the window behind Armstrong. "Ranger, you ever seen a finer six-shooter?"

Armstrong took the Colt from the old-timer, tested the balance, fingered the high-toned hammer and trigger and the glassy silver finish decorated with scrolled oats around the barrel. The initials J.D.M. had been carved into the silver band beneath the pearl butt.

Giving the well-weighted gun an appreciative finger twirl, Armstrong handed the weapon back to Hart. "Nope, can't say as I have. But it doesn't shoot itself, you know . . ."

"Don't worry about me, Ranger," Hart said, standing and wrapping the fancy belt and pistols around his slender waist. He gave a knowing smile and notched the tongue. "I been practicin' in the ravine out back."

He stepped back from the Ranger's table, crouching,

holding both wrinkled hands above the guns. His jaw slackened and his eyes darkened with concentration. Suddenly he jumped, spun, and came down on both feet facing the card players, clawing both pistols from their holsters.

"Pow! Pow! Pow! Pow! Pow!" he barked, extending each gun in turn, snapping off imaginary rounds.

Startled, all the card players except for the gambler, Magoon, had scrambled to the floor, ducking down behind the table.

When old Hart had snapped off a few more shots, he cackled wildly at the three gray faces peering at him over the table top with disgust. Magoon sat calmly holding his cards in one hand, cigar in the other, and regarding Hart with one arched brow.

"You've been out here too long, Mr. Hart. Maybe it's time you and your daughter and grandson returned to civilization."

Big Bill Morgan, who'd been nodding off on the sofa, chuckled and extended his finger to indicate the sheepish look on his partner's one-eyed face. One-Eye DeRosso pushed off a knee, grabbed his chair, and sat down, regarding the old man warily and muttering curses under his breath.

"Crazy old codger," growled the soldier, George Paine. "You're liable to get shot, pullin' such a stunt out here."

Hart only laughed at the lieutenant's indignation and blew at the imaginary smoke curling from his pistols.

Intruding on the old man's merriment, his daughter's voice rose from the kitchen. "Dad, would you give us a hand in here, please?"

Dropping the pistols back into their holsters and letting his laughter simmer to a slow boil, the oldster shuffled toward the kitchen. Grumbling with annoyance, the card players went back to their game while Big Bill Morgan finished his beer, clawed at his bushy beard, and chuckling once more at the old man's stunt, stretched out on the sofa for a nap.

Armstrong stood, donned his hat and coat. "Reckon I'll have a look around," he grunted as he strode to the door.

The wind caught the door, nearly jerking the knob from the Ranger's grip and nearly ripping his hat from his head. Holding his hat down with one hand, Armstrong fought the door closed with the other. When he'd latched it, he turned toward the yard, raising his collar and looking around, squinting against the snow that bit into his face like sand.

It was nearly dark on the ground, the gauzy sky hovering low and spitting gray snow and sleet and occasional rain at the buildings and shrubs. On one of the buildings across the trail or in one of the abandoned shacks flanking the saloon, something had torn loose and was slamming against a wooden frame. The wind howled, cold as though blown across some northern snowfield. It chilled the Ranger right down to his soul.

Seeing no movement but the slanting precipitation, the Ranger ducked his head against the onslaught and ran across the trail to the livery barn. The wind moaned and sighed through cracks between the building's whipsawed boards. When the Ranger got one of the two heavy doors open, pulling hard against the wind, a horse inside whinnied fearfully and knocked against its stall.

Stepping inside, Armstrong pulled the door closed behind him, fighting the wind to latch it. He unholstered his Peacemaker and turned to the barn's musty darkness relieved by four windows, the gunmetal light showing the beams, joists, and stalls—black geometric shapes trimmed with the more ambiguous outlines of shovels, pitchforks, and tack.

The Ranger stood quietly, listening, the pistol extended before him. If and when the gang came to free its leader, they'd no doubt hole up in the barn while they reconnoitered the saloon.

He listened, hearing nothing but the wind rattling the windows and creaking the walls, mice scuttling in the loft. His paint whinnied again, and the Ranger moved down the dark alley between the stalls. The horses were stabled side by side, their heads hanging over the alley, silhouetted by the gray windows behind them.

"Just me, Puma," the Ranger said, running a calming hand down the paint's neck as he peered around the dusky barn. The horse blew and stomped nervously, its withers rippling. The horse shook its head and twitched its ears.

"It's all right, Puma," he said, turning to Renfrow's chestnut. Appearing as nervous as Puma, the chestnut, bobbed its head and whinnied loudly enough to rattle the Ranger's eardrums.

The Ranger froze again, looking around, listening, trying to pick out suspicious sounds beneath the horses' loud breaths and the wind threatening to tear the walls apart.

"What the hell's the matter with you two?" Armstrong

said, puzzled. "Ain't nothin' here to trouble you 'cept the storm. You're safe in here."

He patted each horse gently—long, calming strokes. Probably just the weather. Nothing like a fierce wind and a rickety barn—a strange one to boot—to put horses on edge.

When he'd made sure both mounts had plenty of hay and water, Armstrong fought his way back outside. Head tipped against the wind, he tramped around the barn to the rear, pausing near a dilapidated corral choked with snow-dusted bunchgrass. He squatted down behind a stock trough and squinted against the stinging sleet.

The wind tore and blew at him, throwing him off balance. Snow and ice quickly coated his buckskin, a thin sheen like a metallic finish.

He saw nothing but grass, sage, and creosote tossed about like waves on a storm-wracked sea. The wind sawed at a rotten corral post, adding an eerie creaking to the storm's cacophony.

Armstrong lifted his gloved hand, wiped ice from his brow. In this weather, the gang had probably holed up miles away, if they'd even cut his trail after he'd lost them in the brasada last night. If they were out here, they'd have shown themselves by now.

The cold wind lancing him, making his cheeks burn and his toes ache, Armstrong turned and jogged back along the barn toward the hotel and saloon, the buttery windows beckoning and promising warmth. He was nearly to the porch when he stopped suddenly and turned back to the barn, frowning.

He'd seen only his and Renfrow's horses. Where were the other men's mounts?

A sudden scream from inside the hotel interrupted his thoughts and lifted the hair on the back of his neck. It was no victory yelp from among the card players. It was a man's cry originating from the second story—a shrill exclamation of genuine horror.

Armstrong leapt onto the porch, punched the latch, and pushed through the door.

The heat from the glowing stove hit Armstrong like a gloved fist.

He was crossing the room as the old man, Hart, rose from his chair near the stove, staring toward the stairs. "Ann?"

Confused, his Colt extended before him, Armstrong took the stairs two at a time. He'd taken two strides down the hall now lit by a single smoking bracket lamp when the door to his prisoner's room opened. The boy, Michael, stepped out, Ann behind him. The boy's face was strangely expressionless. Ann saw Armstrong and smiled.

She didn't appear to be hurt. Who had screamed?

"I guess he didn't like my soup." She shrugged, and Armstrong saw the soup bowl in her left hand, a plate of crusty bread in her right. The boy was carrying a black coffeepot and cup.

Hart ambled up behind Armstrong, his raspy voice tremulous. "Daughter, what in blue blazes?"

"I thought I'd see if our Mr. Renfrow could eat anything," she explained to Armstrong in an ironic, humorous tone. "One look at my soup, though, and he let out quite a bellow! I guess you heard."

Armstrong stared at her, amazed she could be so composed when the scream had nearly made him jump out of his boots. Frowning, he peered around the young woman, trying to get a look into the room.

"The soup's good," Hart said, incredulous. "Me and the other men are eatin' it. I ain't heard no complaints."

"He's out of his head," Ann said. "He might be hungry later." She gave Michael a gentle shove, and the two of them brushed past the Ranger, heading for the stairs.

Armstrong nudged the door wide and stepped into the room, aware of Hart shuffling up behind him, wanting to check out Renfrow himself.

The prisoner was cuffed as the Ranger had left him, but now his eyes were open. He looked at Armstrong, gaze brassy and enervated. He opened his mouth to speak, but then his eyes found Hart. His lids snapped wide. His face crumpled with fear.

"Oh, Jesus, *you!*" He twisted, pulling against the cuffs. "Get that old bastard outta here! What the hell's goin' on around here? What're you tryin' to do to me?"

Armstrong felt his face warm with anger. "Hey, watch your mouth, mister, or I'll—"

"That's all right, Ranger," Hart said, glancing down distastefully at Renfrow. He offered a humorless laugh and turned away. "I don't think ole Hatchet Face ever did have much for manners, but 'pears to me he's gone loco to boot."

With that, Hart snorted and shuffled out the door.

Armstrong stared down at the prisoner. "The lady was only offering food, which is a hell of a lot more than most people would have done for you."

Renfrow gazed up at him, his chest rising and falling heavily. "Ranger," he wheezed. He licked his lips, glanced at the open doorway, returned his wretched expression to Armstrong. "This . . . this ain't right. Somethin's bad wrong here."

"Shut up," Armstrong said, turning. "You're out of your head. Nobody's done nothin' to you."

He'd taken two steps when Hatchet Face Renfrow bent his knees and twisted his hips, as though in great pain and making a bizarre noise—half moan, half wail.

"No, Ranger . . . you don't understand."

In spite of himself, Armstrong turned to hear what he had to say. Something about the outlaw's fear was strangely compelling . . . chilling.

The prisoner sobbed, pulled against the cuffs. His eyes slitted, and in a bewitched undertone he whispered hoarsely, *"We killed these people!"*

Armstrong just stared at him. His chest felt tight, but then he realized the man had gone mad, and his mustache rose with a slight grin. When he didn't say anything, Renfrow swallowed and said, "'Bout seven, eight months ago. Me and the boys, we rolled through here . . . killed 'em all . . . took the cattle and horses . . ."

He paused to check Armstrong's reaction. A sudden wind gust slammed against the window, making the curtains billow and the room's single lamp gutter.

"That girl," Renfrow continued, pulling against the cuffs, making the bed shake, the springs squeal, "I took her into the kitchen . . . then slit her throat before I *burned the place down!*"

Armstrong stared down at the man, his broad cheeks pinched up into his eye sockets with disgust. His hands balled into fists as images of his own wife and boy flashed in his mind, murdered by outlaws of the same ilk as Renfrow.

Finally he squatted down on his haunches and swallowed his bile. He regarded the prisoner reasonably. "I don't doubt your sins, Renfrow. That's why you're gonna hang. But obviously you weren't here, or these people wouldn't be givin' us shelter . . . much less bringing' soup to your room."

"She wasn't bringin' me soup cause she was worried I was hungry," Renfrow said, his voice quivering as he stared wild-eyed at the Ranger. "She was tryin' to scare the *hell out of me!*"

Armstrong chuckled and shook his head. There was something satisfying in seeing a man like Hatchet Face Renfrow reduced to a sniveling coward. Slowly the Ranger shook his head. "Man, I did whack you too hard. Just lay here and keep your mouth shut, or I'll whack you again. We'll be pullin' out in the mornin'."

With that, Armstrong turned toward the lamp. He was about to blow it out when the prisoner said in a pinched tone, "Leave it! Leave the damn light!"

Armstrong stopped, shrugged, and strode to the door. "Ghosts, eh?" he said, slowing drawing the door closed behind him. "You know, Renfrow? I think your conscience has finally come callin'. Don't worry. You'll be dancin' with the devil soon."

"Just keep them demons away from me!"

Grinning at the image in his head of Renfrow dancing beneath a San Antonio gallows, Armstrong latched the door and went downstairs.

The Ranger swallowed the last of his antelope stew and dropped the spoon in the empty bowl. Brushing his hands on his jeans and scraping back his chair, he fought down the strange, nettling anxiety he'd been feeling since he'd heard Renfrow's scream, and said, "For a ghost, you sure cook good, ma'am. Thank you."

Ann Coleman stood behind the bar, drawing another beer for Lieutenant Paine. She smiled her baleful smile. "There's more. I made a potful. No tellin' how long this storm will last."

"I'm padded out just fine, ma'am. Much obliged." Armstrong glanced out the window behind him, seeing little but darkness and snow. He crossed the room to one of the two windows in the east wall, saw little he hadn't seen from the window behind his table: darkness and snow through the frosted glass, the silhouette of an ice-encrusted tumbleweed flashing past.

He turned to the room. Hart and Big Bill Morgan were again playing cribbage and sipping whiskey. The other men—Burgenreich, Morgan, DeRosso, Magoon, and Lieutenant Paine—were back playing five-card stud and blackjack . . . for matchsticks now, as Magoon had nearly cleaned the others out.

Tobacco smoke hung in heavy weblike layers, wanly lit by the room's two ceiling globes, two bracket lamps, and a bull's-eye lantern perched on the bar. There was as much shadow as light, and the shadows danced when the wind gusted, causing the flames to flicker.

From the cordwood stack near the stove, Ann and the boy kept the fire humming, so that the stove's black door was mottled gold. The wind howled like wolves just beyond the saloon's creaking, shuddering walls.

Armstrong was edgy. What made him edgier was the fact the others didn't seem edgy at all. But then, none were tinhorns. They knew the dangers of the frontier.

And they were all armed, even Magoon. The gambler may have lost his prized Colts, but he wore a Bisley on his hip, and the sizable bulge under his clawhammer coat bespoke a revolver in a shoulder holster.

Armstrong wasn't so much worried about the men as the woman and the boy. He'd hate like hell for anything to happen to them because he'd led Renfrow's gang to their doorstep. He wished he would have kept riding, held up in a cave somewhere.

"Poker, Captain?" Lieutenant Paine asked. He yawned as the rancher, Burgenreich, was shuffling the cards to deal another hand. "You can take my place. Might put your mind at ease."

"No, thanks," Armstrong said. "Think I'll have another look around outside."

"Wouldn't do that if I was you," Burgenreich said as he dealt the cards and blew smoke around the quirley in his teeth. "McNelly's Viking or not, you run into trouble out there alone, you might pick up the brandin' iron by the hot end."

"Have another drink and relax, Ranger," Big Bill Morgan suggested, picking the pasteboards off the table. "I'll buy."

Armstrong ran his gaze across the men, puzzled by their calm. He'd seen sunning dogs more nervy. Either they didn't think the gang would brave the storm or they were damn confident of their own ability to hold them off.

"I'll take my chances," the Ranger said finally, shrugging into his coat with a rueful snort. "You hear any shootin', douse the lights."

Outside, Armstrong walked to the west end of the

stoop, right of the window. He raised his collar against the cold wind and squinted against the lancing snow.

The snow covered the ground, laying heavily on the sage and creosote shrubs. He looked for tracks. Seeing no hoofprints corrupting the virgin layers of churning snow, he walked to the stoop's east end.

He'd stood there for about three minutes, watching and listening as the wind blasted him, and was about to turn back for the door when he heard something between wind gusts.

A distant horse's whinny.

He turned left, watching, listening, not realizing he'd reached for the Colt until he became aware of it there in his right hand, aimed northeast, into the storm. His pulse throbbed in his temples and his heart leapt in his chest.

He waited, listening hard.

Beginning to wonder if the sound had been only the wind, he stepped off the stoop and walked along the building, passing the two lit windows on his left. The wind was so loud he couldn't hear his boots crunching snow. He kept his hat tipped low as he looked around, catching glimpses of thrashing sage and mesquite branches between dancing snow curtains.

Crouching against the wind, pistol extended in his right hand, he weaved a path through abandoned, dilapidated settlers' shacks, half of them roofless and without doors or windows. The wind moaned through the cracks between the logs, caught at some hide curtains and flapped them hard against the window frame.

He was walking along the west side of a crumbling 'dobe stable when he caught the scent of mesquite smoke. Could be from the saloon but the wind was in the wrong direction. Had to be ahead of him, from one of the cabins.

A woman's voice whispered his name in his left ear.

He wheeled left, expecting to see Ann there, having come out looking for him to convince him to return to the saloon.

But she wasn't there. Behind where he'd expected to see her, a shadow stepped out from a tree—a tall, lean shadow capped with a funnel-brimmed hat tied down with a muffler. Part of the shadow broke away from itself. And then vagrant snow light glistened dully, and Armstrong threw himself behind a post.

The gun flashed and snapped beneath the wind. The bullet was a furious blackfly buzzing over his right shoulder, a thin whistle instantly drowned by the storm. Armstrong heaved himself onto a knee and fired at the flash. He fired again, and then again the Colt jumped in his hand, the powder smoke tearing around his face and gone.

He squinted into the darkness around a wind-battered pecan less than twenty yards away. The shadow was no longer there.

Armstrong looked around, then slowly rose, cautiously stepped forward. When he drew abreast of the tree, the storm-battered branches snapping and cracking above his head, he saw the man on the ground. His hat was gone. Already the snow was dusting him.

Armstrong knelt, saw the two small holes in the gray deerskin coat. The man was wearing too many clothes for the blood to have yet seeped through the layers, but from his open, staring eyes Armstrong knew he was dead. He was in his mid-twenties, with a bushy black mustache and muttonchops, a round, dark face.

Oscar Jiminez, one of the half-breed bandits who rode with Renfrow. Low man on the totem pole, but one of Hatchet Face's boys, just the same.

The blood running wild through Armstrong's veins, he wheeled around. They were here.

Where were the others?

No matter now. They were here. Only thing to do was get back to the saloon, douse the lights, and watch the windows . . . and wait.

The black hulk of the saloon had just come into view before him when he remembered the woman's voice in his ear. He turned and looked behind. Nothing but snow-blown darkness and the whistling, jagged bulk of the derelict barn.

The woman had warned him of Jiminez's presence. He was sure of it. But who was she and where in the hell was she now?

Armstrong leapt onto the stoop drifted with snow and pushed through the saloon's front door, announcing himself. The men were still playing cards.

"They're here," Armstrong said, closing the door on the wind that caused most of the lamps to nearly flicker out. "Let's get these lights blown."

He was heading for one of the bracket lamps when the ceiling creaked as though under a footfall. He froze. The others were moving toward the lamps, Ann and the boy hurrying behind the bar.

"Who's upstairs?"

"Renfrow," Lieutenant Paine said, regarding the Ranger with an incredulous frown.

Armstrong bolted for the stairs, took the steps two at a time on the balls of his feet. The wall lamp was still lit, wavering against the chill drafts swirling about the hall, and belching black smoke. Still treading lightly, Armstrong regarded the outside door at the end of the hall. It was closed, but flakes of melting snow lay before it, glistening in the lamplight. Heart thudding, Armstrong shucked his Colt and moved slowly to the closed door of his prisoner's room, leaning close to listen.

Inside, two men were whispering, voices pinched with concern. "How am I s'posed to get the damn things off?" one said.

Slowly Armstrong turned the doorknob, then brought his right boot back and forward, connecting soundly with the door, just left of the knob.

"Hold it!" he yelled when the two men took shape, one on the bed, the other beside him, turning toward the Ranger now, mouth agape.

The newcomer had a pistol in his left hand. He raised it quickly, but before he could fire, Armstrong shot him, throwing him back against the dresser with a groan. A stone pitcher fell to the floor with a crash.

The man groaned again, clutching his side and again raising his pistol.

Armstrong fired again, taking the man through the middle of his shaggy bear coat. He grunted, twisted, dropped to both knees, and fell on his back with a thud that made the whole room jump.

"*Shit!*" Renfrow shouted, jerking the handcuffs and leg irons and making the bed squawk.

Armstrong was stepping into the smoky room when he felt a sudden, powerful draft. Footsteps sounded on the stairs. The Ranger wheeled back toward the door. A gun popped twice. Lieutenant Paine stood in the doorway facing the opposite end of the hall.

He quickly raised his Colt Army. A man at the other end of the hall cursed loudly. The lieutenant fired three quick, angry shots.

Smoke wafted around the soldier's grinning face.

Wary, holding his own gun down near his belly, Armstrong moved through the door. At the end of the hall, before the open door through which snow swirled, a man lay motionless in a growing blood pool.

"Good shootin', soldier," he said, turning back to Paine. He ran his gaze along the lieutenant's long, lean frame. "You hit?"

Paine bunched his lips and shook his head as he snapped the cover over his Colt. Cool disdain deepened his voice. "He missed me both times. I suspect he's a much better shot when his opponent is unarmed . . . defenseless . . . taken by surprise."

Vaguely puzzled by the soldier's passionate response but with more pressing concerns on his mind, Armstrong turned to the stairs. The other men were grouped about the steps, looking around with wary curiosity. "Y'all go down and keep an eye on the windows and the front door. If there's a back way in, watch it, too. The gang was probably wantin' to get Renfrow out quietly before they hit us. Now that their plan soured, there's no tellin' when they'll hit us next."

When the others had gone back downstairs, Armstrong walked to the end of the hall, cast a cautious glance outside. Seeing little but the swirling snow, he pulled the dead man out of the way, closed the door, and went back into Renfrow's room.

He was unlocking the cuff on the outlaw's right wrist when Renfrow said, "What're you doin'?"

"Takin' you downstairs where I can keep an eye on you."

"Somethin' damn queer's goin' on here, Ranger. You gotta believe me. Damn peculiar. I never used to believe in ghosts—"

"Shut up."

"Jesus, no!" Renfrow's face screwed up. "I don't wanna go down there. No tellin' what they'll do . . ."

"I said shut up."

"Oh, *Jesus!*"

When Armstrong had unlocked the leg shackles, he drew his revolver, extended the weapon at the outlaw's face, and ratcheted back the hammer.

"One attempt to escape, I blow your brains out."

The enervated Renfrow just stared at him, his eyes bulging, lips forming a hard line across his face. "Please," he whispered.

Armstrong backed away from the bed and indicated the door with his Colt's barrel. Renfrow grimaced as he tenderly swung his feet to the floor. Grunting and touching his fingers to his head, he grabbed the dresser, heaved himself to his feet, and moved to the door.

Armstrong trailing him from about six feet away and prodding the outlaw's back with the Colt, Renfrow descended the stairs. At the bottom, he stopped and glared warily across the dimly lit room in which all the lights had been doused but one.

A heavy silence hung while Renfrow stood looking around, pale as a corpse. The wind growled in the wood stove's flue.

"Boo," Lowell Hart said finally, standing with both his pretty Colts drawn, right of the front window. Lieutenant Paine crouched across from him, his long-barreled .44 drawn as he peered into the storm's wrath beyond the frosted glass. Without turning, the soldier snorted.

The others chuckled. Ann and the boy weren't there; they must have been in the kitchen.

Armstrong directed Renfrow to a stout, square-hewn ceiling post in the shadows at the back of the room. He ordered the outlaw to sit, then knelt to handcuff the man's hands behind the post.

Keeping his voice just above a whisper and clutching Armstrong's sleeve with his cuffed hands, Renfrow said, "See those two Colts that old man's got in his hands?" When Armstrong squinted at him, listening, the prisoner continued: "Billy Styles took 'em off the old man's body. Billy, he was killed by a Mex several days later, and his brother, Bob, knowin' how Billy favored them guns, tossed 'em into the grave. Fancy shell belt and all."

Armstrong locked the cuffs and gave Renfrow a skeptical stare. The man was giving him the creeps, and he was tired of it. He didn't have time for Renfrow's madness. His main concern was the prisoner's gang outside in the storm.

He patted the outlaw's shoulder. "Don't worry, Hatchet Face—in just a few days, Judge Pleasants in San Antone's gonna put you out of your misery."

*   *   *

Armstrong went back upstairs, made sure no other hard cases had slipped into the building, and rammed a heavy wardrobe against the door atop the outside stairs. He was pleased to find that none of the second-story windows was accessible from the ground.

Back downstairs, he positioned each of the men at main room windows and before the front door. He made sure Ann and the boy were safe in the kitchen, then returned to the main room and took up his own position at the window nearest his prisoner.

He and the others settled in for what doubtless would be a long night, with only one lamp lit, shunting shadows this way and that as the wind tore drafts about the room. The walls shuddered and the flue knocked, the fire humming, logs thumping against the stove walls as they burned.

In the kitchen, to keep busy, Ann made doughnuts and boiled coffee. She brought the fresh pastries and coffee out to the men, keeping to the shadows so she couldn't be seen from outside. Morgan, One-Eye DeRosso, and Lowell Hart had nodded off when she brought the pot out again around midnight.

"Any movement out there?" she asked Armstrong as she refilled his cup. The Ranger sat on the floor, his back to the wall, rifle between his upraised knees, revolver on the straight-back chair to his right.

Armstrong shook his head. "They probably won't attack until morning, but letting our guard down is a good way to get ourselves killed."

"Yes, it is," she said in a thoughtful tone.

She set the coffeepot on a table and sat down with

her back to the wall, a few feet away from the Ranger. Nearby, Big Bill Morgan snored in a chair backed up to the wall, a beat-up Spencer rifle canted across his chest. Burgenreich and One-Eye DeRosso talked quietly, desultorily, after waking.

"I apologize for bringin' trouble," Armstrong said, rubbing his jaw sheepishly. "I should've kept goin' . . . holed up in a cave somewhere."

"You'd have found no caves for miles. And if you had, you might've had to fight a Comanche for it."

Armstrong opened his mouth to speak again, but she cut him off with, "It was meant to be, Ranger. It was all meant to be." That strange knowing tone again . . . confident, resigned. He didn't know why, but it pricked at the back of his neck. And then he remembered the woman's voice he'd heard outside.

He looked at her across his left shoulder. "Ma'am, was that you outside earlier?"

"I've been out to fetch wood for the stoves." The bridge of her nose wrinkled slightly. "Why?"

"I thought I heard a woman's voice a second before the drygulcher would've drilled me" The chill crept down the back of his neck and along his spine, all the way to his backbone.

"The wind," Ann said. "In this canyon it can sound like many things. Sometimes I think it's my dead husband calling to me from his mine in the foothills."

Armstrong didn't say anything. He was remembering the sound of the voice.

"Your wife is worried."

He looked at Ann, frowning. Had it been a question or a statement? Must've been the former. He shook his head and rubbed a cold-itch on the back of his left hand. "Mary and my boy are dead. Killed by men like him." He nodded toward Renfrow sitting there in the shadows, head tipped back against the post, eyes open, staring at Ann as at a demon flung from hell.

"I'm sorry."

Armstrong shrugged. "It's why I took up Rangerin'." He laughed. "Sure as heck didn't do it for the money!"

Neither of them spoke for a time, just sat listening to the wind and the icy snow tick against the saloon's creaking walls. The heat from the stove radiated nicely. Big Bill Morgan snored.

It felt nice to have a woman this close to him again. If it were only another time, another place . . .

As if reading his mind, she said suddenly, "Of course it is none of my business, but you should marry again. Build another family." She paused, then continued quietly, almost absently, "Your wife would want you to. So would your son."

He hadn't considered the possibility of remarrying, but he found himself considering it now, with Ann sitting here only a few feet away, the soft yellow light and shadows playing about her fair skin and freckles, limning her long, slender neck above the collar of her plaid shirt.

"What about you? 'Pears you're in the same boat."

Ann only smiled, glanced off as though uncomfortable. Armstrong silently cursed himself for his bluntness.

"I best check on Michael," she said, and gained her feet.

She'd started walking back toward the kitchen when

Armstrong remembered the other question he'd wanted to ask her. "Ma'am, where are the other horses?"

She swung half around to him, the coffeepot in her hand—a slender silhouette against the room's swaying shadows. "They're hidden," she said edgily. "We've had problems with rustlers. Men from the area who ride with gangs. Men like him."

She turned her eyes to Renfrow, who jerked against the post now, startled. Apparently he'd been dozing.

"We used to run a few cattle to help make ends meet, but they were taken, too," Ann said. "One night Dad recognized two of the rustlers and rode over to the county seat to report their names to the sheriff."

"The sheriff take care of it?"

She paused, sliding her eyes to Armstrong. "Not yet, but your own mounts should be safe for the night," she added, then turned and headed toward the kitchen.

When the kitchen door had swung shut behind her, Renfrow whispered, "You take me outta here, Armstrong, I'll make you a rich man."

"Shut up," Armstrong growled.

"*Rich!*"

The Ranger picked his revolver off the chair, aimed it at the prisoner, and thumbed back the hammer. "I won't tell you again."

Renfrow let his head fall back against the post.

Armstrong dozed fitfully, keeping his ears skinned for voices and footsteps outside the saloon's wind-wracked walls. His half dreams were haunted by wind and snow and women's voices singing his name. And then the songs were wolf howls and he was running through woods, hearing the beasts panting behind him.

"Daddy!" his son called. "The badmen are chasing me!"

He didn't know how long he'd slept when he woke with a start, grabbing the gun from the chair. He looked around the dim room. Renfrow and the other men were all asleep, slouched against the wall or the sofa or slumped uncomfortably in the Windsor chairs by the front window. A milky sheen pressed through the windows.

Armstrong turned and peered out the window to his right, saw a faint flush of gray in the east, through the canyon's mouth. The storm had cleared, and stars shone, but he could feel a hard chill permeating the whipsawed boards of the wall. Hoarfrost bled through the cracks.

He peered around what he could see of the yard—still mostly dim shadows. Seeing nothing out of the ordinary, he moved toward the front of the room, causing Big Bill Morgan to jerk awake on the sofa, reaching for his Spencer rifle.

"What is it? What is it?"

"Dawn," the Ranger said as he slid a cautious glance out the front window.

In the right corner of his vision, something flashed. The window broke with a glassy pop and rattle. Feeling a glass shard scrape his jaw and hearing the lead slug crack into a tintype hanging on the adjacent wall, Armstrong swung back away from the window and cursed.

He slid another glance around the frame. A man ran along the inside of the front corral rails, crouched low, a rifle in his hand. He ducked down behind a wheelless wagon.

As the other men in the room cursed, scuttled toward the windows, and jacked shells into their rifle breeches, Armstrong quickly stepped to the other side of the window. He edged another look around the frame, gazing east. Two more shadowy figures ran amidst the rabbitbrush, rifles in their hands, positioning themselves for an attack.

Lieutenant Paine kicked a chair aside and shouldered up to the window across from Armstrong, his long-barreled Army Colt in his hand. Armstrong said, "Hold your fire." To Hart, crouched on the other side of the room, he said, "Back door?"

"Through the storage room yonder," the oldster said, throwing a glance to a small, wainscoted door at the main room's rear, where several barrels and crates were stacked. "I barred it, though. They won't get in that-away!"

The old man's sentence was punctuated by another rifle crack. The slug tore through Hart's window and whipped across the room, shattering a bottle on the back bar. Two more quick shots plunked through the front door and through Armstrong's window, both slugs buzzing about the room before smashing into a wall and a ceiling joist.

"Damn their eyes!" One-Eye cried.

"Send Renfrow out, Ranger!" a thick voice called from across the road. "Throw him out or we'll burn the place to the ground!"

Armstrong walked to the door, lifted the heavy wooden bar, and dragged the door open a crack. "Renfrow's tied to a joist, and he ain't goin' nowhere. You burn this place, you burn your leader!"

The man hooted mockingly. "At least he won't be alive to give no judge our names!" A rifle cracked, the slug chipping loudly into the door six inches left of Armstrong's face.

Cursing again, Armstrong slammed the door and barred it.

"Your life ain't worth spit even to your own, Hatchet Face," Jake Magoon said to Renfrow. The gambler was hunkered down behind the freshly stoked stove, mismatched pistols in his hands. He grinned at the outlaw, who spit at him, the spittle falling two feet short.

Armstrong rubbed his jaw and eyed the bullet holes in the door, the broken windows. The saloon's whipsawed plank walls would hold back slugs little better than tar paper. In a fire fight, he and the others would be shredded in minutes. If the outlaws stormed the place and threw a kerosene-soaked torch through a window, the place would go up like well-seasoned kindling sticks.

He eyed the room's rear door thoughtfully. Finally, hurrying down the length of the saloon, he said, "You men stay put, keep an eye on the yard. I'm gonna try to swing around behind 'em."

Renfrow threw his head back and opened his mouth. "Hey, fellas, watch your—!" but the Ranger had anticipated Renfrow's warning yell. He slung his rifle across a table and slapped his open hand across the man's face then quickly lifted the outlaw's bandanna over his mouth and tied it taut behind his neck.

Renfrow kicked and grunted against the gag as Armstrong grabbed his rifle, bolted across the room, and slipped through the wainscoted door. The storage room boasted no windows, so he crossed the cramped cold room slowly, feeling his way, knocking against crates, trunks, old bed frames and other dilapidated furniture. The timbered outside door was a dark-gray frame in the rear wall. He lifted the bar, cracked the door, and peered into misty, snowy shadows, cobwebs clinging to his beard.

Seeing nothing but blue snow drifted against the rabbitbrush and the distant hulks of abandoned cabins and corrals, Armstrong stepped slowly outside and drew the door closed behind him. The cold was like an invisible ice robe closing around him, pinching his lungs and stinging his cheeks. The temperature had to be near zero; he hadn't felt air this cold since cowboying as a youngster up Montana way.

Looking carefully around and deciding that none of the outlaws was flanking the saloon, he ran crouching west, then south through the rabbitbrush, weaving a trail between shrubs and abandoned shacks.

A few minutes later he was jogging behind the corral flanking the barn when a man bolted up from behind a hay crib. Armstrong saw the man's whiskered face and wide, glistening eyes too late. A half second later a brass-plated rifle butt smashed savagely into his forehead.

Armstrong stumbled back in the snow, tripping over his own feet, falling hard on his back. Just before the world went black he heard a man's chuckle and fading footsteps crunching snow.

When the Ranger opened his eyes, the dawn had grown only slightly. He winced against the pain wracking his skull like tomahawks and slowly rolled his head to the right. Must've been out only a few minutes. He rolled his head gently left, trying to determine the damage. Blood trickled from his lacerated temple, made a wet streak on the side of his cheek.

Fetid smoke touched his nostrils, and he froze.

A rifle cracked. Then another and another until a veritable fusillade clamored on the other side of the barn.

He peered that way, and his shoulders stiffened as his eyes widened. Black smoke boiled up above the barn's peak, turning the morning's soft blue sky the color of oily rags.

Lips drawn painfully back from his gritted teeth, he grabbed his rifle, levered a shell, and climbed to his feet. Slipping in the foot-deep snow and pushing off a corral post, he made his way north along the corral toward the barn.

Ahead, the rifles popped and cracked, ricochets twanging. Men whooped and hollered with glee.

He dragged his left hand against the barn's east wall for support as he ambled heavy-footed through the snow, holding his rifle barrel forward in his right hand. His head throbbed, sharp pain lances stabbing down from his temple and into his neck and back. He swallowed down his nausea, squinting and blinking to clear his double vision. The throbbing grew so intense it buckled his knees, and he had to pause for a moment, steeling himself against the onslaught, before willing himself into a labored shuffle forward.

He felt more than saw the front end of the barn. To his left, the rifles made a cacophony that intensified his ear-ringing, tooth-grinding misery. He turned that way, dropping to his right knee, and stared. He blinked, clearing the fog.

Eight or so gunmen stood shoulder to shoulder in the gray-white trail before the barn, firing into the saloon's burning, bullet-pocked facade. Clad in frost-rimed hats and bulky coats, their breath puffing before their faces, they triggered their weapons casually, like boys plucking wooden ducks off a mill pond.

Pine resin popped as smoke and flames stabbed from the cabin's windows, the conflagration roaring as it grew.

Armstrong wheezed as a pain lance stabbed length-wise down his spine. He dropped to a knee, then onto his right shoulder. He cursed and snarled, extended the rifle, tried picking one gunman from the pack.

Something moved before the burning cabin; he slid his gaze that way.

He froze, staring, transfixed.

The front, bullet-riddled, flame-limned door had swung wide, and out stepped Lowell Hart. Behind him was his daughter, Ann, and then the boy, Michael, followed by Lieutenant Paine, Jake Magoon, One-Eye DeRosso, Bill Morgan, and Chess Burgenreich—all lining up shoulder to shoulder, along the smoke-obscured stoop. They carried rifles down casually at their sides—all but Hart, who clutched his pearl-gripped Colts in his gnarled hands, barrels aimed groundward.

Together and all at once, they faced the gunmen, who had suddenly stopped shooting. From this angle, Armstrong couldn't see the expressions on the shooters' faces, only the straight lines of their taut backs as they stood in the trail, frozen in mid-motion, some with rifles to their shoulders, some with the long guns only half raised.

No one said a word. The cabin burned, smoke licking and spiraling up from the windows.

The gunman turned to each other stiffly, eyes wide. Then suddenly they all wheeled back to the cabin and commenced firing.

Armstrong's jaw dropped and his eyes snapped wide, horrified. It was like a firing squad . . . only the firing squad's victims weren't dropping. The eight just stood staring coldly at the shooters as the bullets caromed right through their bodies and smashed into the wall and windows behind them.

One by one the gang's rifles clicked empty, and they stood hang-jawed, backs once again taut, facing straight ahead at the eight people who should be dead.

"Jumpin' Jehosaphat!" one of the shooters yelled suddenly above the humming flames, *"we done killed you people!"*

Another took one step straight back and exclaimed, "I told ye this was the place!"

Slowly Lieutenant Paine raised his rifle to his shoulder. Paine's Spencer stabbed flames as it cracked and jumped in the soldier's arms. The second shooter who'd spoken was blown backward off his feet and landed in the trail with a grunt.

The others virtually jumped out of their boots. One man dropped his rifle. He turned to run as the others on the stoop, including Ann and Michael, raised their pistols and rifles. They extended the weapons with slow assurance, curling their lips, squinting their eyes, taking aim, and firing.

The explosions rose above the thundering flames, the slugs tearing through the shooters as though through rats in a trash heap, blowing blood out behind the men while tumbling the men themselves backward across the snow, rolling them up into snarling, whimpering piles.

Shooting their rifles and pistols over and over, the eight people from the saloon stepped slowly off the porch and closed the gap on their victims, shooting the men again and again while the gang members screamed and wailed and held their bloody hands before their heads as if to shield their faces from the lead.

The bullets cut through the upraised hands and smashed into skulls, smashing the heads back into the snow and silencing the wails with the mouths still drawn. One man, his coat soaked with blood, climbed feebly to hands and knees and crawled slowly toward the barn. Young, towheaded Michael approached him slowly from behind. The boy stopped over the man, raised his rifle to his shoulder, squinted down the barrel, and fired.

The man's head jerked and bobbed. His limbs gave, and he slumped to the trail, dead.

Armstrong spied movement toward the cabin's rear and turned his gaze that way. A man knelt behind the saloon, his back heaving as he coughed. Armstrong's handcuffs hung from the man's right wrist; Renfrow clutched a revolver in that hand. Somehow the outlaw had slipped his left hand free of the cuffs, and he'd grabbed a spare pistol off one of the tables. He turned to look over his shoulder, and it was just light enough now that Armstrong could see Renfrow's wide, impassioned eyes and angular, hatchet face.

The outlaw heaved himself to his feet and scrambled north of the saloon, coughing and disappearing amidst the brush and abandoned shacks. Armstrong pushed to his feet, fighting to keep his eyes open, and tramped wide around the burning saloon, heading north after Renfrow. At the saloon's rear he picked up the scuffed boot prints and followed the trail between two derelict cabins. Beyond a house-sized boulder the tracks turned east and descended a shallow, snowy arroyo.

Armstrong moved heavily along the arroyo, tripping over hidden stones and shrubs, keeping one eye skinned on the fresh boot prints, another on the twisting course of the cut. He brushed at the blood dribbling down his face and winced against the nearly unbearable pain that occasionally caused his vision to double and blur, turning his knees to putty.

"Tim!"

It was a woman's voice, spoken clearly as though from only a few feet away. It was his wife's voice, turning him sharply right.

But it was not Mary standing there on the arroyo's lip, only ten feet away. It was Hatchet Face Renfrow, an old-model Sharps revolver extended toward Armstrong. The voice had frozen Renfrow for a split second.

The Ranger dropped to a crouch as the outlaw's revolver jumped and spoke. Raising his own Colt, Armstrong drilled two closely spaced holes in Renfrow's chest.

The outlaw gave a grunt and crumpled against the base of a tall pecan tree. He ground his heels into the earth as though trying to stand, then collapsed with a long sigh.

Armstrong straightened and, his face a deep-lined mask of pain and anxious expectation, looked around for Mary. He saw nothing but snow-dusted catclaw and piñon. After a quarter hour of searching, the only tracks he found along the arroyo were those of Renfrow.

But her voice had been so real.

Dazed, he slogged back through the shrubs and weaved a course through the abandoned shacks, chicken coops, and falling-down barns, the gray wood turning gold now, the snow sparkling, as the sun rose above the eastern horizon.

As he came around the old stable near the saloon, he looked up and stopped suddenly. His eyes round, he ran his gaze over the charred timbers and mounded ashes of the saloon . . . buried under a foot of fresh snow!

He stumbled forward, dropped to his knees, and shoved his gloved hands into the snow, rooting out a foot-long chunk of charred board . . . as cold as the snow that had buried it.

He looked at the board dumbly, dropped it, and heaved himself to his feet. His heart thudded. His vision swam. He muddled around the saloon's snow-mounded ruins to the trail, paused over the bodies of the outlaws strewn there as though dropped from the sky, blood from the fresh wounds glistening in the brassy light of the rising sun.

He knelt over one of the bodies, placed his hand on a chest. Still warm.

Looking around, his gaze fixed on something amidst the snow-limned shrubs right of the barn. He heaved himself to his feet. Stepping around the bodies, stumbling over a rifle, he moved through the shrubs south of the trail, stopped, and stared at the ground. His mouth sagged. Deep lines cut into the corners of his eyes.

Before him lay eight snow-covered mounds and stone slabs. Heart wheeling, Armstrong dropped to a knee, brushed the snow from one of the stones, and stared at the writing chiseled into the stone's face.

Trembling, he staggered to the next stone and brushed the snow away. He read the inscription, moved to the next stone . . . and then the next . . . until all eight stones stared up at him. Gently he pushed the snow away from the last one and touched the inscription with his gloved fingertip:

Ann Coleman. Killed by the Renfrow Gang, Summer 1874.

In the Line of Duty

Elmer Kelton

—∞∾∾—

This collection would not have been complete without a story by Kelton, who was voted by the Western Writers of America as the greatest living western writer. Beginning in 1999 he wrote a series of novels describing the formative years of the Texas Rangers. The first three books have been collected in *Lone Star Rising,* which includes *The Buckskin Line, The Badger Boy,* and *Way of the Coyote.* The story included here was written in 1967, one of Kelton's earlier Texas Rangers tales. Kelton died in 2009.

The two horsemen came west over the deep-rutted wagon road from Austin, their halterless Mexican pack mule following like a dog, its busy ears pointing toward everything which aroused its active curiosity.

Frontier Texans always said they could recognize a real peace officer a hundred yards away and a Texas Ranger as far as they could see him. Sergeant Duncan McLendon was plainly a Ranger, though he customarily wore his badge pinned out of sight inside his vest. He rode square-shouldered and straight-backed, his feet braced firmly in the stirrups of his Waco saddle. He wore a flat-brimmed hat and high-topped black boots with big-roweled Petmecky spurs. His gray eyes were pinched and crow-tracked at the corners, and they pierced a man like a brace of Bowie knives.

Those eyes moved restlessly, missing little. Quietly, without turning his head, he spoke to Private Billy Hutto. "Two men yonder in that liveoak motte."

Hutto, in his early twenties and as yet simply a cowboy with a commission, let his hand ease cautiously toward the Colt .45 his Ranger wages were still paying for. "I see them. Reckon they're with us or agin us?"

Firmly McLendon said: "We're not here to be with anybody or agin anybody. We've come to arrest one man and stop a feud."

The two men did not follow, but the grim frown never stopped tugging at the corners of McLendon's gray-salted black mustache. It was still there when they skirted the crest of a chalky hill and came in sudden view of the ugly sprawl of picket shacks and rock cabins known as Cedarville.

Disappointment tinged Billy Hutto's voice. "I sure thought there'd be more to it than this."

It was common knowledge from here to the Pedernales River that Cedarville had stolen the county seat by voting all its dogs and most of its jackrabbits in the election. McLendon said: "For what it is, there's more than enough." Maybe next election the courthouse would go to somebody else.

For now, though, the courthouse was here, a frame structure long and narrow, facing a nondescript row of stone and cedar picket and liveoak-log buildings that dealt in all manner of merchandise but specialized in hard drink, by the shot or by the jug. Beside the courthouse squatted a flat-roofed stone jail which appeared more solidly built. The kind of prisoners they brought in here, it had better be. McLendon pointed his chin. "This is where we'll likely find Sheriff Prather."

He swung down and stretched his back and his legs, for it had been a long ride. He cast one wishful glance at a saloon, for it had been a dusty ride, too. But drink had to wait. He looped his reins over a cedar-log hitching rack and pointed at the pack mule, which swiveled its neck as its curious eyes and ears took in the sights. "Tie the mule, Billy. She'll be all over town stirrin' up mischief."

A broad man with the beginnings of a middle-age paunch stepped to the open doorway, darkly eying McLendon and Hutto with a look just short of actual hostility. "Rangers?"

McLendon nodded. "I'm Sergeant McLendon. This is Billy Hutto."

"Where's the rest of you?"

"We're all there is."

"I asked for a whole company. We got bad trouble here."

"The two of us is all that was available. The legislature saw fit to cut the Ranger appropriations. I take it you're Sheriff Prather."

The man was not pleased. "I am. Come on in." He dropped into a heavy chair behind a wooden desk without inviting the Rangers to be seated. Noting the snub and filing it away for future reference, McLendon dragged up a hide-bottomed chair. He gave Billy a silent order with a nod of his head, and the young man stood in the doorway to keep watch on the street.

The sheriff bit the end off a black cigar and lighted it without offering one. "You come to kill Litt Springer?"

"We come to *arrest* him."

"There'll be no peace in this county till he's dead. But I didn't much figure you Rangers would have the stomach for it. Didn't really want to call in the Rangers in the first place, but folks in town pressured me." His eyes narrowed with suspicion. "You're sidin' with him because he was a Ranger himself."

"*Was!*" McLendon put emphasis on the word. "He's not anymore. We'll treat him like anybody else if he's committed a crime."

"*If?*" The sheriff exploded. "Damn right he's committed a crime. Why the hell do you think folks wanted to send for help? He murdered my deputy, Ed Newton."

"Any witnesses?"

"One. Freighter comin' up from Menardville seen the whole thing. You can doubt the citizens of Cedarville if you want to, but that freighter's got no friends here, and no ax to grind. Your friend Litt Springer is a cold-blooded killer."

Billy Hutto turned from the door, face red. "Way I heard it, Sheriff, he had a good reason."

McLendon said sharply: "Billy, you just keep watch. *I'll* talk to the sheriff." He rubbed his fist as if a pain had come in it. "The story we heard was that Litt's brother Ollie was arrested on some jumped-up horse-stealin' charge, and that your deputy turned him over to a hangin' mob."

"Aroused citizens!" the sheriff corrected. His eyes did not meet McLendon's. "Anyway, my deputy tried to protect his prisoner. There was just too many of them."

Billy Hutto snorted, and McLendon had to flash him another hard look. McLendon said: "Sheriff, our information was that Litt has gathered a bunch of friends around him and that there's danger of open warfare between them and the people here who back the mob. Our orders are to arrest him and take him to Austin."

"To Austin?" The sheriff stood up angrily. "If you arrest him you'll bring him here! His crime was committed here. It's the right of this community to see justice done. We'll give him a fair trial."

"And then hang him?"

"You damn betcha. Unless you was to shoot him first and be done with it. That'd be the best thing for all concerned."

McLendon's eyes narrowed. "I understand *you've* been tryin' to shoot him, and you've had no luck at it."

"That's a tough bunch he's got gathered. We can't get close."

"*We'll* get close."

"And fall right in with him, no doubt, seein' as he was a Ranger himself." The sheriff savagely chewed the cigar. "Was he a personal friend of yours, McLendon?"

McLendon stood up and pushed his chair back. "He was sergeant before I was. We rode together."

The sheriff sniffed. "About the way I had it pictured.

Folks ought to've known we wouldn't get no help out of Austin."

Coldly McLendon opened his vest and showed the star pinned beneath it. "We're Rangers, Sheriff. That comes first—before friends, and before enemies. Come on, Billy, let's ride."

He knew the way out to Litt Springer's place on the north end of the county. He had visited there a couple of times after Litt had resigned from the force and had bought it. Litt had tried to talk him into doing the same, and many a long night under a thin blanket and a frosty moon he'd done some serious thinking on it.

He drew his rifle and laid it across his lap. Billy Hutto's eyebrows went up in surprise. "Litt ain't goin' to bushwhack us."

"He's got friends who don't know us. *They* might."

Billy Hutto swallowed and brought out his saddle-gun too.

But they saw no one anywhere along the wagon trail that meandered lazily among the hills and across the mesquite-lined draws. Even so, McLendon was sure their passage had not gone unnoticed. At dusk they drew rein in front of Litt's liveoak-log house. A thin curl of smoke drifted out of the stone chimney. Though he knew within reason that Litt wouldn't be there, McLendon called anyway. "Litt! Litt! It's me, Duncan McLendon!" Nobody could accuse him of sneaking in.

A face showed briefly behind a narrow window. The door opened hesitantly, and a woman stood there, a woman of thirty who looked forty, her eyes vacant and without hope. "He's not here, Duncan."

McLendon swung slowly to the ground and took off his hat. "I don't suppose you'd tell me where he's at?"

She shook her head. "Are you here to visit, or is this official?"

"Official, Martha. I wish it wasn't."

She stared at the Rangers a long, uncertain moment. "Come in, Duncan. I'll fix you some supper."

Billy Hutto dismounted, smiling. He was always hungry. McLendon said: "Billy, you stay out here and watch. I'll tell you when supper's ready."

He followed Martha Springer into the small cabin, hat in hand. It was all one room, kitchen on one side, table in the middle, bed at the other end. McLendon doubted Litt had been in that bed much lately.

"It grieves me to come here this way, Martha."

"They want to kill him, Duncan."

"I know. And they'll do it if he stays out long enough. If I can arrest him, he'll have a chance. He's got friends in Austin."

She shrugged futilely. "What good would it do? This thing has been building a long time. Their stealin' the county seat was a part of it. Then what happened to Ollie. Now this." Her lips pinched. "Litt killed that deputy, just like they say. He doesn't deny it. He rode over there and found him and shot him. What's more, he's got a list of names in his pocket. He says he's going to kill the rest of them too."

"The people who hung Ollie?"

She nodded.

McLendon's stomach went cold. He hadn't heard about the list.

Martha Springer rolled a slice of steak in a panful of

flour. "This country's been like a keg of powder ever since the county seat election. If Litt does what he says, he'll set off the fuse. There won't be a stop to it till they fill up the graveyard."

McLendon's face twisted. "He ought to know better. He was a Ranger long enough to understand how things go wild thataway."

Tears welled up before she blinked them away. "That's just it, Duncan, he *was* a Ranger a long time. Do you have any idea how many people he killed in the line of duty?"

He looked away. Yes, he knew, but he didn't know if *she* did, and he wasn't about to tell her. "Several. It was his job."

"It got too easy for him. The first time or two, it bothered him. After that . . ." She shook her head. "He should've gotten out a long time before he did." Her gaze came back to him. "*You* get out, Duncan. Don't you stay in there till it's too late for you too."

Billy Hutto came through the door. McLendon turned. "Billy, I wanted you to stay . . ." He cut off in mid-sentence, for he saw that Billy's holster was empty. And he saw a tall, gaunt man step in behind Billy, pistol in his hand.

"Howdy, Dunk."

"Hello, Litt." McLendon made no move for his own pistol. He couldn't make it anyway if Litt Springer didn't intend him to. And he wasn't ready to test Litt's resolve. Other people had done that with disastrous consequences.

Springer held his empty left hand out, palm up. "I believe I'd best just take your six-shooter, Dunk. At least till we've had us a little talk." His voice was pleasant, but a hardness showed in his eyes—a hardness some border bandidos had learned they had good cause to fear.

"I'm not in the habit of givin' up my gun."

"You don't need to worry about me. I'm your friend. I wouldn't shoot you, Dunk."

"I'm *your* friend, too."

"But you're still a Ranger. Let's have it."

McLendon eased the .45 out of the slick holster and carefully handed it over butt first. Springer pointed his chin at the chair. "Set yourself back down, Dunk. I'm awful proud to get to see you again. I take it Martha's fixin' you some supper. I'm hungry too."

"You haven't been home much lately?"

Springer shook his head. "We got enough help to keep a posse out, but there's not enough to guard against a single man sneakin' in here in the dark and maybe shootin' from ambush. I'm not ready to die yet."

"You *will* die, Litt, if you stay here and keep this thing goin'. Sooner or later one of them is bound to get you. That's why we've come. We want you to go with us to Austin. We'll get this thing cleared up."

"Too late. I've killed a man now. I'd just as well go on and finish what I've started."

"I heard about your list. You think killin' those men is goin' to solve anything? All it'll do is open up a war."

"*They* opened a war the day they took Ollie and strung him up. Called him a thief, but it was a lie. They hated him because he tried to keep them from stealin' the courthouse. They knew he'd keep on fightin' them and maybe get the election recalled. That'd be the death of Cedarville."

"You didn't have to take it on yourself to start killin' them, Litt. You been a Ranger long enough to know you could go to the law."

"They *are* the law in this country. *You* been a Ranger long enough to know how it goes when a mob like that takes over the law. You know it usually takes force to root them out, and that force ain't always used accordin' to the statutes. These hills are a long ways from an Austin law library."

McLendon studied his old friend regretfully. Litt seemed thinner, older, grayer. There was more of a fierceness in his eyes now than McLendon remembered seeing there before. "We come to take you back with us. I'd hoped I could talk you into it. But if I can't, we'll use force, Litt. You know I mean what I say."

Litt Springer's gaze was level. "I know you'll *try.* But *you* know I got help out there. Even if I didn't have your gun—which I do—you couldn't take me out of here against my will. They'd stop you."

McLendon had no answer to that. Springer's gaze lifted to his wife, who was putting food on the table. She moved numbly as if she had already given up and was shutting the world out. Springer said: "Dunk, you and Billy set yourselves down and we'll eat."

They ate, and the tension lifted a little. Litt Springer's eyes lighted and smiled as he talked of the old days on the Ranger force. "Remember that time we went out to trail those Comanches, Dunk, and you took the midnight watch and saw that Indian standin' in the moonlight and shot him? And shot him, and shot him? And in the mornin' we found that tree stump with all those bullet holes in it?"

McLendon nodded, spirits lighter as he remembered. "And that time, Litt, when you were takin' a nap in winter camp on the San Saba, and a couple of us climbed up on the roof and dropped a handkerchief full of gunpowder down the chimney to wake you up? Like to've blown you through the wall."

Springer laughed. "Remember, they used to say that us Rangers could ride like a Mexican, trail like an Indian, shoot like a Tennessean, and fight like the devil."

They sat there and spun old yarns as if nothing had come between them. Billy Hutto was too young on the force to add to the conversation. He just listened, grinning, holding his silence out of respect for the two older men whose experience was greater than his own.

After a while Litt began recounting the story of his long, dogged hunt for an outlaw named Thresher who had killed a Ranger. His smile died, and his eyes went grim as he recounted the days and weeks and months of tireless searching, the long miles and the hardship and the sacrifice. "They ordered me to quit. They threatened to discharge me from the service if I didn't drop the search and get on to other things. But I told them the man he'd killed was a friend of mine, and I'd go on and hunt him whether I was a Ranger or not. I swore I'd get him, and I did. I shot him like he'd been a wolf. That's what he was, really . . . just a wolf."

McLendon frowned. "This thing now, this thing with the mob from Cedarville . . . it's the Thresher case all over again, isn't it?"

Hatred came into Springer's eyes. "Just like that. I won't quit till the last one of them is dead."

"Nothin' I say is goin' to stop you, is it?"

"Not a thing, Dunk."

"Then stand warned, Litt. I'll be comin' after you. I'll stop you whatever way I have to."

Litt Springer stared at him in regret. "I'm sorry it's thisaway, Dunk. We been friends a long time. But all I can say is, you watch out for yourself. I don't intend to be stopped." He stood up and backed away from the table. "There's a wagon out yonder by the barn. I'll drop your shootin' irons in there where you can pick them up." His eyes lifted a moment to Martha's, then he backed out the door into the night. McLendon could hear his boots pounding across the yard. He moved to the door but couldn't see. He could hear the clatter of the guns falling into the bare wooden bed of the wagon. From out there came the sound of horse's hooves, loping slowly off into the night. McLendon listened, his hands shoved all the way down into his pockets.

Billy Hutto said, "We can't follow him in the dark, can we, Dunk?"

McLendon shook his head. "No. We'll wait till first light and pick up the tracks." He turned back to Litt's wife. "It was a good supper, Martha. I wish I could say I'd enjoyed it. I reckon we'll sleep in the barn. We won't disturb you, gettin' out of here in the mornin'."

Tears glistened in her eyes. "You won't disturb me. I haven't slept since I don't know when."

They were up as soon as the first color showed over the twisted old live oak trees east of the barn. It was still too dark to see the tracks well, but soon as he satisfied himself of their direction, McLendon started out. Billy Hutto followed him silently, and the mule trailed after them. Not until long after sunup did McLendon call a halt by a small creek so they could boil coffee and fix a little breakfast. Billy Hutto had been holding his silence, but it had been an effort.

"Dunk, I always liked Litt. You knew him a lot longer than I did, and you liked him even more. So, what you goin' to do if you finally catch up with him?"

McLendon was slow in answering. "I'll know when I get there."

"You said you'd do whatever you had to. Does that mean you'd even shoot him?"

"I hope it won't go that far."

"But what if it does? Would you shoot him, Dunk? *Could* you?"

McLendon gave no answer. He didn't know the answer.

The tracks bore generally eastward. It didn't take much concentration to follow them, for in the night no effort had been made to cover them up. The morning wore away, the sun climbing into a cloudless blue sky. Riding, watching the tracks, McLendon occasionally took out his pocketwatch, verifying what the sun told him. About ten o'clock he reined up, shaking his head.

"Looks like he's ridin' plumb out of the county, Billy. That don't hardly figure."

Billy Hutto had no comment. He sat on his horse, his face solemn. McLendon stared at him a moment, as if waiting. When he saw Billy was going to have nothing to say, he moved on. Presently he came to a place where the rider had stepped down for a few minutes. McLendon dismounted and examined the tracks, running his finger along the edge of a bootprint.

"Billy, did you notice Litt's boots last night?"

"Don't know as I did. Why?"

"Seems to me he had high, sharp heels—cowboy heels. These are rounder, and flatter." He looked up expectantly. "What does that suggest to you, Billy?"

Billy was slow in answering. A smile played about his lips. "That Litt run in a ringer on us. He never left his place. We been followin' somebody else."

McLendon pushed stiffly to his feet. "It couldn't be that you've known it all along, could it?"

Billy Hutto shook his head. "I begun to suspect it awhile back, but I didn't know."

McLendon's eyes narrowed. "Seems to me Litt Springer slipped up on you awful easy last night. Could it be that you *made* it easy for him?"

Billy tried to appear surprised, but to McLendon he looked more like a kid caught swimming while school was on. McLendon pressed: "Billy, did you talk with Litt outside the house, before you-all came in?"

"A little while, Dunk."

"And he didn't tell you he was fixin' to do this?"

"Not in so many words."

"Where do you reckon Litt would be right now?"

Billy's smile was gone. He took off his hat and wiped sweat from his forehead onto his sleeve. "Could be he's over somewhere around Cedarville, scratchin' names off of that list. With this, on top of the things he *did* tell me, it kind of adds up."

McLendon closed his eyes, a helpless anger swelling in him. "You better tell me all of it, Billy, and tell me quick."

Billy Hutto didn't look at McLendon. His gaze was on the ground. "He said we'd come a day too early for him. Said if we'd come a day later he'd of finished what he intended to do and it wouldn't make no difference anymore. Said he had a bunch comin' to help him. He was goin' to ride over to Cedarville and bait that sheriff to come after him. He was goin' to lead him into a box, him and everybody from town who went with him."

"The sheriff?"

"The sheriff's right at the top of Litt's list. Seems like he told that deputy the mob would be along, and to let them have Ollie Springer."

McLendon's voice was taut. "Billy, I thought you were a Ranger."

"I am. But I'm a friend of Litt Springer's, too."

"Right now you can't be both. Which way is it goin' to be?"

A stubborn anger flared in Billy. "That bunch of rattlesnakes . . . old Litt's got a right to do what he's doin'."

"Not by law."

"Law be damned. There's times the law is wrong."

McLendon turned and looked regretfully over their backtrail. "I know. But it's still the law. You better go to Austin, Billy."

Billy was incredulous. "And leave you?"

"I don't want a man with me unless he's with me all the way. You took an oath, Billy. If you can't live up to it you better turn that badge in."

Billy stared at him, not believing at first. Finally he shrugged. "All right, Dunk. But he's your friend, too."

"You don't have to remind me of that." McLendon unpacked the mule and took what little he thought he would have to have. He tied the meager supplies on his saddle, swung up, and reined toward Cedarville in a long trot, alone.

The temptation was strong to push the horse into a hard lope, to rush for Cedarville. But it was a long way, and a horse ridden too hard might not make it. Years of Ranger experience had taught McLendon restraint. He had spent as much as two days carefully following an Indian trail, always within striking distance but always holding back, waiting for the right place and the right moment. Once he had spent three weeks patiently tracking a Mexican border jumper who, if not pressed or alarmed, would eventually lead him to the headquarters of an entire bandido operation.

All manner of images blazed in his mind, things that could be happening in Cedarville, or somewhere out among these limestone hills. But McLendon held himself back. He would swing into an easy lope for a way, then ease down to a trot, putting the miles behind him much too slowly.

Well past noon, he rode down Cedarville's dusty street and found it quiet. Hearing the ring of a hammer, he reined in at a blacksmith shop. The blacksmith was shaping a shoe against an anvil. Leaning out of the saddle, McLendon called, "You seen the sheriff?"

The grimy blacksmith pointed with the tongs, the hot shoe still gripped in them. "That Litt Springer, he showed up at the edge of town this mornin'. Sheriff got a few men together and took out after him. Last I seen, they disappeared yonderway."

McLendon rode in a wide arc until he came across a trail he took to be the posse's. Spacing and depth of the tracks indicated the horses had been running. He put his horse into an easy lope. Trailing was no effort. He could have followed this one in the middle of the night.

An hour later he brought the horse to a stop. The warm wind had carried a sharp sound. He dismounted to get away from the saddle's creak so he could hear better. Presently it came again. A gunshot. And another.

Litt's working on that list, he thought darkly. He remounted. This time he didn't hold back. He spurred into a hard lope and held it. *Damn it, Litt, why couldn't you have listened?*

Ahead lay a range of broken hills, and amid those hills, a gap. McLendon could see horses, a single rider herding them a short way from the gap, away from the angle of fire. He halted awhile, studying the layout, determining where Litt and his men were scattered, and where the posse seemed to be bottled up in that gap. The firing was sporadic, just an occasional shot fired by one side or the other.

McLendon paused, looking at the gap but not really seeing it, listening to the shots but not really hearing them. He was seeing other battlegrounds, and other times. He was seeing a Litt Springer far different from the one down yonder.

He brought the rifle up from its scabbard, levered a cartridge into the breech, and lay the rifle across his lap. He unpinned the badge from inside his vest and transferred it to the outside where no one could miss seeing it. *Good target,* he thought. But it had been used for a target before. Gently he touched spurs to the horse and moved into an easy trot again.

The horse herder rode forward, six-shooter in his hand. He wasn't a man, McLendon saw; he was only a boy, perhaps fifteen or sixteen. The boy stopped squarely in McLendon's path, the pistol aimed but the barrel wavering. The boy's voice was unsteady. "Ranger, ain't you? Litt won't be wantin' you in there."

"I'm goin' in there, son. I'm going to see Litt." McLendon kept riding, gazing unflinchingly into the boy's eyes. He could see uncertainty. "Son, you move out of my way."

"Ranger, I'm tellin' you . . ."

McLendon didn't slow. He kept staring the boy down. The boy's horse turned aside, the boy trying to rein him back around. McLendon rode past. He never turned his head, but he could feel the gun aimed at his back. He tensed, but he was almost certain—the boy wouldn't fire.

He rode into the opening of the gap. Now he could see Litt's men, perhaps a dozen of them, scattered among the rocks. He couldn't see the sheriff's crowd, for they were keeping their heads down, but he could tell where they would be. A man turned and saw McLendon, and he swung his rifle to cover him.

McLendon said evenly, "I come to see Litt."

"Ranger, you got no business here."

"I come to see Litt."

A call went down the line. Presently McLendon saw Litt Springer moving toward him, crouching to present less of a target to the men bottled up back yonder. Litt straightened when he thought he was past the point of danger. He walked out, flanked by a couple of his backers, carrying rifles. Litt looked surprised. "Wasn't expectin' you, Dunk. Thought you'd still be followin' that false trail. Where's Billy Hutto?"

"I sent him to Austin to turn his badge in."

Litt frowned. "I'm sorry about that. He's a good boy, Billy is. He'd of been an asset to the force."

"Not if he couldn't learn to put duty first. And he couldn't."

Litt's eyebrows knitted. "But you do, don't you, Dunk? Duty always come first with you."

"The day it doesn't, I'll turn in my *own* badge."

"You shouldn't have come here, Dunk. Most of the men we got hemmed down was with that mob the day they hung Ollie. This is as far as they're goin' to go."

"I told you before, Litt, leave it to the law. Lynchin' is a form of murder. We'll take care of them the way it's supposed to be done."

"The law lets too many fish get out of the net. We've got these caught. There ain't none of them gettin' away."

"You're makin' yourself as bad as they are. Worse, even, because you've been a Ranger. I'm askin' you one more time. Let the law punish them."

"The law's too uncertain. *I'll* punish them."

"And start a war. I reckon Martha was right, Litt. You stayed with the Rangers too long."

"What do you mean?"

"You should've quit when it still gave you nightmares to kill a man. Killin' comes too easy for you now."

"When this is over I'll be satisfied."

"No you won't, Litt. There won't be any satisfyin' you because these killin's will lead to more. There'll be other deaths to avenge. There won't be any stop to it till half the men in this county are dead, and you among them. There won't be any rest for you this side of the cemetery gate."

"What do you figure on doin' about it, Dunk?"

"I got to stop you if I can."

Litt held out his hand. "I want your guns."

"Not anymore, Litt. I gave you my gun last night, but I won't do it again. You want it, you'll have to shoot me."

Litt Springer tried to stare him down, but McLendon held against him. Litt shrugged. "Then turn around and ride out of here, Dunk."

"I'm sorry, Litt. Your friendship has meant a lot to me. But from now on I'm not your friend. I'm a Ranger, and I got a job to do."

"Goodbye, Dunk."

"Goodbye, Litt."

McLendon reined the horse around and started away in a walk. The wind had stopped, and the still heat seemed to rise up and envelop him. Another shot came from the gap, but McLendon didn't hear it. He was hearing muffled echoes of old voices and old laughter from beyond a door he had shut behind him.

Gripping the rifle, he suddenly reined his horse around. He spurred him into a run. Ahead of him, he saw Litt Springer stare in surprise, eyes wide, his mouth open. Litt started bringing up the pistol he had held at arm's length. One of the men with him shouted a warning and dropped to one knee.

McLendon leveled the rifle. He saw fire belch from Litt's pistol but knew Litt had missed by a mile. McLendon squeezed the trigger and felt the riflebutt drive back against his shoulder. Through the smoke he saw Litt Springer stagger backward, the pistol dropping from his hand. McLendon leaned over the horse's neck as the man on his knee brought his rifle into line.

Litt coughed an order, and the man lowered the rifle. McLendon levered a fresh cartridge into his own and stepped to the ground, letting the horse go. Litt Springer was on his knees, arms folded across his chest, his face going gray. He stared at McLendon in disbelief.

"Dunk . . . I didn't think you could."

Some of Litt's men came running, and McLendon could see danger in their eyes. One grabbed at the Ranger, and another shoved a pistol into his belly.

Weakly Litt said, "Let him alone, boys. . . . He's a friend of mine."

"Friend?" one of them shouted angrily.

"A friend," rasped Litt. "He done what he figured he had to."

Litt crumpled. McLendon let his rifle fall and eased Litt onto his back on the ground. Throat tightening, he said: "I didn't want to, Litt. I kept tellin' you . . ."

"And I ought to've known. You're a better Ranger than I ever was, Dunk."

Litt's friends were gathering, leaving their places around the men they had trapped in the gap. Litt started to cough. McLendon could see blood on his lips. "Litt," he said, "call them off. Let this be the end of it."

Litt blinked, his vision fading. "You told me you'd see that the law took care of them."

"I meant it, Litt. I'll see that every one of that mob pays."

Litt nodded. "And you ain't never lied to me. Boys, go on home."

A few of them wanted to argue, but Litt waved them away with a weak motion of his hand. "We got his promise. Go home, boys."

Litt was gone then. Slowly the rest of the men came down from their positions. Openly hostile, they honored Litt's order. They caught up their horses and soon were gone, the dust settling slowly behind them.

Cautiously the sheriff crept out of the gap, rifle in his hands. Behind him the others followed, some still crouching, suspicious. Finally satisfied, the sheriff straightened and let his rifle arm hang loose. He strode over and looked down on the still form of Litt Springer.

"I seen what you done, Ranger. To be honest with you, didn't think you would. I reckon we owe you."

Curtly McLendon said, "You owe me nothin'."

The sheriff shrugged. "Have it the way you want it. Takes a special breed of a man who can shoot down his own friend thataway. I'll remember it. If ever I got another cold-blooded job that needs doin', I'll call on the Rangers."

McLendon didn't even think. In sudden rage he swung the riflebutt around and clubbed the sheriff full in the face. The lawman fell, surprised and cursing, the blood streaming from his broken nose.

The others stood frozen in shock. "Get him up," McLendon shouted. "Get him up and out of here before I kill him!" As they hauled the sheriff to his feet, McLendon said, "Wait!" They paused. McLendon gritted: "I'm takin' Litt home to bury him. But I'm comin' back. I got his list, and every man on it is goin' to answer to a judge. Now git!"

They caught their horses and helped the sheriff into his saddle and rode off toward Cedarville. Looking down on Litt Springer, Duncan McLendon unpinned the Ranger badge from the front of his vest and put it back on the underside, where he usually wore it. They wouldn't need it to know who he was.

THE BLUE BURRO
L. J. WASHBURN

—◦◦◦—

L. J. Washburn is a past winner of the Shamus
Award for Best Private Eye Paperback Novel.
She won it with a Lucas Hallam novel called
Wild Night. There were other Lucas Hallam
novels, but of late she has been keeping the
character alive through short stories. Here one
of Hallam's old Texas Rangers buddies asks a
favor that gets Hallam involved in much more
than he bargains for. Livia's Hallam stories
always illustrate that she is at home with not
only the western genre, but the mystery and historical genres as well.

The night before, Hallam had said, "The Blue Burro is
the sort of place a fella with enough money can buy
anything his heart desires . . . 'cept maybe an honest
drink."

Tonight, before his eyes, that assessment had been borne out. He'd been sitting at a table in a corner of the smoky cantina for a couple of hours, nursing a succession of watered-down drinks, and during that time he had watched the ownership of stolen jewelry, packages of dope, and underage girls change hands a dozen times or more. Most of what he saw filled him with anger and the desire to haul out the hogleg under his coat and let daylight through the innards of the skunks responsible for it.

But he was here to do a favor for an old friend, a friend who had once saved his life, and until that job was done, Hallam had to rein in his temper.

Besides, Race had hinted that there was a lot riding on this assignment, a whole hell of a lot. Things that maybe affected the whole blamed country . . .

Both men had worn the star-in-a-circle badge when they rode together in South Texas, hunting outlaws in the brush country along the border. Jim Race had been a sergeant in the Texas Rangers, and so had Lucas Hallam. Eventually Hallam had left the force and hired on with the Pinkertons, but Race had stayed in the Rangers and made captain. More than fifteen years had passed. Roads were paved now, and automobiles chugged and clattered along them. Nary a horse was tied up in front of buildings lit up by electricity. Over in Europe, nation fought against nation using metal behemoths that lumbered along through bloody mud and flimsy contraptions of wood and canvas that soared overhead through smoke-filled skies. Everything had changed in the world.

But when Hallam got the telegram from Jim Race

asking him for help, Hallam had come without hesitation. Some things, it seemed, did not change.

They met in a room in the Camino Real Hotel, in downtown El Paso. When Hallam opened the door and saw Race standing there, memories came rushing in on him.

The two of them pinned down in a shack on the banks of the Nueces River, their horses dead . . . Hallam with a bullet in his leg, unable to run . . . standing off rush after rush of the outlaws who wanted to kill them, until night finally fell . . . the way Jim Race had hoisted the much larger Hallam over a shoulder and gone out the back of the shack under cover of darkness, carrying him across the river and a couple of miles to an isolated ranch, where they had gotten help . . .

It had been a heck of a thing to do, especially since Hallam had urged Race to slip out alone after dark. He would stay there, he had said, and keep the gang busy until Race was long gone. Race hadn't even considered the idea. He'd grinned and said, "You wouldn't do that if the tables were turned, now would you, Lucas?"

Hallam hadn't been able to say honestly that he would have, and so that was that.

Now as they faced each other in the hotel room, Race took off his hat—a fedora, for God's sake, not a Stetson!—revealing a lot of gray in his reddish hair. He stuck out a hand and said, "Lucas, it's mighty good to see you again."

Hallam shook with him and looked at the brown tweed suit. "I thought you was still a Ranger."

"I am. Captain, in fact. Reckon you could say I'm undercover."

Hallam grunted.

"Too many people in El Paso know me," Race went on. "This getup's not going to fool anybody for very long, but at least I won't draw as much attention to myself dressed this way. I don't want anybody to know about you and me talking."

Hallam nodded. During his time as a Pinkerton operative, he'd had clients who needed to keep everything between them secret. This wasn't really the same thing, but in a way it was. If he took the job, whatever it was, he wouldn't get paid, but he'd be working for the Texas Rangers anyway.

"I got a bottle and some glasses. Sit down and tell me about the trouble you got."

Race laughed humorlessly. "You mean a fella can't want to get together with an old trail partner without having anything else in mind?"

"That telegram sounded to me like you needed a hand with something," Hallam said as he splashed whiskey into the pair of glasses on the night stand. He handed one to Race, took the other himself. "You want to drink to old times?"

"Hell, no," Race said. "Mostly they weren't near as good as we remember 'em."

"Probably not."

"I'll drink to the future instead."

Hallam shrugged and clinked his glass against Race's. "To the future."

"Let's hope there is one."

Now that was a damned odd thing to say, Hallam thought. He tossed back the hooch, licked his lips. "Tell me about it," he said again.

Without being asked, Race sat down on the edge of the bed and put the fedora on the spread beside him. "I'm looking for a fella named Kenneth Langham. He's supposed to be somewhere over in Juárez."

"Young fella?"

"Twenty-three."

Hallam nodded. Young Americans went missing in Juárez all too often. Most of them stumbled back over the river bridge sooner or later, once they got their fill of whatever fleshpot or dope den that had swallowed them up for a while. Some of them landed in jail on the wrong side of the border, and that was just too bad. A good number wound up dead, and that was worse, but still, there wasn't a whole hell of a lot you could do about it. Somebody bound and determined to wreck their life would usually find a way to do it.

"I didn't think the Rangers handled missing persons cases."

"Young Langham's father has money."

"Oh," Hallam said, but that still didn't really explain anything. In his experience, the Rangers didn't do favors for rich men. But he had been away for a while. Maybe that was something else that had changed.

"Normally, all we'd do is contact the authorities in Juárez and let them look into it," Race went on. "You know how much good that would do, though."

"More than likely not much," Hallam said.

Race nodded. "And we can't operate across the border ourselves." He smiled faintly. "It's not like the old days, Lucas, when jurisdictional lines could be . . . bent a mite every now and then. Relations between the U.S. and Mexico are especially strained right now, what with

Carranza taking over and Villa raising such a ruckus all over the place and nobody much knowing who's going to be in power from one day to the next . . ." Race shook his head.

"So what you need," Hallam said, "is for somebody who's a civilian to go over the river and look for Langham."

Race looked squarely at him and said, "Yes. That's exactly what we need."

"Got any idea where to start lookin'?"

That was when Race had said, "Have you ever heard of a cantina and gambling den called the Blue Burro?"

The Blue Burro was owned by a man named Gonsalves, who also owned a ranch a dozen miles or so below the border. Hallam had heard plenty about him but had never met the man. Most of what Hallam had heard was bad. Gonsalves was said to have personally killed at least eight men and ordered the deaths of many more. In the old days he would have been a bandido. Now he was just a businessman who was somewhat more ruthless than normal.

"Good luck, Lucas," Jim Race had said the night before when he left the hotel room. "And thanks. There's a lot riding on this. More than I can say. Walter Langham is a mighty important man. Important to the whole country."

The name had been a little familiar to Hallam. He had gone to the El Paso Public Library during the day and read some newspapers. Walter Langham was Langham Steel. He could probably get away with calling President Wilson "Woody" if he wanted to. How in blazes had the son of a man like that gotten mixed up with a polecat like Rico Gonsalves? Then he remembered all the other rich men's sons who had gotten themselves in trouble. Yeah, there was always a way. And Race had been pretty positive about the tip the Rangers had gotten that Kenneth Langham was spending a lot of time at the Blue Burro, one of Cuidad Juárez's most notorious dives.

Being a civilian, Hallam could grab the kid, drag him across the river to El Paso, and turn him over to the Rangers, who could then ship him back to his daddy. Of course, if Kenneth raised a big enough ruckus before Hallam got him out of Juárez, the Mexican police might arrest him for kidnapping, and he'd probably never see the light of day again. Hallam would do his best to see that that didn't happen.

"Señor, *por favor?* You like a girl, señor? You like me?"

Hallam turned his head and looked up and saw a girl standing there at his shoulder. She was a dark-haired, dark-eyed beauty, no doubt about that, but Hallam figured she wasn't over sixteen. She rested a hand with long red fingernails on his shoulder and leaned over so that he could get a good look down the low neck of her blouse.

"No thanks, honey," Hallam told her, feeling even older than his forty-four years. He wished he could tell her to get out of this hellhole, but he knew that even if he did, it wouldn't do any good.

She leaned even closer, breathing into his ear in English, "I think they're going to try to kill you soon."

Hallam wasn't expecting that. She hadn't sounded Mexican at all when she said it, and as he glanced at her again he decided that despite the dark hair and eyes and the olive skin, she was American. And maybe a mite older than he had first thought, too.

"Who?"

"The two at the bar ... *there* ... I heard them talking about you. They work for Gonsalves."

Hallam looked where the girl indicated with a flick of her eyes. Two men stood with their backs to the bar, watching the room. Hallam had already pegged them as a couple of Gonsalves's enforcers. One was Mexican and about as wide as he was tall. The other one had pale hair cropped short and a face like a wedge. His eyes were pale, too, and they lit on the table where Hallam was sitting.

The girl leaned in still more, twined an arm around Hallam's neck, and kissed him. She put a lot of feeling into it. She sure as hell didn't kiss like a sixteen-year-old, Hallam thought, and then reminded himself that it had been a long time since he had kissed a gal that age. He didn't really know how a sixteen-year-old would kiss in these modern times.

"Who are you?" he asked between his teeth when she pulled away.

"Just somebody trying to do a fellow American a favor. I think you'd better get out of here while you still can, mister."

"They're watchin' me. If they want to kill me, they won't just let me leave."

She reached down and took his hand. "Come with me. I know a way out."

Hallam's mind worked fast. This might be a trap. Assuming that the fellas at the bar really did want to kill him, the girl could be working with them, trying to lure him someplace where they could dispose of him without too much fuss. Or she could be telling the truth about wanting to help him. Of course, that left unanswered the question of why an American girl was pretending to be a whore in a Juárez cantina.

If he played along, he might find out, Hallam decided.

He held the girl's hand as he came to his feet. "Lead the way," he said.

She tugged him toward an arched doorway with a beaded curtain over it. Hallam had seen girls taking customers through here all evening, so there shouldn't be anything suspicious about what they were doing. The girl glanced back at him and said quietly, "They're still watching. I don't like the way they're talking to each other. I think they've realized that I'm not one of the regular girls."

"Best not waste any time, then."

The beads rattled as they pushed through them. The hall on the other side was lit by only a few candles stuck here and there. It was narrow, with a lot of doors on both sides and a door at the far end. The girl let go of Hallam's hand and hurried toward that door.

"It'll be locked," she said over her shoulder. "Can you break it down, or pick the lock?"

"Comes down to it, I'll shoot it open."

She looked at him again. "You've got a gun?"

"Yep."

"Good. You may need it."

One of the doors on the left side of the hall opened. A heavyset American stepped out, grinning back into the tiny room at the girl who sat nude on the bed, counting the money he had left her. "You did fine for your first time, darlin', just fine," the man told her.

Hallam bumped him hard with a shoulder as he went past. "Hey!"

The beads rattled loudly.

"Get back in there," Hallam said.

"Who the hell do you think you are, bud?"

Hallam thought about leaving him there in the line of fire—anybody dumb enough to think he'd found himself a virgin in the back room of a bordertown cantina was pretty close to being too stupid to live—but instead he put a hand on the man's meaty shoulder and gave him a hard shove that sent him flying back onto the bed. The nude girl jumped out of the way.

"Go!" Hallam said to the girl in front of him.

She ran the last ten feet to the door at the end of the hall. Hallam was right behind her. He reached under his coat and drew the .45 revolver from the holster canted on his left hip. Somebody yelled, *"Alto!"* but didn't wait to see if he was going to stop. A gun roared, the sound deafening in the narrow confines of the hallway.

The bullet spanked past Hallam and gouged a big hole in the cheap plaster on the wall. He twisted, saw the two men who'd been at the bar coming after them. It was the pale-haired man who had fired; smoke drifted from the barrel of the gun in his hand. His Mexican compadre had a knife with a long, heavy blade. The thing was damn near a machete. There wasn't much room to do it, but Hallam put a bullet between them that made them jump in opposite directions and run into the walls.

"Get out of the way," he said to the girl as he turned back toward her.

She huddled in a corner as he launched himself

against the door. It was sturdier than it looked, but Hallam was a big man and knew how to hit a door. The wood around the lock splintered.

Hallam stumbled a little as he went through the door, but he was still able to reach back with his left hand, grab the girl's arm, and drag her after him. Two more shots blasted. Hallam flung the girl down the alley toward a distant spot of light and then dropped to one knee. Since he always carried the hammer on an empty chamber, he had four rounds left in the Colt. He slammed all four of them down the hall, hoping none of the whores or their customers would pick that moment to step out.

The pale-haired man went down, clawing at a bullet-torn thigh. The Mexican pitched forward, too, but Hallam sensed that he wasn't hit, just getting out of the way of the lead. Hallam got to his feet, feeling a twinge in his bad knee as he pushed up, and then he ran after the girl. His boots splashed through muck in the alley, and he thought he stepped on a rat or two.

"Over here," she called as he reached the mouth of the alley. She was behind the wheel of a Model T with the top pushed back. Hallam ran over and cranked the engine while she held down the starter. The engine caught.

"You know how to drive this thing?" Hallam asked over the coughing and sputtering.

"Just get in!"

Hallam used his long legs to step over the passenger side door without opening it. He dropped onto the seat as the automobile lurched forward. He put the Colt back in its holster and then hung on.

In the lights from the buildings they passed, he saw her grinning at him. "First time in an auto, cowboy?"

"No," Hallam said. He frowned as the contraption swerved around a corner. "I'm just not real fond of 'em, that's all."

"Well, we'd better hope Gonsalves's boys don't have one handy, or they'll come after us."

"The gringo won't. I put a forty-five through his leg."

"Good for you."

There were fewer automobiles over here in Juárez than across the river in El Paso. At this time of night, Hallam and the girl pretty much had the streets to themselves. She drove past the big downtown *mercado,* which was closed, and stopped in a small park. The place was deserted.

"I'm obliged for your help," Hallam said.

"Why did Gonsalves's men want to kill you?"

"Don't know. Why did you decide to give me a hand?"

"I couldn't stand by and let a fellow American be murdered."

"That's another thing," Hallam said. "What was an American girl doin' at the Blue Burro?"

She laughed. "A girl has to make a living somehow—"

"No," Hallam said, "you ain't a whore. Who are you, lady?"

"I'm the one who helped you, remember? I don't think you have a right to ask questions."

Hallam opened the door of the Model T. "All right, then, I reckon I'll be movin' on."

She hesitated, but only for a second, before saying, "Wait. Please."

Hallam had figured from the first that she wanted something from him. He had no idea what it might be, but either she would tell him now or he would walk away. He had business of his own over here, and it meant that he would probably have to venture back to the Blue Burro before this night was over.

He sat there with the door half open and waited in silence. After a moment, the girl said, "My name is Jacqueline Southwick."

"Fancy name."

"This is where you're supposed to ask if I'm one of the Philadelphia Southwicks."

"I reckon you must be," Hallam said, "or else you wouldn't've brought it up."

"Yes, I am. I came down here to look for someone. A . . . a young man."

"Your beau?"

"That's right. At least . . . I thought he cared about me. Now I'm not so sure. He . . . he abandoned me on a trip through Texas, while we were in Dallas. I should have gone home, I know . . . I could have wired my father for a train ticket . . . but I was afraid something was wrong, that my friend might be in trouble. I heard he was in El Paso, so I came out here. I had enough money for that. Then I heard that he had been seen in Juárez, at a place called the Blue Burro, so I dressed myself like the sort of . . . the sort of woman who would frequent such a place, and I came to look for him."

Hallam thought about the story. It was just oddball enough to be true, but he wasn't sure yet if he believed her.

"You're rich?" he asked.

"Well . . . my family is. My money is actually in a trust fund that I can't touch until I'm twenty-one. That's still two years from now."

"And you ran off on a lark with a young fella and came to Texas. Did the two of you elope?"

She shook her head. "No, we're not married. I know, it's positively scandalous—"

Hallam held up a hand to stop her. "But the whole adventure got fouled up when the young fella dumped you in Dallas, and you're a mite too ashamed to go slinkin' back home to your folks."

Her chin lifted angrily. "If you have to be so crude about it, I suppose that's a reasonable assessment."

"How long have you been hangin' around the Blue Burro lookin' for the young fella?"

"This is the third night."

"You been posin' as a soiled dove for three nights and ain't had to . . ."

"Young women of my class are quite adept at promising more than they ever intend to deliver," she said.

Hallam just shook his head. Jacqueline Southwick had no idea how lucky she had been. He was going to have to see to it that she took herself back across the river and stayed there. He didn't need that headache on top of his job for the Rangers, but he couldn't just leave her to wolves like Gonsalves and his boys, either. She thought of herself as an adventuress, but really she was just a lamb waiting to be gobbled up.

"You didn't ever find your beau, did you?"

"No. But I think I know where he is. I overheard Gonsalves talking to some of his men." She leaned toward Hallam, excited and animated as she spoke. "I think they took Kenneth down to Gonsalves's ranch."

"Kenneth?" Hallam said.

"Yes, that's my friend's name. Kenneth Langham. Of the Pittsburgh Langhams."

Hallam was still digesting that when she grabbed his arm and said, "The minute I saw you, I knew you were the man to help me. Will you take me to Gonsalves's ranch and help me rescue Kenneth? I know that awful man is holding him prisoner! He probably intends to demand some sort of ransom from Kenneth's father."

That sounded likely to Hallam, if indeed it was true that Kenneth Langham was at Gonsalves's ranch. Having Jacqueline Southwick fall into his lap, so to speak, had filled in some of the blanks for Hallam. Even without meeting Langham, Hallam had him pegged as a wild young man, too full of himself for his own good, the sort who would drag a gal halfway across the country and then desert her and run off to gamble and whore his way into trouble on the wrong side of the border. Easy pickin's for a man like Gonsalves, who was always in the market for a fast, dirty dollar. Langham probably never expected his girlfriend to try to track him down, and he probably hadn't figured that his father would use the influence of power and money to set the Rangers looking for him, either. Those strands had intertwined and brought Hallam and Jacqueline together.

Had Jim Race known about the girl? Hallam doubted it. Race would have warned him about that possible complication. And even though she had given him a hand, she *was* a complication, one that he didn't need.

"Maybe I'll go and look for your fella," Hallam said, "but you got to get back across the river to El Paso."

"Oh, no," she said instantly. "I'm going with you, mister—What *is* your name, anyway?"

"Lucas Hallam, and if I'm goin' to pluck your beau away from Gonsalves, I can't be lookin' out for you at the same time, Miss Southwick."

"You won't have to look out for me. I can take care of myself. In fact, *I* helped *you* get away, back at the Blue Burro, remember?"

"And I said that I'm obliged—"

"Besides, if I go along we can take my car, and we can be at Gonsalves's ranch before morning. I have a pretty good idea of how to get there. If you go alone, you'll have to either walk or find a horse, and it'll take you a lot longer."

Hallam tried not to sigh in frustration. "You don't know what you're gettin' into—"

"I can shoot if I have to." Her hand dipped into the folds of the long skirt she wore, and from somewhere she came up with a small pistol. It gleamed in the faint light that penetrated the shadows under the trees. "Just give me a chance, Mr. Hallam. I . . . I have to help Kenneth if I can."

Hallam knew it was the wrong thing to do. He knew he ought to take her across the river by force if necessary and make her stay there. But once he was gone, how could he stop her from following him? If she was bound and determined to be part of this, maybe it would better to keep her close by, rather than having her blunder around and maybe cause even more problems.

Besides, there in the rear hallway of the Blue Burro,

she had seemed pretty coolheaded. She drove the automobile good, too, he thought. Better than he could, that was for damned sure. And if they succeeded in snatching Kenneth Langham away from Gonsalves, they would need to rattle their hocks out of there in a hurry.

"All right," he said, hoping that he wouldn't regret it. "You can come with me. But you got to do what I tell you to do."

"Of course." He couldn't really see her face in the shadows, but he could hear the smile in her voice as she added, "Should we seal the bargain with another kiss?"

"Just drive," Hallam told her.

Hallam had a pretty good idea where Gonsalves's ranch was, and Jacqueline had overheard enough to confirm the location. They found the main road leading south out of Juárez and followed it.

Hallam thought about what had happened at the Blue Burro. Why had Gonsalves's thugs come after him? They shouldn't have known who he was, and they sure shouldn't have had any idea that he was there on a job for the Texas Rangers. And yet the girl had overheard them plotting to kill him, and they had come after him as soon as he'd made a move to get away. Had someone found out about his meeting with Jim Race and put two and two together? An even more disturbing question occurred to Hallam. Did Gonsalves have an informer working inside the Rangers?

He would worry about that once he had rescued Kenneth Langham, Hallam told himself. He felt a stirring of resentment. Not only was he risking his own life on the young man's behalf, but a beautiful young woman like Jacqueline was putting herself in danger because of him. It sounded to Hallam like Kenneth Langham needed to grow up a whole heap. Somebody ought to shake some sense into his head. Maybe, if he had the chance, he would give the boy a good talking to.

Not that it would accomplish much, more than likely. Youngsters like that thought they had the world by the tail, just because their fathers had money. They might grow old, but they seldom grew up.

Kenneth Langham would at least have the chance, if Hallam had anything to say about it.

Jacqueline talked quite a bit, raising her voice over the rattle of the engine. She complained about the way her folks treated her, always prodding her to do things she didn't want to do and telling her she couldn't do the things she really wanted to. Hallam figured out pretty quick that she was a smart girl, smart enough so that a life of sitting around drinking tea and going to society parties bored the hell out of her.

"I think I'd like to learn how to pilot an aeroplane," she said. "Don't you think that would be fun, Mr. Hallam?"

Hallam had seen a few of those flying machines, and they bothered him more than automobiles did. "I reckon I'll stay on the ground," he said. "I never wanted to be higher up than the back of a good horse."

"Oh, pooh. You're a spoilsport, just like my father. He thought it was completely improper for me to learn how to drive. Young ladies just don't do such things, according to him."

"Well, maybe they shouldn't."

"Despite your rough exterior, you're just like him. I can tell that now."

That was the first time anybody had ever told Hallam that he was just like some rich man from Philadelphia.

"I'm going to learn how to pilot an aeroplane," Jacqueline went on, "and someday I'm going to fly off in one and visit all the jungles and deserts in the world and have all sorts of thrilling adventures. And if my father doesn't like it, that's just too bad. I'll be a grown woman soon, and I'll do what I want."

Hallam hoped she lived through this night, so that she would have a chance to be a grown woman. It hadn't seemed to occur to her that she was in the middle of one of those thrilling adventures right now.

That was because it didn't seem so thrilling while it was going on, Hallam mused. When your life was actually in danger, everything seemed a mite confusing and frightening, and usually you had to be both lucky and good to survive. Especially lucky.

"Of course, once Kenneth and I are married, he'll probably try to tell me what to do, too," Jacqueline went on. "But will I listen to him?"

"Probably not," Hallam said.

She laughed. "That's right. Probably not!"

The road was rough, and the ride shook up Hallam's insides more than any horseback ride he had ever taken. The Model T rattled so much he didn't see how it held together. But somehow it did, and along about three in the morning, they came to the side road that led to Gonsalves's ranch. Jacqueline turned west, toward a range of low hills. Hallam saw the faint twinkle of lights a couple of miles away. That would be the ranch.

The sound of the automobile's engine would carry quite a ways in the night air. When they came to a small gully with gently sloping sides, Hallam said, "Drive down in there, over behind that clump of mesquite. We'll go the rest of the way on foot."

"We're not going to drive all the way to the ranch?"

"Not unless you want them to know we're comin'."

"Oh. Yes, that makes sense. We'll hide the auto here and come back for it once Kenneth is with us." She drove down into the wash.

Hallam didn't intend to walk back here. He figured they could get their hands on some horses, there on Gonsalves's ranch, and ride back to the automobile. If need be, they could just forget about the contraption and horseback all the way to the border. Wouldn't be the first time he had ridden across the Rio Grande that way, Hallam thought with a faint smile. Wouldn't even be the first time he had crossed the border with somebody chasing him.

"I don't reckon there's any chance I could talk you into stayin' here and waitin' for me?"

"Of course not."

Hallam gave some thought to tying her up and making her wait here. But he knew she'd put up a fight, and more important, if anything happened so that he couldn't get back to the automobile, then she really would be in a fix. Like it or not, he was stuck with her. In a way, he had been ever since she had sidled up to him in the Blue Burro.

"Come on," he said.

His boots had low heels, so walking wasn't too bad a chore. Jacqueline wore slippers, though, and they didn't give her feet much protection from the rocks and gravel on the road. She didn't complain, but she couldn't help but say "Ouch!" from time to time. Hallam was glad they didn't have that awful far to go.

They were about halfway to the lights that marked the ranch when he heard something. He stopped and turned and looked to the south. Another automobile was coming up the main road from that direction. Its headlights cast yellow cones in the darkness. Those beams of lights bounced up and down as the automobile hit rough spots.

Hallam figured the vehicle would go on past the ranch trail, but the lights slowed and then swung to the west. "Somebody's comin'," he said. "Get off the trail."

Jacqueline didn't argue. She hustled off into the scrubby brush with Hallam following her. "Squat down," he told her when they were about fifty yards off the road.

"I don't believe anyone has ever told me to squat before. That's another of those things proper young ladies of Philadelphia society don't do."

"We're a hell of a long way from Philadelphia," Hallam said. He hunkered on his heels and waited with the Colt in his hand.

There was enough moonlight and starlight for him to be able to see the automobile as it approached. It wasn't a Model T, he saw. This contraption was somewhat bigger and heavier. He leaned toward Jacqueline and asked, "You know what kind of automobile that is?"

"I think it's a Mercedes-Benz touring car." She sounded puzzled. "That's a German automobile. I wouldn't expect to find one down here."

The Mercedes-Benz, if that's what it was, rumbled on past the spot where they waited. "Well, it looks like it's goin' to Gonsalves's ranch, just like us." Hallam waited until the red lights on the back of the automobile had vanished, then stood and motioned for her to follow him.

They resumed walking toward the ranch. Hallam didn't holster the Colt, and he noticed that Jacqueline had the little pistol in her hand, as well. "You sure you can shoot that thing?"

"I'm an excellent shot. I've been to a target range in Philadelphia several times."

"Ever shot at anybody who's shootin' at you?" Hallam asked, already knowing the answer.

"No, but if I have to, I will."

"Before the night's over, you'll probably have to."

There were a lot of lights burning at the ranch, Hallam saw as they drew closer, more than should have been at this time of night. In fact, it looked like the whole place was awake. That wasn't good. He had hoped they could slip in, locate Kenneth Langham, and get out with him before anybody noticed. Hallam figured the young man would be guarded, but he wasn't worried about taking care of a couple of guards. If he had to fight all of Gonsalves's men, though, it would be a different story.

The house had been there for a long time, a sprawling two-story Mexican hacienda made of whitewashed adobe, with red slate tiles on its roof. There was an outer wall, also of adobe, with a black wrought-iron gate in it. The house would have an inner courtyard with a fountain in it, overlooked by a second-floor balcony that ran all the way around. Once the place had been owned by a real ranchero, a don who raised fine cattle and horses, instead of a whoremonger and dope smuggler like Gonsalves. Hallam wondered how Gonsalves had gotten his filthy hands on the ranch. It was probably an ugly story.

The big German touring automobile was parked in front of the gate. A man wearing some sort of uniform leaned against the front fender, smoking a cigarette. That would be the driver, Hallam thought. Another man strolled over from the gate. He wore a town suit and a peaked sombrero. One of Gonsalves's guards. Hallam and Jacqueline watched the two men for a moment as they crouched behind some brush; then Hallam whispered, "Give me a few minutes to work my way around closer to them, then you walk up bold as brass."

"I'm going to distract them while you attack them, is that right?"

"I reckon that's the general idea," Hallam said. "You up to it?"

"Of course!"

He squeezed her shoulder for a second, then moved off into the darkness, circling closer to the wall so he could come up behind the two men. For a big man, he moved with a quiet grace that made his passage through the shadows nearly soundless. He wound up kneeling beside the adobe wall about a dozen feet from the driver and the guard. They didn't have any idea he was there.

Hallam had been waiting only a moment when Jacqueline strolled into the light and approached the automobile. "Hello, boys," she said in a sweet, lilting voice. Both men turned sharply to stare at her, startled to see anyone come walking out of the night, let alone a beautiful young woman. Out of habit, they reached under their coats, and Hallam knew they were reaching for guns.

He was on them before they knew what happened. His big hands closed on their heads and smashed their skulls together with a sound like a watermelon being dropped on the floor. The two men collapsed without any chance to raise an alarm. Hallam didn't think either of them would wake up for quite a while.

Jacqueline ran lightly over to him. "Did you kill them?" she whispered, sounding a little awestruck.

"They ain't dead . . . I don't think," Hallam told her. He took her arm. "Come on."

The gate was half open. They slipped through. Hallam led the way along the wall of the hacienda until they reached a corner where a stairway led up to the second floor. As quietly as possible, they climbed the steps, went through a narrow passage, and found themselves on the balcony overlooking the interior courtyard. A railing of black wrought-iron that matched the exterior gate ran along the edge of the balcony. The fountain down in the courtyard laughed and gurgled, and a man laughed, too. It wasn't nearly as pretty a sound.

Hallam catfooted along the balcony toward the voices he heard. Jacqueline followed him, and he certainly couldn't complain about her making too much noise. She was as quiet as an Apache.

The trees growing around the fountain had lanterns in them. Hallam and Jacqueline stayed well back so that the light from the lanterns didn't reach them. It spilled over the two men who sat in comfortable chairs beside the fountain, though. Hallam recognized Gonsalves, a slender, narrow-faced man with a mustache. The other man was shorter and thicker, with close-cropped gray hair and one of those monocle things stuck in his eye. He wore an expensive suit and toyed with a heavy walking stick made from some sort of gnarled wood.

"When the time comes, you will have my country's gratitude officially, Señor Gonsalves," the gray-haired man said. "Until then, you have my gratitude, unofficially, for your assistance in this matter."

"It was my pleasure, Excellency," Gonsalves said. "You will speak to the Kaiser on my behalf?"

"Most assuredly."

Hallam frowned. The Kaiser? That was the fella who was the big boss over in Germany, and the gray-haired man in the courtyard below looked and sounded German, as far as Hallam could tell, not being an expert on such things. Why was somebody who worked for the Kaiser paying a visit to a cheap Mexican crook like Gonsalves?

And where was Kenneth Langham?

"Will the young man be here shortly?" the gray-haired man asked. "It is a long journey back to Mexico City, and I wish to delay it as little as possible."

"I sent one of my men to wake him," Gonsalves said. "He should be here soon."

A door opened somewhere down below. Footsteps rang on the flagstones that paved the courtyard. A voice said, "Herr Rammelman, it's good to see you."

Jacqueline's fingers dug into Hallam's arm. "That's Kenneth," she hissed.

Hallam had already figured as much. And as Kenneth Langham strolled up to join Gonsalves and the German, it was obvious that he wasn't a prisoner after all. He wore a lounging jacket, and a cigarette dangled from his lips. He shook hands with Rammelman.

"What's he doing?" Jacqueline hissed. "What's going on here?"

Hallam didn't know the answers, but he figured if they kept quiet, they might learn them. He put a finger to his lips and touched Jacqueline's shoulder lightly with his other hand.

Kenneth sat down with Gonsalves and Rammelman. A jug of tequila sat on a small table, along with some glasses. Kenneth poured a drink for himself. The other two men already had glasses in their hands. Kenneth lifted his glass and said, "My father sends his regards, Herr Rammelman . . . along with a more tangible token of his esteem."

Rammelman grunted. "More than a token, Herr Langham. Half a million dollars is a great deal of money. More than enough to persuade Señor Villa to assist us."

"Here's to war," Kenneth Langham said.

Hallam's head was spinning. Kenneth Langham hadn't been kidnapped. He had come here to Gonsalves's ranch voluntarily, and he had brought half a million dollars with him, delivering it on behalf of his father. Walter Langham had built a fortune in steel . . . and that fortune would only grow larger if the United States became involved in a war. But a war with who? Mexico?

The men tossed back their tequila. Gonsalves licked his lips and said, "Herr Rammelman, you must make it clear to Villa that I will be the territorial governor once he is in power. That is my fee for arranging this meeting."

"Of course," Rammelman said. He reached inside his coat and brought out a sheaf of papers. "Everything is set forth in these documents. General Villa will attack the United States and draw them into a war in their own backyard, so to speak, so that the Americans will have neither the time nor the inclination to interfere with our affairs in Europe. Then, once we have been successful, we will assist Mexico in turn to reclaim all the territory stolen from her by the Yankees. Everyone profits by this arrangement . . . including, of course, Herr Langham and his father."

Kenneth smiled. "The money's in my room. Why don't I go get it before Villa gets here?"

"An excellent idea," Rammelman said. He laughed. "I must admit, I am a bit curious to see what half a million American dollars looks like."

Kenneth stood up and walked under the balcony, out of sight. Hallam glanced over at Jacqueline. Her face was drawn tight, and her eyes were wide with shock and anger. He took her arm and drew her back into a darkened alcove.

"He . . . he's a traitor!" she whispered, her voice shaking a little from the depth of her feelings. "I thought I knew him, but I didn't know him at all!"

"Take it easy," Hallam said. "This changes everything. We got to figure out what to do."

"Well, I don't want to rescue him anymore, that's for sure! He made his own choice to join up with these . . . these hoodlums."

"Yeah, but if we leave him here, he's goin' to turn over

half a million bucks to Pancho Villa, and Villa's goin' to try to start a war with the United States. I don't know about you, but I don't care much for that idea."

"Neither do I," Jacqueline said. "How do we stop them?"

Hallam's rugged face creased in a grin. He had hoped she would see things that way. "Come on."

They found some more stairs and hurried down to the first floor. Speed and stealth were their most important allies, Hallam thought. He looked along the covered walkway where several doors were located. Kenneth Langham had come out of one of those rooms. Beyond them, Gonsalves and Rammelman were visible sitting next to the fountain, but the two men weren't paying any attention to the shadowy corner where Hallam and Jacqueline lurked. They were still drinking and talking.

Hallam and Jacqueline peered around the corner of the adobe wall at the doors. Hallam talked in a swift whisper, and Jacqueline nodded. When one of the doors opened and Kenneth Langham stepped out carrying a small leather suitcase, Jacqueline stepped around the corner and softly called his name.

Kenneth stopped and looked, staring at her in surprise. If he yelled, they were in for a fracas, Hallam thought, but instead, the young man was so shocked to see the girl he had left behind in Dallas that he took a step toward her and said, "Jacqueline?"

Hallam couldn't see Kenneth Langham from where he stood, but he could see Jacqueline just fine. He watched her smile and beckon to Kenneth, and as pretty as she was, dressed in that long, colorful skirt and low-cut white blouse, it would take most young men a lot of willpower to turn down that invitation. Kenneth didn't have that much willpower. He hurried along the flagstone walk, bringing the suitcase with him. Jacqueline retreated around the corner. Right about now, Kenneth had to be wondering if he had imagined her. He had to find out.

He stepped around the corner, right into Hallam's fist.

The punch landed solidly on Kenneth's jaw, jolting his head back and making his eyes roll up in their sockets. At the same time, Hallam used his other hand to grab Kenneth's coat and keep the young man from falling. He jerked Kenneth's limp form deeper into the shadows.

"Did . . . did you hurt him?" Jacqueline asked as Hallam lowered Kenneth to the ground. She might claim she no longer cared for him, but some habits were hard to break.

"Just knocked him out," Hallam said. "Grab that bag."

Jacqueline picked it up. "It's heavy."

"Blood money usually is." Hallam risked another glance around the corner. Gonsalves and Rammelman were still sitting by the fountain, drinking and smoking. They didn't seem worried that Kenneth Langham hadn't returned yet.

Even though Hallam had seen only the two men he had knocked out at the gate, he figured Gonsalves had at least a dozen more men at his beck and call, and all of them would be hardened killers. It would take only a shout to summon them. The smart thing to do would be to throw Kenneth over his shoulder and get the hell out of here. He and Jacqueline could slip back to the Model T and light a shuck for Juárez. Once they made it over the border to El Paso, Hallam could dump the kid and the money in Jim Race's lap and let the Rangers sort out everything.

And yet he couldn't help but think of those documents Rammelman had placed on the table next to the tequila. The papers detailed the whole German plot involving Pancho Villa attacking the United States. It seemed to Hallam that it would be a good thing for the American authorities to have those papers.

"Take the suitcase," he told Jacqueline. "Get back to the automobile and wait for me. If you hear a bunch of shootin', though, you better take off and get back to El Paso as fast as you can. When you get there, take the money to a Texas Ranger named Jim Race and tell him everything that happened."

"A Ranger? Are you a Ranger, Mr. Hallam?"

"Used to be. Right now I'm just givin' them a hand."

"I knew as soon as I saw you I could trust you to help me. That's why I said what I did about Gonsalves's men plotting against you."

"Wait a minute," Hallam said. "You mean they weren't talkin' about killin' me?"

"Well . . . no. As a matter of fact, they were after me. I thought if I pretended to help you, then you would help me."

So when the two gents had chased them down the hallway in the back of the Blue Burro, they had been trying to get their hands on Jacqueline, not him, Hallam thought. He had figured it was the other way around. It looked like just about everything in this business had turned out to be something different than it appeared to be at first glance.

"I'm sorry," Jacqueline said. "I shouldn't have lied to you."

"That's all right," Hallam said. He hadn't spilled the whole story of his involvement to her, either. "Take the money and get out of here."

"Please . . . be careful. And bring Kenneth with you, if you can."

"If I can," Hallam promised.

She slipped off into the night, taking the suitcase with her, and as soon as she was gone Hallam used Kenneth's belt to tie the young man's hands behind his back. He found a handkerchief in Kenneth's pocket and crammed it in his mouth to serve as a gag. Then Hallam left him sitting there against the wall, still unconscious.

He didn't know much about those newfangled automobiles, but he knew they ran on gasoline. When he got back to the Mercedes-Benz parked in front of the hacienda, he found the two men he had knocked out still lying slumped beside the vehicle, out of sight from the house. Hallam caught them under the arms and dragged them farther away from the automobile. Then he went back and poked around the contraption until he found the spout where gasoline was put into it. He unscrewed the cap, sniffed to make sure he had the right place, and made a face at the stink. People claimed that automobiles would eventually do away with the smell of horse shit, but as far as Hallam was concerned they weren't really much of an improvement.

He pulled the tail of his shirt out, tore some strips of

cloth off it, and knotted them together. Then he lowered the makeshift fuse down into the gasoline tank, letting some of it dangle out. He waited a minute to allow the fabric to soak up some of the gasoline and then fished a match out of his pocket. He snapped it into life on his thumbnail and held the flame to the cloth. It caught fire and began to burn. The lower it went, the faster it would go.

Hallam turned and ran back toward the house.

Kenneth Langham was gone when Hallam got to the place where he had left the young man. Hallam bit back a curse and drew his gun. Kenneth must have come to and managed to get to his feet. He had stumbled off looking for help, which meant that any second—

Out in the courtyard, Gonsalves started yelling in Spanish.

A second later, the Mercedes-Benz blew up, lighting the night sky with a brilliant splash of flame.

Hallam ducked around the corner and broke into a run, heading toward the fountain. He saw Rammelman trying to untie Kenneth. Gonsalves was gone, no doubt heading for the front of the house where the explosion had just rocked the place. Kenneth saw Hallam coming and let out a yell. Rammelman spun around and jerked out a gun.

Hallam didn't see a German diplomat, didn't think about the possibility of an international incident. He just saw a fella pointing a gun at him. After that, instinct took over, and the revolver bucked in Hallam's hand as he fired.

The bullet spun Rammelman around and dropped him to the flagstones. He hunched over, badly wounded. Kenneth's hands were free now, and he made a dive for the gun Rammelman had dropped. Hallam lunged forward and kicked him before he could get it, breaking his jaw. Kenneth sprawled on the ground, knocked senseless again.

The documents still lay on the table. Hallam scooped them up with his free hand and jammed them inside his coat. He bent, picked up Kenneth Langham, and tossed the young man over his shoulder. The boy was skinny and didn't weigh too much. Hallam headed for the back, knowing he couldn't go out the front. That was where Gonsalves and his men would be congregating, where the Mercedes-Benz still burned fiercely.

Hallam was half right and half wrong. Gonsalves's men might be at the front of the hacienda, but Gonsalves himself came trotting out of the rear wing, carrying a shotgun. When he saw Hallam coming toward him, he jerked the greener up and fired.

Hallam felt the bite of buckshot, but he also heard the deadly thud of lead into Kenneth Langham's body. Kenneth jerked and slipped out of Hallam's grasp as Hallam fell to one knee. The Colt came up and roared as Gonsalves tried to reload. The Mexican cried out as Hallam's bullet tore into him and drove him backward. He dropped the greener and tumbled onto the flagstones, barely twitching when he landed.

Hallam looked at Kenneth and saw that the lounging jacket was sodden with blood, as was Hallam's coat. Most of the blood on Hallam had belonged to Kenneth. The young man had caught the brunt of the shotgun blast, and it had pretty much blown him in half, although Hallam's life had been saved in the process. Hallam hadn't meant for it to happen that way, though.

He didn't hide behind any man, and sure as hell not a traitor.

Traitor or not, Jacqueline was going to be upset to hear that Kenneth was dead.

But she'd never hear about it if he didn't get away from here, Hallam told himself. He lurched to his feet, ignoring the hot, wet pain where a few of the lead pellets had ripped through his side, and ran out the back of the hacienda, kicking open a rear gate.

He circled the place and headed for the gully where he and Jacqueline had left the Model T. He hoped she was still there. The idea of walking all the way back to Juárez, shot up as he was, didn't appeal much to him.

Lights bloomed in the darkness in front of him before he got there. An engine roared and clattered. Hallam leaped aside, but the automobile skidded to a stop before it reached him. "Mr. Hallam!" Jacqueline cried.

Hallam tumbled over the side door and gasped, "Go!"

She hesitated. "Kenneth?"

"He didn't make it," Hallam said through his teeth. The pain in his side was getting worse.

Jacqueline hesitated only an instant to let that soak in. Then she spun the wheel and tromped the foot feed. The wheels threw sand and gravel in the air as the automobile slewed around and took off. Shots banged from the hacienda, but none of the bullets came close.

Hallam figured they were about halfway to Juárez before he passed out.

He was sitting at the bar in the Camino Real when Jim

Race slipped onto the stool beside him. The tightly wrapped bandages around Hallam's torso didn't keep him from lifting a glass of whiskey to his lips.

"Nobody can raise quite as big a ruckus as Lucas Hallam," Race said quietly. It was the middle of the afternoon and they were alone at the bar, it being siesta time for the locals.

"You sent me down there," Hallam pointed out.

"To look for a missing kid, not to uncover some German plot to start a war."

Hallam shrugged. "I found the kid."

"And he wound up dead, too."

"Gonsalves did that, not me."

"Yeah." Race signaled the bartender for a drink. When the man had brought it and gone, the Ranger went on, "Those papers had too much blood on them to be legible, you know. Kenneth Langham's blood."

"I told you what they said. And you got the half-million. That's got to be proof of something."

"Yeah, but what?" Race shook his head. "The word is, we're letting the whole thing drop. As far as the Rangers—and all the rest of the authorities on this side of the border—are concerned, we don't know a damned thing about it."

Hallam grunted. "What about Walter Langham?"

"What about him? All he knows is that his boy went into Mexico and didn't come back. A damned shame, but these things happen."

Hallam sipped his whiskey. "Why did Langham pretend to want Kenneth found in the first place?"

"It was just a formality, a report so that if anything happened to the boy, Langham would look like an innocent concerned father. He didn't really expect us to *do* anything about it. That's my guess, anyway."

A hard smile touched Hallam's face. "So in a way, it was Langham's own fault that his plan got ruined and his boy got killed."

"If you want to look at it that way. Unofficially, Langham will be investigated . . . but a man with that much power and money . . . don't expect too much justice, Lucas."

"Not too much," Hallam said, thinking about Kenneth Langham. "Just enough."

After a moment, Race said, "What about the girl? Can she be trusted to keep her mouth shut?"

"I reckon. She's pretty smart. Got me back here in one piece, didn't she? Anyway, she's goin' to be busy for a while." Hallam grinned. "She's goin' to buy herself one o' them aeroplanes and learn how to fly it. Says she wants to take me up for a spin."

"Lucas Hallam in an aeroplane?" Race snorted. "I don't believe it!"

"You never know, Jim," Hallam said. "You just never know."

A couple of years later, Mexican rebel troops under the command of Pancho Villa crossed the border and raided the town of Columbus, New Mexico, killing sixteen people and prompting the United States to send a punitive expedition into Mexico after him, commanded by General John J. "Blackjack" Pershing. That failed expedition did nothing to stop the United States, and Pershing, from a year later entering what was then known as the Great War. Hallam sometimes wondered what, exactly, had prompted Villa to attack Columbus. One thing was certain: If the attack was part of a German plot, Walter Langham didn't have anything to do with it. The steel magnate had blown his own brains out three months after his son's death in Mexico. It was in all the papers.

Jacqueline Southwick learned how to fly an aeroplane, one of the first women to do so, but she didn't fly off and have any more adventures. She married a rich young fella back in Philadelphia instead. Before that, though, she spent some time in California with Hallam, and she probably would have stayed longer if he had just said the word, which he didn't. He was too old for her, whether she wanted to believe that or not.

So when it came time for her to leave, she kissed him one last time and then got on the train, and as Hallam watched it pull out of the station, he smiled and said softly to himself, "Oh, pooh."

A BORDER DISPUTE
ROD MILLER

—◦◦◦—

Rod Miller is a cowboy poet and fiction writer who has had stories in the anthologies *White Hats* and *Black Hats*. This story is an impressive feat from any writer, let alone a fairly new one, as he tells the tale very effectively . . . in reverse.

The walls of the gorge lit up briefly in the lightning flash. Although it was but midafternoon, heavy clouds and high cliffs blocked enough light that it was dark as late evening along the river's course in the canyon's bottom.

Knowing it was a matter of minutes until the clouds burst, the man in the canoe started watching the walls for a place to put ashore.

Not that he minded getting wet. But the tons of water the storm was dumping on the desert were already pouring down feeder gorges and into the river, and the coming high and white water was more than he cared to tackle in a cheap open canoe. His cargo was much too valuable to risk. And so he scanned the shore as he slid along on the current.

Not that there was shore to speak of. But that was why he was on this stretch of the Rio Bravo—Rio Grande, the gringos called it. Smuggling drugs across the border wasn't the cakewalk it once was, so the commerce was forced into ever more inventive avenues and isolated places.

The so-far-successful method that brought him here was simple. Get to a place on the Mexican side of the river where you can get yourself, your cargo, and a cheap canoe over the rim of one of many canyons downriver from the Big Bend country and float lazily downstream for a few days or even a week to reach another semi-accessible prearranged place on the American side, set the canoe adrift, and climb out of the canyon with the cargo.

So far, it had worked. The buffoons in the Border Patrol and the DEA idiots could not comprehend this offset fashion of fording the river and so concentrated on more conventional crossings. But, he feared, the *Rinches*—the derogatory border-Spanish term for the Texas Rangers—were wising up and he might soon have to come up with a new and equally devious plan or he could wind up in some Texas *juzgado*.

His eyes picked up a dark cleft in the cliff's face just a few feet above the water. He backpaddled to slow and turn the canoe, pushed himself back upstream a few yards with a dozen deep strokes, then pivoted again and allowed the canoe to drift downstream as he used the paddle to force it against the wall.

When he again spied the slender opening he grasped jagged rock and stopped for a closer look. The canyon hereabouts was riddled with caves, but not many were accessible without serious climbing and he had neither the time nor inclination for that. So he sought shelter that was above the high-water mark and no higher.

This should do fine, he thought.

With a couple of lengths of bright yellow plastic braided rope he lashed the canoe securely fore and aft to rock outcroppings. He rummaged through one of the watertight plastic chests that filled the canoe and selected a blanket, a battery-powered fluorescent lantern, a water bottle, and a lunch sack full of cold tamales and tortilla-wrapped frijoles. He fashioned a makeshift sling from the blanket and with the food and lantern in its pouch scrambled the few feet up the cliff to the narrow opening.

Once through the crack, he sat back against the wall for a moment to catch his breath. As he sat, a thunder-clap rolled through the canyon shattering the sky, knocking the storm loose into the gorge. The sound of heavy raindrops splattering off rocks and pocking the river made him glad he was out of it.

Even in the dark he sensed the cave was a small one and sang a few lines of a favorite *corrido* to see if the echo agreed. It did.

The smuggler slid a few feet further into the moun-tain before unslinging the blanket. He set the lunch sack aside and stowed the lantern between his thighs and wrapped the blanket around his shoulders before punching the button to activate the lamp.

He did not realize how accustomed his eyes had become to the dim until he squinted in the painful glare of the light. A hand raised instinctively to shield his eyes. Then his vision cleared and an inadvertent gasp, nearly a scream, filled the cave when he saw what he saw.

Sitting next to him, no more than a foot away, was a rack of bones and stack of litter that had once been a man. Another skeleton lay on the floor nearby. The smuggler, whose line of work had occasioned his seeing no small number of dead bodies and even watching a goodly number who were alive become dead, was nevertheless startled and shocked and left temporarily lacking the ability to breathe.

Calderón died instantly in a powderflash and since he saw it coming it would be incorrect to say that he never knew what hit him. Another cliché often applied to such instances may, however, be true: He never felt a thing.

That cannot be said of the other man, Butts, whose death was both lingering and painful.

And although it violates the order of their dying, it is yet true that Calderón killed Butts, and then Butts killed Calderón.

The smuggler considered bolting the cave and braving the storm, but curiosity got the better of him once composure returned. He studied the bodies—corpses, skeletons—and wondered how they came to be dead in this out-of-the-way place.

It was clear they had been dead for a long time. A long, long time. Little remained in the way of flesh—the odd strip of jerky clinging here and there the only evidence that meat and skin once covered the bones.

Since the skeletons were largely intact, the place must be protected from predators, at least large ones. He assumed bugs and worms and rodents had done the scouring.

A sizable chunk of bone was missing from the upper forehead and top of the skull of the man seated beside him. The side of the head of the other man, the one curled on the floor next to the black smudge that must have once been a fire, was dented and cracked. That says something, he thought.

Butts knelt next to the small fire, kindled from rats' nests and twigs and a few pieces of driftwood he'd collected from where they'd been lodged in the rocks near the cave's entrance. The fire would never burn long enough to dry them, but the spindly flames provided a bit of light and took the edge off the chill.

It wouldn't matter if they were still wet come morning, anyway, he thought, since it would be back in the river for the both of them until they could find a place on the left bank to climb out of the canyon. He fed the fire a few more twigs and turned toward Calderón in time to see the rock in the Mexican's fist the instant before it smashed into his head with a dull crack like a stick of wood snapping underwater.

The blow rattled Butts to the soles of his boots, but as his eyes blurred and his ears buzzed and his brain bled, he managed to unholster his Colt and with the last remnant of strength in his arm and hand bring the weapon to bear and fire. Calderón, weak from the flight and the fight and the fall and the float, had barely managed to lift the rock, no bigger than the crown of his lost sombrero, for a second swipe at the fallen Butts when the heat of the muzzle blast withered his eyelashes and the bullet ripped a peso-sized chunk out of his head.

As soon as Butts fired the shot, the weight of the gun carried his hand to the cave floor and he instinctively curled into a fetal position. The noise inside his shattered head drowned out the sound of his whimpering. Pain squeezed at his skull and the blood poured both into his head and out of it, eventually washing away all awareness and finally life itself.

Not much left in the way of clothing, the drug runner noticed. Practically all the fabric, it appeared, had been unraveled and hauled away string by strand. Most likely, he thought, to line rodent nests. Dried and cracked remnants of leather boots remained. Rusted spurs said both had been horsemen.

Other metal objects survived. Corroded buckles and tarnished brass cartridges in a gun belt around the body on the floor. A rusty old revolver wrapped in finger bones. And, still surrounding the thin bones of the men's wrists, a pair of handcuffs.

The cuffs linked the right wrist of the man leaning against the wall to the left wrist of the man on the ground. That, and the fact that the downed man held the gun, led the smuggler to the obvious conclusion that the one seated next to him had been the prisoner of the other.

But what the hell were they doing here, in this miserable cave in the bottom of a river gorge with no way out? As he mulled it over, his eye caught something else. There, wedged in the dust under a rib bone, was a dull metal disk. He wiggled it out of the dirt and brought it closer to the light.

He could see, after rubbing off a layer of grime, that it had once been a silver peso. But its face had been crudely hammered smooth and a series of wedges punched out to create the shape of a star within a circle, around which was stamped the words TEXAS RANGER.

Rinches! he realized. This dead *pendejo* was one of the *Rinches!*

Butts clung to the rocks with one hand while the other fist held a twisted handful of Calderón's shirt collar. He was further encumbered by the Mexican's heavy *mochila,* an oversized set of saddlebags slung over his shoulder. Both men sputtered and spat volumes of water back into the river where it belonged. Calderón had the worst of it, in turn hacking water from his lungs and spewing it from his stomach.

"Stay afloat, Calderón. I can't keep you from drowning by myself."

"Why don't you just let go?"

"You ain't getting off that easy, you thieving son of a bitch. I'll watch you rot in a jail cell and enjoy every minute of it."

The Mexican made a halfhearted attempt to tread water while the Ranger looked over the rocks above. The canyon walls were rough and jagged, nearly vertical. Caves and shelter rocks were visible in the cliffs, but he could not see a way to get to them. Then, just before casting off to float downriver and try again elsewhere, he spied a dark cleft in the rock a few yards upstream. Maybe, just maybe, he thought, it was within reach and might offer shelter from the coming night.

"Come on. Upstream," Butts said.

"*Qué?* What do you want?"

"There," the Ranger gasped, pointing out the cave. He hacked up and spit out another gob of slimy water. "Climb. Get out of this damn river."

Butts pulled Calderón through the water and spun him toward the rocks. The Mexican clawed for holds, and between the two of them pushing and pulling, they reached the spot below the cave. The Ranger jerked upward on Calderón's shirt, lifting him higher in the water.

"Up," he said. "*Arriba.*"

The Mexican barely had the strength to struggle the few feet up the face, and it was almost more than Butts could do to pull himself along behind and prod the prisoner at the same time. As Calderón disappeared into the narrow crevice, the Ranger called out to him.

"Calderón!"

He waited a moment, stuck to the rock like a lizard, then called again, louder this time.

"Calderón! Poke your ugly face out that hole!"

The Mexican's face slithered out the crack like a tortoise poking its head out of its shell.

"*Qué?*"

"Here. Grab these."

Butts pulled as many sticks and twigs of driftwood as he could find out of the rocks and shoved them upward one at a time. Calderón took them and pushed them into the darkness behind him. Having scavenged all the wood at hand, Butts scrambled that last few feet up through the rocks and followed his prisoner into the cave. Before he even sat down, he clamped handcuffs around Calderón's wrist and fastened the other end to his own.

"What the hell, man?" Calderón said. "You think I'm going somewhere?"

Butts did not reply, merely dropped to the ground in a heap of fatigue and sucked in a few ragged breaths.

"Unhook these bracelets. I don't want to spend the night chained to no damn Ranger."

"Shut up. It ain't like you got any choice in the matter."

"Where am I going to go? I been chased halfway across *Tejas.* I been beat up. Fell off a cliff. Nearly drowned. I ain't got the strength to break wind and you think I'm going somewhere? Besides, you know I can't hardly swim anyhow."

Butts ignored Calderón. Or pretended to. He did not believe for a minute that the Mexican was anywhere near as bad off as he let on. Besides, the Ranger had experienced all the same troubles his prisoner had and doubted he himself had the strength to stop an attempted escape.

After a brief moment of blessed silence, the prisoner piped up again. "Hey, Ranger—what's your name?"

"Butts."

That drew a chuckle. "Butts? What kind of name is Butts?"

"My name. The one I got from my daddy. The only one I've got."

"What, gringo, you don't got a first name? Everybody just calls you Butts?"

"That. Or C.W."

"*Qué?*"

"C.W. Them's my initials. I go by C.W. Butts."

"What's that stand for, C and W?"

That drew a chuckle from the Ranger. "Clarence. Clarence Winthrop. Clarence Winthrop Butts."

Calderón laughed. "*Madre de Dios!* No wonder you like C.W. How come you know my name?"

"Hell, you're famous, Calderón. Either a hero of your people or the most hated man in West Texas, depending on who you ask. I've known your name these ten years since I been with the Rangers."

A fruitless chase after the Mexican had, in fact, been the first assignment Butts was given as Ranger. Butts was detailed to the Rangers' Frontier Battalion, which had but a few years earlier captured the notorious murderer John Wesley Hardin and killed the outlaw Sam Bass. The day of his enrollment in July of 1882, the tenderfoot Butts was sent out with a posse to chase down Calderón and his bandido gang after they had robbed an express shipment out near Marfa.

But the robbers won a long, hot miserable race across the desert and crossed the border before the Rangers could overtake them. Butts had spent a goodly portion of the intervening decade trying to stop the Calderón gang's robberies and killings across West Texas, but the Rangers always seemed to be a day behind the bandits.

"I been on your tail now and again over all that time."

Again Calderón laughed. "You must not of got too close, Butts, or I would know who you are."

"Maybe so. You are a slippery little bastard, I'll give you that."

"*Claro.* But outsmarting gringos is no big thing. It has been an easy life, robbing those who stole our country. It is like—how do you say it?—taking candy from a baby. Beating you people is almost too easy."

"That maybe was true once, but those days are over now. You make the same mistake my daddy said caused the Confederacy to come out in second place—thinking that winning battles is the same as winning a war."

"What are you talking about, Butts? I have good English, but I do not understand what you say."

"I'm saying you may have won some battles by getting away up till now. But now you're mine, and that means you done lost the war."

Both men sat quietly for a time; then Butts unslung the heavy saddlebags from his shoulder and tossed them back into the cave, where they lit with soggy clink. As his eyes adjusted to the dim light, he spied a wad of grass that had once been a nest for rats or mice and picked it apart into a small pile in front of him. Other similar wads were within easy reach and he retrieved a few of those and piled them nearby.

Finding a likely looking piece of rock, Butts next pulled his pistol from its holster and glanced the stone against the metal at the bottom of the grip to see if he could raise a spark. He could. Soon the dry grass sparkled and smoked and glowed and a few gentle breaths coaxed out a flame.

"Thank God for Samuel Colt," Butts said, holstering his revolver as he added progressively larger twigs to the fire. He knew the fire would be short-lived. But he did not know that within minutes more than a fire would die in this cave.

*   *   *

Curious about the rest of the story, the smuggler hoisted up the lantern and cast his eyes into the dark corners of the little cave. At first he saw only evasive movements of rodents and insects hiding deeper in cracks and crannies, but in due course his eyes picked out a curled and cracked hunk of leather in the shadows.

Stepping gingerly to avoid splintering the bones on the floor, he followed the lamplight to the discovery and dragged the heavy bag away from the wall and into the cave's center. It looked to be of the same vintage as the bodies and about as intact. It was, he decided, a *mochila* of the type he still saw used occasionally by the vaqueros of his homeland on the opposite shore. Smaller than a kyack for a packsaddle but bigger than the saddlebags of Texas cowboys, a *mochila* was cut to fit over a saddle horn and cover all or part of the seat. Pockets or pouches were sewn on the sides for carrying whatever the rider wanted to take along.

And what, exactly, the smuggler wondered, was this one carrying?

The *mochila* was dried out and some of the leather strings that stitched it together had rotted through. Parts of it were gnawed away. But the pouches still held whatever they had held. He shifted it around to get to one of the buckles to find out what, and as he tugged the strap to free the buckle prong, it broke in his hand. Peeking in through the lifted flap, he caught the dull glint of metal.

His heart skipped a beat and his lungs involuntarily gasped for air. In the exuberance that followed, he tore loose the other pocket flaps and shook free a trove of tarnished silver coins and glowing gold coins that clinked into a pile on the floor of the cave, followed by the dull thud of a quartet of shiny, good-as-new gold ingots.

Butts knew the bandit was his when he saw Calderón abandon his spent horse, leaving the broke-down animal quivering and dripping sweat and sucking wind at the rim of one of the many rocky canyons hereabouts that dropped into the bigger canyon of the Rio Grande.

From a distance, he watched the robber strip the *mochila* and head down the deepening gully afoot. Calderón attempted to spook the horse away, but the scrub had hit bottom and stood unfrightened, spraddle-legged with head sagging. The Ranger's horse was also tired, but being accustomed to better feed, had held out just enough longer to run the Mexican mount into the ground.

Turning his horse in the downhill direction of the gully, Butts pushed hard along the rim for better than half a mile, figuring to get ahead of the bandit before dropping into the canyon for a surprise attack.

The plan worked. Concealed behind a rock outcrop at the side of the narrow draw, Butts watched for some minutes as Calderón hustled downhill, dodging boulders and scrambling over drop-offs into the shallow hollows at their bases where storm runoff would puddle and churn before heading again downhill to the next short fall.

Having been the object of the Ranger's pursuit for several long hours and many hard miles, Calderón assumed Butts was still coming after him, so he spent as much time looking behind him as ahead. And so it was unnerving when Calderón turned from one such backward glance to find himself stood up by the barrel of a revolver mere inches from the end of his nose.

Too startled to react, the Mexican did not even breathe until Butts spoke.

"Don't you move, you greaser son of a bitch, or I'll shoot you dead sure as you're born. Get them hands up, real slow."

As Calderón complied, Butts pulled the bandit's pistol from its high-riding, cross-draw holster and threw it into a jumble of rocks on the steep side of the canyon.

"Now sit down. Drop right straight down on that skinny butt of yours and don't try anything cute."

Keeping his pistol trained between the man's eyes, Butts squatted before him and patted around for the knife he knew would be concealed in his boottops. He found it and tossed it away.

Butts then holstered his pistol and looked to where he had tucked a pair of handcuffs under his gun belt, his brief inattention prompting the prisoner to reach behind his head and slide a thin-bladed knife out of a scabbard concealed between his shoulder blades.

Calderón's sudden movement caught the Ranger's attention and he instinctively took a backward step. The resulting accident is the only thing that saved his life. Butts stumbled and tripped when his heel caught on a rock and he fell flat on his back. Unable to stem or shift the momentum of his thrust, the bandit's blade sliced only desert air as he followed its path over the top of the fallen Butts, likewise stumbling and landing half in the dirt and rocks and half atop the lawman.

Quick as spit on a hot griddle, Calderón scrambled off Butts and to his feet and looked around desperately for the knife jarred loose in the fall. Butts saw it first, and grabbed it up from where it had landed almost in his hand. He flipped quickly to his knees and braced for the Mexican's next attack, but Calderón instead turned and loped off downhill. The knife clattered in the rocks as Butts flung it away and took after him.

Even with the heavy *mochila* Calderón carried, Butts figured he must have a thirty-pound advantage over the outlaw, who while short and skinny was likewise wiry and cagey. And had it not been for dumb luck, he knew the Mexican's knife would already have cut him to ribbons. So while his pursuit was vigorous, it was not without caution.

It took another accident to again stop the chase. An unfortunate step wedged Calderón's foot between boulders, impeding his stride just enough to stretch him out facefirst among the muddle of rocks in the bed of the dry watercourse. Butts was upon him before he could recover, and with all the force the lawman and gravity could muster, Butts dropped a knee into the middle of the man's back.

Rather than disabling the desperate bandit, the capture inspired him and Calderón flipped to his back and unleashed a vicious knee, which landed swift and square in the Ranger's crotch, expelling his breath more effectively than the Ranger's knee to the Mexican's back had.

Calderón exploited his advantage by crabbing out from under the Ranger and landing another ferocious kick to his ribs. Butts automatically reached for his pistol as the blow rolled him, but could not accomplish the draw as he had affixed the safety strap over the gun's hammer to secure it during the chase.

Now it was his turn to scramble out of the way on elbows and boot heels as the Mexican attempted to brain him with a rock. Again, Calderón's momentum carried him to the ground, and again Butts took the opportunity to leap astraddle his back. He immediately grabbed Calderón by the wrist and wrenched his arm behind his back, forcing the hand painfully upward. Then, for good measure, he landed a few kidney punches.

The Ranger relaxed slightly when the Mexican sagged limp below him and again he reached for the manacles. In the instant he loosened his grip on Calderón's wrist to replace it with the grip of a cuff, the bandit exploded upward and again scrambled out of his grasp and down the draw.

He did not get far, soon skidding to a stop. His next step would have carried him into empty air with nothing between him and the river below but a sheer drop of some thirty-five feet. Lacking the Mexican's knowledge of their current situation, Butts did not stop as Calderón had, instead launching himself with a mighty leap, the force of which barely diminished as he wrapped his arms around the bandit and carried them both out into the chasm.

Although Calderón knew what was coming and so his scream came first, Butts soon overcame the disadvantage and his yell surpassed the Mexican's on all counts—length, intensity, and the quality of the profanity. And he did not stop the scream until it was replaced in his mouth by river water.

The shock of the landing tore the pair apart and when Butts surfaced he saw that Calderón was in a bad way, his slight frame lacking the buoyancy to keep himself and the heavy *mochila* above water. Besides, the bandit evidently lacked swimming skills beyond the ability to thrash around enough to break the surface from time to time and gasp a breath as the river pushed them along downstream.

A few powerful strokes carried Butts across the current to where the Mexican floundered and he wrapped his arm around Calderón's neck to hold his head above water. Calderón, of course, misinterpreted the action as another attack and objected violently. Butts increased pressure on the bandit's throat to dampen his struggling and yelled into his ear instructions to hold still. Either fatigue or lack of oxygen or the Ranger's yelling finally calmed Calderón, and he relaxed and allowed Butts to keep him afloat.

"Damn it, man, here I am trying to save your life and here you are trying to drown us both. You're going to have to shed them saddlebags or they'll drag you down."

"Are you loco? This *mochila* is why I have been running from you and why you have been running after me. And now you want me to dump it in the river?"

"No, you fool. I'll carry it. It won't weigh me down near as much as it does you, you skinny little bastard. Give it over then we can figure how to get out of this damn river and back on dry land."

Quarter eagles. Half eagles. Eagles. Double eagles. Spanish *reals*. Silver dollars. Gold dollars. Silver pesos. Other curious coins the smuggler had never seen nor heard of. But he knew enough to know that the metal the coins contained far exceeded their worth as minted currency.

And then there were the gold ingots, whose value he could not, dared not, even imagine.

He passed the time stacking, restacking, dividing, subdividing, combining, separating, shuffling the coins.

There were worse ways to pass a rainy night, he thought.

All the success Calderón had enjoyed eluding the Rangers over the years ended by sheer happenstance, one of those ugly coincidences life throws at one from time to time in order to keep one humble.

Butts and a couple of other Rangers happened to be laying over in the railroad town of Sanderson on a trip from Fort Stockton to Langtry. Word came down while the men were enjoying a rare hotel breakfast that a bandido gang had waylaid the morning eastbound a few miles outside of town and made off with a bank shipment—not a tremendous haul, but a significant one.

Even before their abandoned breakfasts had gone cold, the Rangers were armed and mounted and on the trail.

Calderón did not imagine that pursuit would come so quickly, so the Rangers surprised the bandits squatting around empty money sacks dividing the take for easier transport. Had they done so in concealment, it is likely the lawmen would have captured them then and there. But the Mexicans had stopped on a wide and dusty dry lake bed and so saw the Rangers coming from a good way off.

They quickly stuffed the loot back into bags, into pockets, into pouches, into saddlebags, into *mochilas,* even inside shirts and the crowns of sombreros and clambered aboard their horses and lit out across the flat. But the Rangers were better mounted and the gap between the three of them and the five bandits closed with every stride.

The pursued and pursuers started exchanging optimistic gunshots while still outside pistol range, and kept up the fire until the distance closed to effective range. Whether the Ranger riding next to Butts meant it or whether it was a fluke—a subject of much discussion in Ranger circles for years to come—the fact remains that he placed a bullet directly through the back of the neck of one of the retreating bandits, evening up the odds some by making it three after four.

Shortly after the bandit fell, the group split in two, with three staying together and the other striking off alone. Butts signaled the other two Rangers to continue after the group of three, knowing they could improvise in the likely event the bandits split up again later. He veered sharply southward following the lone rider. Already he sensed victory—sensed, at least, that the chances of catching the bandit were heavily in his favor. What his chances might be once he caught up with him he could not say.

Off the flats and onto more rugged terrain, the pace of the pursuit slowed. But still Calderón drove his mount furiously. He knew the river was ahead. And he knew it cut through one deep gorge after another through this country, most likely putting it and the border beyond reach. But if his horse held up, he knew the off chance that he would hit the river at a place he could cross was the only chance he had.

The rain had stopped sometime during the night and by midmorning the worst of the gullywasher had passed and the Rio Bravo was back to its normal flow.

He was nervous, tense, wound tighter than his usual state of alertness while at work. Which is to be expected, perhaps, given that yesterday's unlikely events had made this far and away the biggest payload of his career—even if he jettisoned the contraband drugs. So even though the chances of someone in law enforcement spotting him on this rugged, lonely stretch of river were practically nil, the smuggler nonetheless kept a sharp eye on the cliffs above the left bank. He did not think he would spot a Border Patrol officer up there, or a DEA agent.

But those *Rinches*, he thought. Those damn *Rinches*. It's hard to get the best of the *Rinches*.

DEAD MAN'S GUN
ED GORMAN

—◆◆◆—

Ed Gorman's credits are well known. He won numerous awards in multiple genres, including a Western Writers of America Spur Award for Best Short Story. His last western novel was *Backshot*. Here he infuses his western story with just a touch of the eerie quality you'd find in his horror stories. The results: another signature Gorman tale.

In all my active years as a Ranger, I fired my gun for official business only twice, once to startle a couple of drunken cowboys away from firing any more shots into a store-front window. I don't have to tell you how cowboys are when they've come to town for a weekend of fun.

The other time was to kill Clayt Monroe. Yes, *that* Clayt Monroe . . . I took his Colt .45 from his dead hand.

I'm retired now. Retired earlier than I wanted to be because a neighbor of mine, a man named Av Caulder, was caught one night in my barn making love to my wife. I was the one who caught them. For three days I was cold. I don't mean that in just an emotional sense, either. I mean in a physical sense. Even though it was a boiling Texas summer, when I went to the line shack to get away from my house and my wife, I couldn't get warm. I felt as if I was dying. A part of me didn't mind that prospect at all.

Mae and Caulder had seen me come into the barn. They jumped up, throwing clothes on, Mae calling out to me, pleading, begging for me to listen. But I hadn't even had time to unsaddle after six hot days and nights of tracking a pair of bank robbers. I just got on my horse and rode off to the line shack.

When I finally did return home, I told Mae that I never wanted to talk about it, that I knew I had to be at least partly responsible because of my long absences from home—a few times I'd been gone two months into the vastness—and that for the sake of our boys, we needed to stay together. She said that it had only happened twice and happened out of loneliness rather than any love for her part for Caulder and that she prayed that someday I could forgive her.

Caulder . . . well, he was the sort who told everybody. He slept with a lot of married women and loved to brag on it. Everybody knew within twenty-four hours that he'd slept with Mae. In town I was looked at either as a fool who wouldn't defend his honor—a Ranger has enemies and they delight in the misery and humiliation of others—or such a pathetic fool I'd believe what a lying slattern of a woman told me just because I loved her so blindly.

It wasn't easy walking those streets at first, but winter came and then spring and then another summer and it was someone else's bad luck to play the fool for the town ... and so my circumstances began to fade.

While the marriage wasn't what it had been, we shared the same bed again and there were those blessed days when I didn't once have a picture of Mae and Caulder in the barn that night.

Then Mae died from heart disease. I took her to three different docs in the area, but not a one of them could do anything for her. At least she went fast. This time I wasn't cold. In the middle of the full moon night, the cry of the coyote a kind of forlorn music, I'd kneel by her grave and weep because I missed her so damned much and loved her so damned much, and blamed the both of us for what had gone so wrong back there with Caulder.

A few weeks before she died, she asked me to sell, bury, destroy—she didn't care which—the Colt .45 I'd taken from Clayt Monroe's dead hand. She said she never felt comfortable being around a gun that had killed so many people. I said I couldn't I said that it was worth a lot of money and that was money our two sons, now grown, could split up when I passed, which probably wouldn't be all that long. I also said there wasn't any doubt that this was Clayt Monroe's Colt .45—got his initials carved on both sides of the barrel.

You know about Clayt Monroe, the gunfighter who didn't want any law on him after he killed a man, so he always asked a sheriff or a deputy to be present when the gunfight took place. Right before Monroe and his opponent squared off, Monroe always asked the sheriff to pronounce this a legal gunfight. And the lawman always did. Hell, he wanted to see the great, grand Clayt Monroe in action as much as everybody else did.

Clayt Monroe officially killed thirty-eight men in nine years. He killed them in Missouri just after the war, in Nebraska and Colorado over a three-year period following that. And finally in Texas, where he spent the last four years of his life with a pretty dark-haired wife named Linda. Folks who knew Monroe said that he killed at least six men because of Linda. They will tell you, and I have no reason to disbelieve them, that Monroe's jealousy was a sickness with him. That he would tear apart saloons, picnics, baseball games, and any other public gathering if he suspected that anybody had slighted Linda in some way. Or, God forbid, had made some sort of flirtatious advance toward her.

Monroe ended up his life in cattle country, owning a large operation with his brother Deke. When he'd grown up, cattle country had been open range, the way the Spaniards had preferred it, but now he saw that the fenced-range type had its advantages. He settled down with Linda. But it didn't take long for Linda to realize what Monroe actually had in mind.

Now, for this time and place in Texas, Linda was a cultured girl. She'd spent several years in a finishing school before her daddy, a man who was at best marginally respectable, went broke in a gold-mine scheme he'd set up himself. She played piano and painted quite seriously; and the ballet lessons she'd taken had left her with a love for dance of just about any kind. She was a proper girl and a devoted Methodist, and while she wanted children and a responsible life, she also wanted, upon occasion, to have fun. To travel the ten miles to the nearest town and do a little shopping and maybe spend time with some of the women she saw only on Sundays at church. And there were Saturday-night dances. Nobody could say barn dances were immoral or improper—well, there are probably some who would, but cranks and crocks are just something you have to suffer in this vale of tears—and so she saw nothing wrong with dragging her husband along to them.

Monroe saw a lot wrong with barn dances, a friend of his told me, repeating what Monroe had once told him one drunken night. No matter how modestly she dressed, and she always dressed modestly, Linda was going to attract the male eye. She attracted the female eye too, but that was out of jealousy. Monroe, as I understand it, had two fears. One was that she would dance with another man and this would make Monroe look like a cuckold. Another man was dancing with his wife and the great grand Clayt Monroe wasn't doing anything about it? The fact that at barn dances everybody always danced with everybody else didn't make a difference to Monroe, apparently. He wanted to be absolute master of everything around him, and that certainly included his wife. For this reason, he had instructed Linda to never dance with any other man except when everybody was working through a do-si-do.

His other fear was that she would fall in love with somebody else. Monroe was twelve years older than Linda and was beginning to look it and act it. The

Monroe family curse was arthritis and it was beginning to slowly but definitely hobble him.

This was around the time I met him on the first of two occasions. It was in a saloon in the small town of Osley. He was there with some of his ranch hands and was enjoying his liquor. When somebody pointed out that there was a Texas Ranger present, he swept over to my table and dramatically shook my hand. He sat down uninvited and began to tell me of all the times the Rangers had helped him out. He was most appreciative. This was also the first time I saw Linda. She was at a lone table in the shadows of the back. Monroe went on and on about the Rangers—I figured he'd produce a trophy of some kind and he'd hand it to me—when I saw one of the bartenders lingering at Linda's table. Monroe's gaze followed mine.

With no warning and no excuse to me, he was up and stalking to the rear of the place. The bartender's back was to him. Monroe spun him around and slashed downward with his Colt, cutting the man's face as surely as he would have with a knife. The man screamed—not shouted, screamed—and covered his face with his hands, apparently realizing even then that he would be scarred for life. Linda did the shouting and all of it was directed at her husband. Now it was her turn to do that stalking. She went straight outside, through the batwings. I never saw her again.

Nearly three years to the day, Clayt Monroe killed his brother. And not in a fair fight, either. After having convinced himself that Deke and Linda were seeing each other on the sly, he drunkenly wobbled from the house to the stable, where he found Deke in a dark corner. By this time, Monroe had no doubt that his wife and brother had betrayed him. He took his Colt from its holster and opened fire.

We need to stop right here and readjust the picture. Because I'm in it, too. I'd been in the kitchen, finishing up a meal with Monroe. We were alone because Linda, he said, had a headache and was upstairs resting and Deke was tending to chores.

That time we'd had a few beers together in the saloon where he attacked the bartender, Monroe had invited me to stop by his spread if I was ever in the area. Well, I was in the area. I rode out and spent a pleasant afternoon touring the ranch with Deke. He told me that he and Linda were throwing a big surprise birthday party for Clayt the next day. He invited me to sleep over and enjoy the fun. He said that the gift was a bronze statue of Clayt in his gunfighting days. Very dramatic. They'd had the statue made in Houston. They were hiding it in the barn.

I could have told Monroe all this—told him how silly and wrong he was being about his brother betraying him—but at the last of our meal, he suddenly jumped up, just as he'd done in that saloon that time, and headed out the back door. No word of explanation. No word of apology. I noticed he was wearing his gun. I wondered why.

I waited a full two minutes before going after him. I shouldn't have waited at all. By the time I found him in the stable, his gun was drawn and he was in the process of shooting his own brother several times in the back.

By then I had my own gun drawn, standing there in the lantern-shadows and sweet roadapple smell of the hay, calling for him to stop, the animals in their stalls gentling down in the hours of early night.

He did more than stop. He dropped down a foot and spun around on me. I didn't have much choice but to fire on him. I didn't have time to choose my shots. In another circumstance, I would have shot to wound but not to kill. He was obviously crazy, booze-crazy, jealous-crazy. In that millisecond that we faced each other, I glimpsed behind him the bronze statue that Deke and Linda had had prepared for his surprise birthday party.

I fired. He moved to the right just as I did so. Maybe if he hadn't moved, the bullet wouldn't have been fatal. But he did move and the bullet was fatal. He paused a moment, firing a shot over my shoulder, and fell sprawling to the stable floor, his blood staining the golden hay immediately. He died at the base of the life-size statue.

Deke was dead, too.

I went back to the house to get Linda. I found her upstairs in their marriage bed. She wasn't merely sleeping. She was dead. She'd been beaten badly about the face—the bruises ugly to see—and then strangled. My guess was that she'd been dead for some time.

At first I didn't mind being The Man Who Shot Clayt Monroe. Oh, I said I minded, wanting to sound humble and all, but being interviewed and photographed was a pretty exciting way to fill up the hours of a widower and retired Ranger. I sent my sons the newspaper and magazine clippings, and they in turn showed them to their own children, who, they said, were greatly impressed with Granddad.

Not until a year of articles and interviews and a few personal appearances—and I was pretty damned bad in front of an audience, let me tell you—did I began to understand that the interest was not so much in me as it was in the Colt I'd taken from Monroe's cold, dead hand that evening on his ranch. People wanted to see it and touch it. It was like a religious ceremony, the way a priest venerates a chalice that has been blessed, the way mourners pass by an open coffin. Sure, it was interesting enough that I'd brought down Monroe, but the weapon was the fascination. More than a hundred newspaper photographers probably took pictures of it; more than a thousand people walked past it on display.

I didn't realize how much of a legend the Colt had taken on until the first time it was stolen. I'd gone to the county fair that blazing hot afternoon, only to come home to find my house a mess and the gun gone. Turned out later that a local man named Kenny Blaine had taken it. Seems he believed that the gun would give him the power to kill a man who'd cheated him out of some land thanks to a crooked judge. He'd been afraid of the man until he got the idea that with Clayt Monroe's Colt, he could kill anybody, no matter how fast they were on the draw.

I learned all this when Blaine's widow came in tears to my place one night to report that her husband's enemy had shot her husband dead. She was returning the weapon. She cursed it. Said that its legend had filled her husband's head with nonsense. I felt sorry for her. I didn't know what to say.

A pair of brothers stole the weapon the next time. They were the Hartson brothers, Dub and Andy, and it was their idea to challenge a gunny named Burt Swander to a fight that would avenge their father's death. Their father had drunkenly drawn down on Swander one night. Swander had shot him dead with a single bullet. Burt was the first to challenge Swander. How could he lose when his hand was filled with Clayt Monroe's Colt? Well, he did lose. Swander killed him in front of a saloon full of witnesses. Then Andy grabbed the Colt. Swanders killed him too, even though most of the witnesses seemed to agree that Andy had actually drawn first.

The third man to steal it was a Mexican laborer who wanted to win back his losses from a rigged card game. His fate was no different from the others who believed it had magical powers. The man who'd cheated him cut him down even before the laborer could quite clear his holster.

This was when I went to the local newspaper and had the editor witness me flinging the Colt into the big fast muddy river from which it would never return. I hadn't told anybody about the men who'd lost their lives using it. That would only enhance the legend—more and more people would try to beat what was clearly what so many people saw as "the curse." The Colt had stood Clayt Monroe in good company so long as his fights were fair. But whatever blessing the Colt had bestowed on him ended when he shot his own brother in the back. Now there was a curse on it. Or so it seemed, if you were inclined to think that way, which in my serious moments, I wasn't.

I'd gone to the editor so that people would stop bothering me about the gun. The whole thing had become a burden. I was tired of having my house broken into and tired of seeing foolish men throw away their lives on the belief that a gun had magical powers.

This was what appeared to happen, anyway. The editor didn't examine the Colt, so he didn't see that the initials Clayt Monroe had carved in the real gun were missing. He just assumed that my story about being tired of the whole thing was true.

The real Colt was actually in my bottom desk drawer. I wouldn't be having any more problems with it. Or so I thought.

Most folks, not having much interest in the Colt anyway, accepted my story at face value. That I'd thrown the gun away. That I regretted ever having it. That I didn't want to talk about it ever again.

But there were true believers. There always are, aren't there? The people who make their dull lives interesting by dreaming up all sorts of fanciful notions? To these people, the gun had taken on the reputation of a religious icon.

They continued trekking to my house over the next year or so. A lot fewer of them than there used to be. But still annoying. The wink and the nudge: *C'mon now, old-timer, you know you've still got that gun and so do I. How about just letting me get a glimpse of it?*

I never strayed from the official story. I always invited them to dive to the depths of that dangerous river if they were so eager to find the magical gun. I suppose a few of them were foolish enough to do so. And I imagine that a few of them drowned for their foolishness.

There were a few break-ins, too. I was always home. I chased them off with a shotgun, just like a farmer in a farmer's daughter joke.

And then finally, finally, they stopped coming. The ones who knocked on my door and made pleas; the ones who broke in and tried to steal.

I was left alone. At last.

Or, thought I was, anyway, until the day when I was down in the barn when I heard footsteps and swung around to find Av Caulder standing in the sunlight while I was lost in the shadows while sweeping out one of the stalls.

"I talk to you a minute?" he said.

It was kind of funny how Caulder and I had ended up treating each other after I'd found him in this very barn with my wife all those years ago. Very formal. Not friendly, not unfriendly. Formal, as if we'd just been introduced and were sort of watching the other man to get a sense of him.

I rested the broom handle against the stall, dipped my hands into a bucket of soapy water, wiped my hands on a rag, and walked up toward the light.

The formal feeling was gone. At first I wondered why. Here all these years I'd seen Caulder at church, at the general store, at baseball games, at horse auctions, I'd been able to make my peace with him. I could never forgive him, but at least my rage was under control.

But as I said, that control was gone suddenly. I suppose it was being in the same barn where it had happened, my wife and Caulder. My mind started making pictures I didn't want to see. Her there naked, shocked and sad when our eyes met—that afternoon she'd changed, and so had I. But Caulder never had. Now as I approached him, I saw the same arrogance that was always on that face. Not even the fear in the eyes could quite disguise the arrogance.

I knew about the fear. He'd slept with one too many married woman. A man named Soames, a man who'd killed his share of gunfighters in New Mexico and had moved here a few years back, was known to be somewhat unhappy about the fact that his wife had confessed to sleeping with Caulder several times. Well, this Soames was more than "somewhat" unhappy. He had let it be known that he was going to find Caulder and force him into a gunfight.

Caulder said, "I hate to bother you."

I shrugged. *He was in the barn with my wife. I'd heard what she'd said to him in the jubilant moment of her ringing pleasure. I felt shame for her, rage for him.* "What can I do for you, Av?"

"I guess you heard about Soames."

"Yeah," I said.

He tried a smile. "One too many married woman for ol' Caulder, I guess."

"Yeah, sounds that way."

There were tears in his eyes. *He was in the barn with my wife.* "I hear things, Jake."

"What sort of things, Av?"

Must've been one hundred degrees in that sun. But that wasn't the only reason he was sweating so hard.

"Things—you know—about that gun. Clayt Monroe's gun."

"I threw it in the river, Av. Couple years ago, in fact."

He licked parched lips. "That's not what I heard, Jake. I heard—well, that you still have it."

"Now who told you that, Av?"

"It don't matter. The thing is—he's gonna kill me, Jake. He won't even hesitate. He'll just kill me right off."

"Maybe you shoulda thought of that."

"I shoulda, Jake. I sure shoulda. But that don't matter now. All that matters now is—" He started to draw the makings out of his shirt pocket. But he was trembling too hard to roll a cigarette. "I just need that gun, Jake. It's my only chance. Maybe some of the good luck Clayt Monroe had—maybe it'll rub off on me, Jake." He had no shame left in him. The tears bloomed full and silver now. "Please, Jake. I don't blame you for hatin' me—for what I done, I mean—but you're my only chance. You and that gun of Clayt's."

I couldn't do it. Much as I hated him, much as I could no longer even pretend that I had made me peace with what he'd done—I couldn't hand over the bad-luck gun that had gotten so many other men killed. I tried to think of myself as a decent man. And I wanted to be able to keep *on* thinking of myself that way. I wouldn't mind seeing him killed, that was for sure, but I didn't want to have a hand in it.

I nodded back to the stall where I'd been working. "I need to get back to work, Av. I'm sorry."

He was on me before I could stop him, wrenching the front of my chambray shirt in his hands, spitting in my face as he shouted at me. "You can't just let me die, Jake! You gotta let me have that gun!"

What I did next felt pretty damned good, let me tell you. I'd waited long enough to do it, that was for sure. I planted a fist so deep in his belly that he not only doubled over, he began puking up whatever food he'd had in the past few hours.

I left him doubled up on the dusty hot ground there and went back inside to the shadows. I picked up my broom and went back to work.

I kept an eye on him, of course. He lay there for what seemed like a long time. I suppose he didn't want to move. He probably felt safe there. Soames wouldn't come looking for him here. He could be pretty sure of that.

His horse was just a few feet away.

When he finally got to his feet, he rocked a little on his heels. He looked hollow and unsteady. There was no arrogance left in his face. And then he started to walk his unsteady way over to his horse. Halfway there, he let out a sob that was probably as much for my benefit as his. Caulder was the dramatic sort. A lot of women liked that in a man.

He got himself up into his saddle and then just looked at me. He shook his head, as if I'd just betrayed him, and then turned his mount toward the west.

I looked back at the stall. The same one I'd found them in.

Mae was crying out again. Crying out in pleasure. And then I was seeing those beautiful eyes of hers in that ugly moment—those shamed and frightened and saddened eyes. And the rage was on me now and I wanted to feel Caulder's throat under my hands.

I was barely aware of it. It was one of those things where you seemed to be guided by some external force.

I went running out of the barn and shouting Caulder's name.

He hadn't gone far. He turned around in his saddle and looked back at me.

"C'mon, Caulder!" I said. "I'll give you that gun. I've got it inside."

It didn't take long to find it in my bottom desk drawer. Nor long to carry it outside and put it in his waiting hands.

"Oh, God, Jake, I wanna thank you so much. I really need all the luck I can get."

"Yeah," I said and I was smiling at him and thinking of the two of them in the barn that long ago day that the worms will someday eat out of my memory. Smiling at him. "Yeah."

Then he was on his horse and riding away.

ONE HUNDRED AND TWO DAYS

MARCUS GALLOWAY

———❦———

Marcus Galloway has built up an impressive list of anthology credits. He's had stories in *Boot Hill, Desperadoes,* and *How the West Was Read,* among others. His latest novel is *It All Comes Around,* the third in a series.

This story describes the 102-day pursuit by the Texas Rangers of Bonnie and Clyde, with just a touch of personal involvement.

Dallas, Texas
February 10, 1934

It had been going on for years.

Ever since he'd seen her that first time, he knew he had to have her. It had only been a glimpse, but that one glimpse of her was all it took. Of course she'd been with someone else at the time. That's what made it so hard to get her. That other man was always there. That skinny, prissy little prick was always around and guarding her as though he had that right.

Jon Morris hadn't been with the Texas Rangers for more than a few months at the time, but back in the summer of '32, he saw something that most Rangers never did. In fact, what he saw was something most Rangers prayed to the good Lord above that they would never have to witness.

On the other hand, it had also been one of the finest moments of Jon's life.

Jon had been working with an old man named Varley at the time. Ol' Cam Varley had been with the Rangers ever since he could fit the hat. He'd been with them so long that he took on the attitude that a lot of the old-timers got where they started paying attention more to their own rules than any others.

They'd crossed state lines into Oklahoma because of the two criminals they'd been chasing. Varley didn't think twice about it, and Jon had been too wet behind the ears to question him once they'd wound up in the wrong place at the right time. He heard the shots like they were thunder, and when he heard that car come barreling toward them, Jon would've sworn that it was the earth itself trembling beneath his feet.

Varley was old, but he'd still had enough gumption to get that old Packard into gear and pull into the road just as those two lawbreakers came blazing past. Thinking back on it, Jon could see the both of them in that car just as clear as if they'd stopped and posed for a picture.

That skinny bastard Clyde was leaning out the passenger window with a pistol in each hand. He was perched on the edge so his head and shoulders were above the top of the car. From there, Clyde popped off a few rounds toward whatever they'd left behind and even sent a piece of lead flying toward Varley's Packard.

Just as Jon pulled himself down into his seat and fumbled for his own .45, he got a look at Bonnie. She was all beaming smiles and whipping strands of golden hair. She'd looked over at him at that same moment and put on a smile that was even brighter than the one before. Such a slight little thing and still she handled that car without so much as twitching at the sound of gunfire.

It was a moment that the hunter got his first look at his prey. It was a moment that took away his innocence and turned Jon Morris into the man he'd never thought he could be. He thought about that moment every day since it had first happened. And he was thinking about that moment when he was suddenly snapped back into the present by the slap of paper against polished wood.

"Hey there," said Will Ames, another Ranger working in Dallas. "Better straighten up and look sharp. We got company coming."

"Company? What the hell are you talking about?"

"We're getting a visitor. He should catch your interest since he's coming to talk about those two right there." When he said that last part, Will jabbed a finger down toward the newspaper that he'd slapped onto Jon's desk.

The paper was filled with the normal fare. There was news about the hard times and enough misery to make the black print seem even darker. But the last thing Jon noticed was the letters. The first and only thing to catch his eye was the all-too-familiar pictures spread across the front page. They were the same two snapshots that had been plastered all over every paper across the country. One was of Bonnie putting Clyde at arm's length while pointing a shotgun at his chest. Oddly enough, they were both smiling in the picture. Even odder was the fact that Jon smiled whenever he saw that picture too.

The other snapshot was of Bonnie all by herself. She was standing in front of a car with one foot propped up on the bumper. Scowling at the camera in a way that still couldn't hide her mischievous beauty, she chomped on a cigar and held a pistol up near her face.

With the Depression and all, there were plenty of people out there saying that Bonnie was a beauty or Clyde was some kind of modern-day Robin Hood. There were stories out there about how those two only stole the bank's money, which was why common folks didn't mind helping them out every now and then.

Well, Jon didn't have much to say about stories like that. When he saw those pictures and read stories like the one in that newspaper, there was plenty more going through his head. Plenty more, indeed.

"You believe that?" asked Ames.

"Believe what?"

"They printed another one of them god-awful poems that Bonnie wrote."

Jon turned the folded paper over and skimmed down to the poem. " 'The Story of Suicide Sal'? I already read this one."

"Good. I'm glad to see that someone's been reading up on those two. I like a man who does his homework."

The man who said that wasn't the same Ranger who'd dropped the paper. Ames was standing at attention as though he didn't know whether to salute or shake hands. Jon turned toward the direction where the other gruff baritone voice had come from and found himself looking into a pair of sharp eyes embedded in a face that might have weathered a thousand storms.

With skin as tough as rain-beaten canvas marked by wrinkles older than a few of the Rangers' newest recruits, Frank Hamer stood glaring at the younger Rangers as though he'd just read their entire lives by staring them down. He was a big man and wore old-fashioned clothes that reminded Jon of one of those grainy photographs from the hallway in the front hall of the field office building. On second thought, he realized that Hamer actually was a prominent figure in more than one of those pictures.

Jon shot up out of his chair and straightened his posture. "Jon Morris, sir."

Looking over to the man who'd brought the paper, Hamer said, "If you'd be so kind as to excuse me and Jon Morris here."

"Oh. Uh. Sure. I mean, yes, sir."

Although Hamer didn't smile, he didn't frown, either. His face was like the front of a thick oak tree. Thick, bristly white hair sprouted from his scalp, but somehow didn't make him look old. The mustache on his upper lip was so thick that it covered a good portion of his face, making his expression even more unreadable.

"He's a bit jumpy, ain't he?" Hamer asked, nodding toward Ames, who was beating a hasty retreat from the office.

"It's just that . . . well . . . you're kind of a . . . well . . . legend."

"I'm just an old Ranger who's caught his fair share of badmen. Until just recently, I wasn't even that much."

"I heard you were retired."

"Retired and fixin' to start a garden, that's right." Pausing for a second, Hamer's face scrunched up slightly and a slight smile could be detected through all the whiskers, wrinkles, and leathery skin. "Well, I was relaxin' anyhow. The garden wasn't my idea. I got the call to come back into service by the same folks that've been trying their best to keep me out. I guess they figured I was less trouble than those two devils."

Hamer tapped his meaty finger against the picture of Bonnie and Clyde. Looking down at the snapshot, his eyes narrowed slightly as he studied those two young faces. There wasn't any malice in his stare. Instead, he seemed to just commit every line and curve to memory.

Watching the older Ranger, Jon couldn't help but feel like he was present at the start of some real piece of history. Every time a report came in about the two bank robbers, he'd gotten that same feeling. It was almost as though he could hear the scratch of pen against paper as events were being recorded for posterity.

"When do you plan on getting started?" Jon asked.

Hamer shook himself out of his thoughtful silence, tapped the picture one last time, and pushed the paper away. "No better time than the present. That's what I say."

"You're starting today?"

"Any reason why I shouldn't? It seems to me that I've sat by and watched this job get botched for too long. I wanted to ask you something, Morris. You caught sight of those two a few years back, didn't you?"

"Yes, sir." The vision of Bonnie driving that car was still fresh in Jon's mind. All he had to do was close his eyes and she was there, smiling at him. "I chased them after they robbed a general store in Atoka, Oklahoma, back in '32."

Now, it seemed that Hamer was studying Jon's face every bit as carefully as he'd studied the faces printed on the paper in front of him. "Two lawmen died that day in Atoka. Clyde killed 'em both like they weren't anything but dogs."

That was another memory that Jon could never forget . . . no matter how hard he tried.

"Yes, sir."

"One of those men was riding with you at the time."

Jon could feel the color drain from his face, leaving his skin cold and clammy. Every time he thought about how that day had ended, he felt a pain that was like an icy little fist clenching at the bottom of his stomach. "His name was Cam Varley."

"I know," Hamer replied, reaching out to place a beefy hand on Jon's shoulder. "That's why I came to you today. They told me to pick out someone to help me, and on a case like this, that could mean big things for an up-and-comer like you. I didn't want to give this opportunity to just anyone, so I figured I'd give it to someone who's earned it. I thought I'd give it to someone who's got a genuine stake in the matter."

Hearing that, Jon felt the fist in his stomach start to loosen. "I'd be honored, Captain Hamer. Thank you."

Tightening his grip on Jon's shoulder, Hamer added,

"This ain't about revenge. This is about you puttin' those demons to rest that've been tearing you up inside. I've worked with plenty of men and have had more than my fair share of them die right in front of me. I know what it can do to you, and I know that it never feels truly over until you set things straight. You understand me?"

"Yes, Captain."

"The moment I see you acting less like a Texas Ranger and more like someone who's out for blood, that's the moment I send you right back to this here desk."

Jon's mind opened up to a world of possibilities that he hadn't even known existed. In the blink of an eye, he'd gone from reading about the headline cases to stepping into one of them. No longer was he walking by the pictures of lawman legends in the entrance hall to the Rangers' office building. Now he would be working right alongside one of the biggest legends the Rangers had to offer.

"So what do you say?" Hamer asked.

Jon got up from his seat and offered his hand to the burly captain. "I won't let you down."

Hamer's hand enveloped Jon's and squeezed with enough force to push the bones in the younger man's hand together. "You better not. I intend on tracking them two down, but it's gonna get rough. You can bet on that."

Rough, it turned out, was an understatement.

Clyde Barrow and Bonnie Parker continued to cut a swath through several states, changing up their partners in crime with no discernible reason behind it. Clyde's brother, Buck, and Buck's wife Blanche rode with the couple on a fairly steady basis. There was a gunman and thief named Ray Hamilton who rode with the gang until he parted ways with them on his own accord.

After Ray, the bank robbers took out a filling station and even robbed the place of its attendant, a man by the name of William Daniel Jones. It turned out that Jones, much like Bonnie herself, welcomed the chance to tread the path of the lawless instead of scraping by within an honest life.

Hamer and Morris pieced these things together by diligently tracking the robbers and sifting through the bloody remnants left behind. The gang wasn't particularly skilled, but seemed more blessed by the youthful attitude that they could walk through fire and come out with just a tan to show for it. Sheer audacity and plenty of ruthless disregard for human life allowed the gang to keep robbing. Whatever slack remained was taken up by the public perception that the youths were somehow in the right and were wild reflections of the frustrated populace trapped reading newspapers in their sweltering homes and offices.

The next couple of months dragged by with leaden feet. Morris felt like he was in a war, struggling toward his singular goal while Hamer kept plucking away, seemingly unaffected by the insanity around him. It was early April when both Rangers were sitting in the Ford V-8 that had become their new home.

The interior of the car smelled like salty sweat and ham sandwiches. Every inch of the interior as well as the two men on the seats was covered with a thick layer of dust and grit. Hamer sat behind the wheel, staring intently out the window while Morris fidgeted restlessly beside him.

"I heard they weren't coming anywhere near here," Morris said nervously.

"They'll be here."

"But that skinny fella at the diner said—"

"I don't care what he said," Hamer interrupted. "That doesn't matter. What matters is how he said it."

"What?"

"He was scared. And since I was askin' him about them devils that blazed through here, I think he's scared because I might find out he was lyin' to you and me both."

Jon felt his stomach drop and his heart skip a beat. "I don't think he was lying."

"Don't worry about it. Being able to tell these things comes with experience. I've been lied to by the best of 'em, and that fella at the diner wasn't anything close to the best. Besides, Clyde's about due to come through here."

"Where'd you hear that from?"

"Didn't have to hear it. I just kept my eyes open. Since this hunt started, that boy has played a circle from Dallas to Joplin, Missouri, to Louisiana, and back to Dallas. We just been to Joplin, so that brings us here." Looking over to Jon, Hamer asked, "And where do you think they'd hole up if they were in this here town?"

Jon closed his eyes and tried to think while so many other things were going through his head. "We passed a few houses for rent, but they've got Buck, Blanche, and that other kid with them, so they'd need somewhere bigger. Clyde's got his guard up, so I'd say they'd either be at that motel on the outskirts or that barn we passed on the way into town."

Hamer's eyes lit up a bit. "And what made you think of those places?"

"That guy in the diner. He twitched when you brought them up."

"Now you're thinking like a Texas Ranger," Hamer said with a proud smile. "Let the rest of the boys know where we're headed. We'll split up and each sit on one of them places." Pausing for a second and nodding once, he added, "I'll even let you pick which one you'd like to watch."

It may have been a small thing to someone listening to the conversation from the outside, but Jon knew better than to discount that particular allowance. Coming from a man as precise and persistent as Hamer, letting someone else choose his own assignment was one hell of a step. So far Hamer had yet to relinquish much of the control over his operation, and now that he had a choice to make, Jon almost forgot what he wanted to do.

He remembered real quickly, however, when he thought about who he was after.

"I'll watch the motel," Jon said.

Hamer nodded once and handed Jon a flare gun. "Then that leaves me with the barn. We won't be able to see each other, but whoever spots those kids just needs to fire this in the air. That way's gonna be quicker than any other and we'll be close enough that we should be able to see that flare right quick. You sure you're ready for this?"

"I've been ready for this for a long time."

*   *   *

Jon had half of the support officers with him as he rolled to a stop just down the street from the motel where he knew the gang of robbers was staying. The flare gun was stuffed in the pocket of his jacket where it would stay no matter what. After all, he'd been the one to get approached by a frightened informant who pointed to someone she saw with a gun sticking out of the front of their coat. Hamer had been talking to another local at the time. That armed man turned out to be William Daniel Jones, and he was with a young blonde woman carrying enough groceries to feed four or five other hungry lawbreakers.

Jon listened to what the informant had said, but didn't know quite what to do with it. The only thing he was certain of was that he didn't want to tell Hamer. If he did that, then he'd be putting too much at stake. Jon had come too far to risk ruining it now.

Well, the two were due back from the grocery store any moment now. Jon knew now that he'd done the right thing in pointing Hamer in the wrong direction. Sometimes, when things dropped into someone's lap, it meant they were meant to be.

"Meant to be," Jon whispered as he got out of his car and signaled the others to stay behind.

The closer he got to that motel, the more it felt like he was finally meeting his destiny. No longer would he be just some lonely Texas Ranger working toward a bullet or some anemic pension. He didn't have to dream about how things could be as he sat at his desk, and he didn't have to pretend what it would be like to get close to her while staring at her picture.

Jon Morris was turning his fantasy into a reality. His desk was collecting dust hundreds of miles away, and Bonnie was so close that he could smell the wildflower scent of her soft golden hair. He waited until the former filling station attendant had passed before hastening his steps toward Bonnie.

"Oh," she said in a soft voice that sounded like something just short of a song. "You frightened me. I didn't see you sneak up on me like that."

She was beautiful. Jon had studied every line of her face and every curve of her body from those pictures, but not one of them had done her justice. Even the few glimpses he'd caught of her, which had fueled more sweet dreams than he could count, seemed like nothing compared to this.

Doing his best to act the way he'd planned, Jon smiled at her and immediately worried that she would see right through him, all the way down to the pure aching love in his heart. "Sorry about that. Are you, uh, staying here?"

She nodded quickly, every inch of her body infused with joyous, youthful vigor. "I sure am. Me and my husband."

For a moment, all Jon could do was look at her. He wanted to do so much more, but knew that if he didn't take care of certain things first, than nothing else would ever follow. Her eyes glittered with life and her tight little body practically begged to be in his arms.

"Are you staying here too?" she asked.

Jon took a breath, hating the fact that his time with Bonnie was so damn short. "I think someone's been following you," he said abruptly.

Her expression became concerned and she looked around. Shrugging, she said, "I don't see anyone."

"I know there's someone. Look there in those cars parked across the street."

She glanced in the direction he pointed and suddenly lost her smile.

"I know who you are," he told her.

"What? Who are you? Is that the law in those cars?"

"I've seen you in the newspaper and I . . ." No matter how many times he'd imagined having this conversation, it could never prepare him for the actual moment. "I, well, I don't want to see anything happen to you."

Bonnie cocked her head to one side and fixed her gorgeous eyes upon him. "Aww, that's so sweet." For a couple seconds, she just looked at him. Somehow, it seemed that she was having just as hard a time trying to find the right words as Jon was. The longer she waited, the more she wanted to get moving. Bonnie shifted from one foot to another and even started hopping as though it took all her strength to keep from running back to her rented room.

Finally she dropped her groceries, lunged forward, and wrapped both arms around Jon's neck. She had to lift herself up onto her tiptoes to get her face close to his, and when she did, she planted a kiss on his lips that would have melted steel.

Her mouth was soft and tasted like honey. When Jon pulled in a breath, his nose was filled with Bonnie's scent. She smelled like wildflowers and a fresh breeze. Her hair was soft against his cheek. Without thinking about it, Jon put his hands on her hips and responded to her kiss. That little bit of encouragement was enough for her to respond as well.

Just when Jon thought the kiss couldn't get any better, he was proven wrong. Bonnie opened her lips slightly and let her tongue slip out just enough for the moist tip to brush against his lips. Jon's breath caught in his throat, and when he extended his tongue to taste her, Bonnie took him all the way inside, wrapping her lips around him and sucking just enough to curl his toes.

As it was happening, that kiss seemed to last for a lifetime.

When it was over, Jon swore that it had been done in the blink of an eye.

She stepped back from him and hopped a few steps away on the balls of her feet. She moved like a leaf being tossed on a breeze and got a look on her face that made her appear to be a naughty little girl.

"Thank you, mister," she purred. "I won't forget you."

In Jon's mind, those words became etched in stone. If he thought about it just a little bit, he could still taste her on his lips and could still feel her little tongue sliding into his mouth.

It was perfect.

It was one of the few perfect moments that any man could ever have. The only bad thing about it was that it was now over.

"You'd better go," Jon told her.

"You too. Things might get a little noisy." And with that, Bonnie twirled around and dashed straight for room 5. "Clyde! Clyde! We've got to get out of here! Clyde!"

The rest of what Bonnie shouted became muffled beyond recognition as she went into the room and slammed the door shut behind her.

The next minute or two were a blur. Jon gave Bonnie a few moments to tell her story to the others and then he broke into a run back toward the cars. He took a longer way around the motel just to buy a little more time, but when he got back to the rest of his team, he did the only thing he could.

"Well?" one of the officers asked. "Are they in there?"

Squeezing every bit of juice out of the time he was buying, Jon looked back to the motel and nodded. "Yeah. They're inside."

"Should we call in Hamer or go after them ourselves?"

That was no choice at all in Jon's mind. "We've got to move on our own. Hamer will come once he hears the shots."

Jon led the officers toward the wrong side of the motel, still feeling Bonnie's lips upon his own and her body against his. All the times he'd stared at her picture and read about her exploits, Jon had imagined himself holding Bonnie, smelling her hair, tasting her skin. Her smile was even prettier up close and her eyes were more beautiful than he could have ever imagined.

He thought he'd waited long enough. For Jon, the seconds after Bonnie's kiss had dragged by and he'd done his best to give them as much time as they needed to get clear of the motel. When the door to room 5 popped open and William Daniel Jones came scurrying out, Jon didn't even hear what the officer said, but he knew that the robber had been spotted.

Although he did his best to keep anyone from rushing in, Jon was unable to hold the other officers back completely. They were too anxious and too high-strung to wait another second. Rather than draw any more attention to himself, Jon drew his pistol and started running toward the motel. The least he could do now was try to control the damage.

Buck Barrow came out next, and the moment he got a look at the oncoming officers, he pulled the triggers of the two pistols he was holding. The guns roared and spat toward the Rangers, filling the air with lead that hissed and tore at whatever flesh they could find.

Clyde was next and he didn't even look for a target before turning a Browning automatic rifle toward the commotion and pulling his trigger. With the addition of that firepower, the front of the motel turned into a war zone. There were screams coming from the other rooms as well as shouted orders coming from both Jon and the robbers.

Jon felt like his head was underwater, since all the chaos was diluted to a low rumble thanks to the pounding of blood in his head. Certain sounds came through clearer than others, such as the thunder of the Browning as well as the song of bullets whipping past his head.

Next came the wet slap of lead against flesh as one of the bullets hit an officer and sent the lawman straight to the ground. Jon looked over to see one of the youngest and most eager of his men spin around on one foot wearing an expression on his face that was oddly blank. The kid's eyes had already glazed over. Actually, only one of his eyes had glazed over, since the other eye had been turned to a pulpy crimson mist along with that half of his face thanks to the automatic fire from the Browning.

Acting on impulse, Jon took a few shots toward the robbers as blood from another of his men sprayed across his face. Jon's finger froze upon his trigger when he saw Bonnie come running from the motel room. She was dragging Buck's wife Blanche, who was covering her eyes and screaming loud enough to be heard over the gunfire.

Jon leveled his gun at her, but was unable to pull his trigger. Even as the lead flew around him, he couldn't bear the thought of harming one golden hair upon Bonnie's head. That moment of hesitation was all it took for her and Blanche to make it to the car that William Daniel Jones drove up between the robbers and the officers. Buck might have been limping, but other than that, the robbers piled into the car and kept shooting from the windows as they tore away from the motel.

"Jesus Christ," one of the officers said. "Matt's dead. They got Matt and I think Kyle might be hurt real bad."

Jon stood there and watched as the getaway car drove toward the line of cars the Rangers had positioned to block the main exit that led to the street. He could feel the other man's blood on his cheek and could still see Matt's head exploding in the split-second darkness every time he dared to blink his eyes.

"They're coming back!" another of the officers shouted.

Jon's training kicked in and he chucked away his pistol so he could get to one of the shotguns laying on the ground. "Form a firing line! Get ready because they'll be coming this way."

Sure enough, the getaway car slammed into one of the parked cars but was unable to move it. From there, they turned around and pointed their grill straight toward the officers and started rolling their way.

Jon worked the shotgun's lever and placed the weapon against his shoulder. The men around him followed suit, and when the car got in range, every gun went off to tear a chunk out of the front of its grill.

Every gun went off, except for Jon's.

Just like that day in '32, Jon got a look at Bonnie's face as that car sailed by and the only thing he could think about was how beautiful she was. She wasn't smiling this time or laughing, but he had their kiss to warm him up and that was enough to keep his finger from pulling that trigger.

The whole skirmish was over in less than a minute.

The car had gone by, leaving a trail of smoke behind it thanks to the damage it took from the gunfire. Another of the officers had been hit by someone shooting from the car's window, but it was just a nasty-looking wound in the man's shoulder. As the car rolled into the street, the driver gunned its engine and forced another oncoming car to the side of the road.

Jon recognized that car immediately and wasn't surprised in the least when he saw it try to right itself and take off after the getaway car. About ten minutes later, the familiar Ford V-8 came back to the motel and Hamer jumped out faster than Jon thought the older man could move.

"What the hell happened?" Hamer shouted. "Why the hell didn't that flare go off? What happened to my men? How many got hurt?"

"We tried to close in on them," one of the other officers said. "Jon even went up to Bonnie and tried to get a handle on where they were, but when we came back to make the arrest, they flew out of there with guns blazing."

Hamer nodded, but was unable to stand still as he looked back and forth between the dead body and wounded men laying on the ground. "You talked to Bonnie, Jon?"

"Y . . . yes, sir, Captain."

"What'd she say?"

"Not much, sir. I . . . I was trying to . . ."

"It's not your fault, Jon." Hamer's face darkened and he walked toward his car while sirens filled the air. "They're animals. I'd hoped to sneak up on them and catch them by surprise, but I guess they won't be taken quietly. All right then. I'll keep this in mind. Next time I won't try to be so polite."

There was plenty Jon could say, but nothing that would help. Slowly, almost without thinking about it, he reached up to wipe the blood from his face. Even now, with his pulse racing, the taste of gunpowder in the back of his throat, and the stench of death in his nostrils, he couldn't help thinking of Bonnie's kiss.

"That bitch."

Jon's eyes snapped over to Hamer, who'd been the one to say those words.

The big Texas Ranger was kneeling down beside the body of the dead officer, his face catching the light of the approaching ambulances. There were no tears on Hamer's cheeks, but the grim line of his mouth said so much more than any words that could have come from them.

"Those murdering sons of bitches," Hamer whispered.

Jon went over to put his hand on Hamer's shoulder,

but stopped just short before making contact. "I'm sorry, Captain," he said while pulling his hand back.

"It's all right, Jon. You did all you could."

Those words hit him like a punch in Jon's gut. They almost made him forget the soft, sweet touch of Bonnie's lips upon his own.

Almost, but not quite.

Gibland, Louisiana
May 23, 1934

Hamer had been right about Clyde's pattern. Once he'd gotten it down, all Hamer had to do was put himself ahead of Clyde on that track and wait for the train to arrive. Truth be told, Jon learned a hell of a lot about manhunting from Captain Hamer. Through the use of contacts, finely honed instincts, and a few lucky breaks, Hamer had narrowed down his search to a lonely stretch of road not too far from the Texas border.

In the end, Jon got the feeling that Hamer found out about him as well. The captain had become distant over the last couple of days, but the final blow came when he refused to tell Jon who'd tipped him off that Bonnie and Clyde would be driving down that particular road at that particular time.

Hamer hadn't really been talking much at all lately. It seemed that he and Jon had both gone through changes over their time together. Hamer had become more intent on bringing the robbers to justice and Jon had fallen in love. After that kiss, Jon decided that love wasn't too strong a word anymore.

He was in love and all he needed was to wait for the perfect moment to make his big move. That moment came when he, Hamer, and five other lawmen were camped out on an embankment on the side of that dirt road. The Rangers were armed with two rifles, three shotguns, and a Browning automatic similar to the ones that the robbers themselves enjoyed using.

Hamer sat amid all that firepower like a spider calmly waiting for the flies to get stuck. The other officers fidgeted somewhat, but had been handpicked by Hamer for the task and behaved more like soldiers than lawmen. As for Jon, he sat with his shotgun in hand knowing full well that he would be with his girl once and for all by the end of the day.

"Here they come," Hamer whispered, intruding on Jon's constant flow of plans and fantasies. "Get ready, and remember, these devils killed plenty of good lawmen. Don't cut 'em one damn bit of slack."

The others signaled their acknowledgment without words, but with the metallic crackle of guns being cocked and safeties being snapped off.

Jon watched as the car came around the bend and into view. Even before he could see through the dirt and grit being kicked up, he knew Bonnie was in that car. He could feel her nearby and apparently wasn't the only one. Hamer tensed beside him, shifting in his position so he could settle the butt of his rifle against his shoulder.

It wasn't said that they would start shooting when the car got in range, but it was somehow understood. Hamer had discussed taking out the tires or disabling the car, but the others had just mentioned punching the vehicle and anyone inside of it full of holes. Jon had seen too many plans fall apart to take any chances with this one. That's why, despite all the protests he heard, Jon got up and started running straight down the middle of the road.

The car rolled to a stop and Bonnie's smiling face looked out through the window to meet Jon's eyes. Jon felt his own smile come and ran over to the side of the car.

"Bonnie! Remember me?"

Sticking his head out the window, Clyde squinted toward him with his beady rat's eyes. "Who the hell are—"

But Clyde's question was cut off by the sudden belch of smoke and fire erupting from Jon's shotgun. The first blast caught Clyde in the neck and upper chest. If Jon had been a few steps closer, he might have severed the skull from that skinny bastard's shoulders. As it was, he put enough lead into Clyde to erase him from the face of the earth.

The next shot was just to make sure.

"I know this is bad, Bonnie," he said desperately while walking around to her side of the car, "but I can get you out of this. We can be together."

Tears streamed from her eyes and Clyde's blood soaked into the pretty dress she wore. Shock and horror mixed upon her face like mud that had swirled into a once-clean pool. Those eyes fixed first upon the shotgun in Jon's hand and then upon the badge he wore.

"Go to hell!" she spat. "You goddamn son of a bitch!"

Footsteps approached the car as Hamer and the other men closed in. "Stick 'em up!" Hamer shouted.

Jon didn't notice Hamer or any of the others. He didn't even notice as Bonnie went for one of the several guns packed into the car between her and Clyde. He was too busy trying to figure out how she could talk like that after what they'd been through. After all he'd done for her.

"But I tried to help you," he said, unaware of the Rangers moving in nearby. "I only wanted to help you."

"You killed Clyde!" was all she could say as the blood flowed from the body of the skinny young man slumped half behind the wheel and half out the window. "Go to hell!"

"Stick 'em up," came Hamer's order one more time.

"But don't you see? Now we can be together. I love you."

It was the moment he'd been waiting for. He'd waited one hundred and two days for that moment to arrive and now it was here. When it came, he'd imagined Bonnie to react several different ways.

Laughing at him was definitely not one of them.

"You . . . love me?" she asked. "Are you crazy?"

And now that smile came once again. It was the smile that had given him the will to go on just as the gang's lust for blood had driven Hamer onward during those same one hundred and two days. Only this time was different. This time Bonnie wasn't smiling at him. She was laughing at him.

"You bitch," Jon snarled as his rage blotted out everything but the wicked smirk on Bonnie's sweet little mouth.

She was trembling as she lifted one of the revolvers

laying on the seat beside her and pointed it toward Jon. She wasn't smiling anymore, and for that, Jon practically welcomed the sharp, pinching pain that stabbed right through his chest and flared up like a fire inside of him.

With Hamer and the rest of the Rangers in position, once Bonnie took aim at Jon, the air around that car exploded as though the gates to hell had been knocked open. Rifle shots cracked through the once-tranquil air, and the sputter of the Browning was like a deadly pulse beneath it all. Next came the chilling sound of breaking glass and cracking bones and bullets punching holes in steel.

The hiss of punctured tires mixed with the thump of lead punching holes through flesh and the rattle of two bodies going through their final motions within the confines of that car.

Outside the car, Jon stood looking into Bonnie's vacant eyes. The blood ran down from where he'd been shot, and despite all the smoke in that stinking coffin on wheels, he swore he could only see the smoky wisp curling from the barrel of Bonnie's revolver.

Hamer was there to catch him as Jon fell over. He could feel the other man die in his arms without giving so much as a sputtering breath to fight off the Reaper.

"Jon's name stays out of the papers," Hamer said to the closest officer. "I don't want him bandied about in that circus."

The other Rangers gazed upon the scene not quite knowing how to react. All they knew was that they didn't want to disobey the man who'd calmly led them straight into the history books.

*   *   *

Captain Frank Hamer retired from the Texas Rangers in 1949. Regarding the pursuit of Bonnie and Clyde, he was quoted as saying simply, "On February tenth, I took the trail and followed it for exactly one hundred and two days. Like Clyde Barrow, I used a Ford V-8, and like Clyde, I lived in the car most of the time."

Jon Morris remained unknown, his story untold.

Until now.